Skyward Ascension

Book 3 of the Shadows of Rebellion series.

by David Lingard

A note from the author

I just wanted to say here, thank you, whoever you are for however you have arrived at this book and my story. It makes a big difference to authors like me, who like to feel as though their hard work and dedication is appreciated when our work is read.

Your investment of your own time and money is as always, well appreciated. It takes a long time and a lot of effort to write, edit and release a book, so please, I ask that you **rate** and **review** everything that you read – and not just this book, so that lesser-known authors can grow their audience and gain the credibility that they deserve.

Also, I have a website that is usually kept up to date with current works, reviews and a few extra little bits. You'll find it at: www.davidlingard.com

Chapter 1 - Forgotten

Theodore. It was the single word that he could remember when he awoke in the smoking crater. Still, beyond that, everything was a mystery. Looking down at his body, he could see that he was burnt, cut and bruised, but more than that, his clothes had been burnt or scorched away to nothing, and every hair on his body, legs, arms, face and head had disappeared too. Assuming that he used to have hair, that was.

Theodore was alone, with no memories and no clue of who he was, what he had been doing, or what he was supposed to do next.

As he struggled to make sense of his situation, attempting to prove his mind for any lost memories, Theodore could do nothing other than panic. Or did he prefer 'Theo'? No, Theodore was definitely right.

His palms turned immediately sweaty, and his heart rate began to race.

But then he looked at the sand surrounding him and saw something that made him fall to his knees and empty the contents of his stomach; the ground around him was littered with bodies, blackened and burnt, almost unrecognisable. He shut his eyes tightly and wished more than anything else for this all to be some terrible nightmare, that he hadn't really seen what he had just seen, that he was really away somewhere else, safe and sound in bed, and this would all just simply disappear.

But when he opened his eyes again, the world was still as it had been. He remained on all fours, not wishing to fully appreciate the scope of the death and destruction surrounding him, but he knew that eventually, he would have no choice.

"Come now, brother," a low-pitched, dark-sounding voice reached

Theodore's ears, and he peered behind himself to see a man approaching in long, purple robes.

"I knew it would take more than a few holders of the Eternal Flame to take you down… tell me, how many did you send along to the afterworld?"

The man had a long black beard and long black hair, and both were streaked with a silvery white. His eyes were so purple that they were almost black, and the sight stirred something within Theodore, a memory perhaps? Or a recognition of the man, he couldn't be sure.

"What… what happened?" Theodore asked slowly, trying his best to focus his gaze on the man rather than the bodies surrounding them.

The man peered down at Theodore curiously for a moment, apparently trying to assess why he would ask such a question. Then something flickered in the man's eyes, an understanding of sorts, and Theodore didn't like it at all.

"When you return to yourself, you will know where to find me. Until then, rest, recover, and soon it will all become clear, my brother."

"What?" Theodore repeated, still having no clue what was happening.

But the man did not answer; he simply turned away from Theodore and appraised the battlefield, now talking to himself.

"It would be such a shame to leave these souls out here, wouldn't it? It is my duty to set them free, to allow their passage to the afterworld so that they can be at peace," he said softly.

The man then moved out of the crater that Theodore stood in, unmoving, and began to wave his hands in a slow yet mesmerising pattern, his dark purple robes billowing around him as though they were caught in some unfelt breeze. As he moved, Theodore felt the air become heavy with whatever power this was that the man wielded, and a luminous violet aura surrounded his outstretched palms. Theodore watched, captivated by the spectacle unfolding before him.

A surge of power emanated from the man, pulsating with an eerie brilliance. Arcane symbols materialised in the air, glowing with a vibrant purple hue. The ground beneath him trembled, responding to the raw magical energy being channelled through the man's fingertips and with a swift motion, the man thrust his hands forward, and a purple shockwave rippled through the air. A vortex of swirling energy formed before him, crackling with a bright, intense purple light. Somehow, The vortex seemed to draw the essence of the fallen souls scattered around the battlefield.

As the vortex expanded in a wide circle, ethereal wisps of light began to detach from the lifeless bodies littering the ground and were pulled toward it. Each wisp clearly representing a lost soul, glowing faintly with a mixture of anguish and longing as though they wanted this to happen. They floated through the air, gravitating toward the centre of the vortex like moths drawn to a flame.

Theodore's heart sank as he witnessed the souls being gathered. He could somehow feel the weight of their sorrow, their unfinished stories seeking closure. The man's spell acted as a conduit, harnessing the energy of death itself to grant these souls passage to the afterworld.

Theodore felt deep down that he wanted to stop this, but he had no idea why, how, or why he felt so guilty, as though all of this was somehow his fault. But in the end, he did nothing. The spell simply expanded, gathering more and more souls from the battlefield.

Watching with his mouth hanging slightly open, Theodore raised himself to his full height until the spell had run its course, and the battlefield that once stank of death and loss now seemed empty, somehow like it was now void of the memories of the past. In a way, it was calming, but Theodore felt that what he had just witnessed was not a normal situation.

"I will see you soon," the man said to Theodore once his work had been completed and the spell had disappeared to nothing. "But do try not to take too long in your recovery. We do despise waiting, brother."

And with that, the man simply turned and walked away. Theodore thought about chasing after him, to ask him what any of this meant or what he was supposed to do next, but something within him was scared. Scared of what this man was, but more than anything else, scared of what he would tell Theodore about himself if he did indeed call this man a brother.

Eventually, When Theodore was sure that he was alone again, he managed to calm himself and looked about the sands to see if there was anything that he could use to cover himself with, but on closer inspection, everything had been too severely damaged to be of any use at all. There was something, though; near him and lying on the ground, there was a shining silver sword with a golden handle and a blackened tip. He didn't know who it had belonged to, but to survive the intense heat that must've caused such death and destruction, he could only assume that it was forged by some master craftsman and probably worth a small fortune.

Theodore picked up the sword, and it felt surprisingly light and well-balanced. It didn't awaken some deep-seated memory of him being an expert swordsman or anything of the sort, but just holding onto something made him feel a little less naked. The problem now, though, was that he was still very much naked, and that was something that he very much wanted to change. He may not have had his memories any more, but he still had a sense of embarrassment, it seemed.

Theodore stood amidst the desolate battlefield, clutching the gleaming silver sword tightly in his hand. The blade reflected the muted light of the surroundings, casting a faint shimmer against the backdrop of destruction. Though he had no recollection of his past or skills, he felt a vague sense of reassurance holding the weapon.

With resolve in his eyes, Theodore began to amble out into the battlefield, searching for anything that could offer him cover or protection. Most of what he found were shreds of former robes of black and red, a few pieces of broken armour and leather, and a handful of swords that had either been snapped entirely or had their handles either melted or burnt away. He again could not comprehend the intensity of whatever battle had occurred here and how he alone had managed to survive. Had the crater in the sand protected him somehow? Or had he simply been lucky?

Theodore's mind was clouded with questions, but he pushed them aside for the moment, focusing on his immediate needs. Eventually, as he made his way further from where he had started, he found the body of a young man lying amongst some scattered debris. The boy was still wearing a tattered black and red robe, though it had seen much finer days, and Theodore knew that even though just the thought of it sickened him, he could put the robe to far greater use than the fallen boy was going to.

With a mixture of gratitude for the boy and the thought of self-disgust, Theodore carefully unravelled the robe from the body and, lifting it slightly, pulled it free. He was happy to note that it was indeed in one piece.

Theodore quickly wrapped the cloak around himself, tying it securely in the middle, allowing the robes to drape loosely off his shoulders to offer a semblance of modesty and protection from the elements if it was so required.

Though the robes were tattered and singed at the edges, they did provide at least some cover from the elements and the prying eyes of anyone who might stumble upon him in this desolate wasteland. Theodore adjusted the robes, ensuring they provided enough freedom of movement to wield the silver sword he still clutched tightly in his hand. He now had two things to his name: an old tattered robe that he'd stolen from a dead man, and a shining silver sword, which he'd found without an owner.

Feeling slightly more composed and covered, Theodore turned his attention to the next most important things that fell flatly onto his mind: shelter, food and water. There was nothing all around him as far as the eye could see; he had no idea which way would bring him to the closest civilisation and even if they would be friendly towards him or not. He could've kicked himself for not asking the strange dark-haired man which way to walk, but something inside him told him that he really didn't want to strike up a conversation with that man.

Not being able to remember anything past his name was an inconvenience. He didn't know if he had been on the winning or losing side of some war, and if he simply walked into an enemy city, they would surely not take to him kindly. What he needed to do, was find out if he could fend for himself and lay low. But in an arid desert wasteland, the chances of surviving alone were slim.

He felt thirsty and hungry. Not like he hadn't eaten or drunk in days, but he knew that he needed to find something before the end of this day at least, or he was going to get weaker and weaker until he would eventually just lay down and die.

At least he was equipped with his makeshift attire and the gleaming silver sword.

Theodore surveyed the expanse of the battlefield once more. His nakedness had been replaced by a rough semblance of clothing and protection, and while he still lacked memories, the sense of vulnerability that he had been feeling had certainly lessened.

Spending a little time to see if any of the fallen combatants carried water flasks or the like, it was eventually clear to Theodore that this place would offer him nothing more than what it had turned into, willingly or not: a graveyard for the fallen.

Taking a deep breath, Theodore decided to venture away from desolation, his steps cautious yet purposeful. The remnants of his former life were scattered around him, an enigma he was determined to unravel one day, but for now, he had more important things to take care of.

He walked with a newfound resolve, each footfall a testament to his resilience and his refusal to be defined by his lost memories, but in reality, he had simply chosen a direction at random; they all seemed the same, and no matter how hard he tried to look, nothing seemed to offer any difference to any path that he could take.

The sun beat down mercilessly, intensifying his thirst and hunger as he walked. The landscape stretched endlessly before him, an unforgiving desert of sand and scorching heat. His resolve was tested with each step, but he pressed on, fuelled by the basic primal instinct to survive.

He scanned the surroundings, searching for any signs of life or resources that could sustain him. But the barren wasteland offered little reprieve. There were no signs of vegetation, no sources of water, and no visible paths to guide him towards potential salvation.

Theodore's mind swirled with frustration and doubt. How had he come to be in this forsaken place? What events had led to the devastation that surrounded him? The answers remained elusive, buried deep within his forgotten memories.

As the hours passed and he continued along his aimless journey, Theodore's energy waned, and the weight of his predicament bore down upon him. The silver sword felt heavy in his grip, a constant reminder of his only tangible possession. He had no choice but to rely on his determination and the faint glimmer of hope that kept him moving forward.

With the sun beginning its descent towards the horizon, Theodore's senses heightened. He strained his ears for the slightest sound, hoping to detect any signs of life or civilisation. But the desert remained silent, save for the occasional gust of hot wind that swept through the arid landscape.

The thirst that gnawed at Theodore's throat grew greater and greater until it was unbearable, while hunger gnawed at his stomach. Each passing moment deepened his understanding of the challenges he faced and the urgent need for sustenance. But his resilience persevered, pushing him forward despite the odds stacked against him.

As twilight painted the sky with hues of orange and purple, Theodore's footsteps grew weary. He knew he couldn't continue much longer without replenishment. Just when despair threatened to consume him, a faint glimmer of light in the distance caught his attention.

Heart pounding with a flicker of hope, Theodore quickened his pace towards the source of the light.

He pushed everything he could into his legs, urging them to pump over and over into the ground so that he could reach whatever salvation this was. It seemed so far away, but he had hope, a purpose and a direction, and that was what he clung to as his weary body moved.

Eventually, he saw something that he hadn't been expecting. The glimmer of light had been coming from a kind of farmhouse, sat against the backdrop of a forest that seemed to grow into existence and span away as far as his eyes could see. Theodore could only thank his lucky stars that he had picked a direction that eventually led out of the dry and arid desert sands and into a place that he instinctively knew would be water and perhaps even food.

As Theodore closed in on the farmhouse, he could see that there was a large wooden storehouse not far from the main building, and everything in his being told him that this place was where he needed to go.

As he moved, he kept his eyes open in case anyone would appear to watch his approach, but to his relief, Theodore saw nothing out of the ordinary, so he simply kept moving.

The storehouse was a wide open building with walls on three sides and no doors, and he entered without hesitating. Immediately he was greeted by a few farm animals separated into pens, and to his delight, he could see water barrels that were clearly for the animals and some crates of fruits and vegetables. They weren't in the best shape or even the cleanest, but Theodore was simply so hungry, and he knew beggars couldn't be choosers.

Theodore wasted no time as he hurried towards the water barrels, his thirst overpowering any sense of caution. He reached out and dipped his cupped hands into the cool water, bringing it to his parched lips and drinking greedily. The water revitalised him, soothing his dry throat and renewing his depleted energy.

With his immediate need for water satiated, Theodore turned his attention to the crates of fruits and vegetables. Though they were past their prime, showing signs of decay and all of them at the very least were badly bruised, they still held the promise of nourishment. He rummaged through the crates, salvaging what he could — a bruised apple, a slightly wilted carrot, and a handful of withering berries.

Though meagre, the food was a lifeline. Theodore bit into the apple, savouring the sweetness and juiciness as he chewed. It was a taste he had forgotten, a reminder of life's simple pleasures. The carrot provided a satisfying crunch, and the berries burst with a tangy flavour that invigorated his senses.

As he ate, Theodore's mind began to clear, his thoughts less clouded by hunger and thirst. Which reminded him that he was not alone in this farmhouse. The presence of the farm animals in their pens indicated that someone tended to this place, someone who could return at any moment.

But he was just so tired. He'd pushed his body past its comfortable limits, and all he wanted to do was lay himself down and sleep until he could think about what he should do next with a clear mind.

Seeing that at the back of the storehouse were large piles of hay, some bound and some left free, he knew that he would have the opportunity to rest, to conceal himself and afford himself the opportunity to refresh his broken mind.

So that is exactly what he did.

Pulling the hay all around and over himself as he sank into its soft embrace, Theodore buried himself at the back of the storehouse, and within just a few moments, he had fallen into a deep and much-needed slumber.

Chapter 2 - Found

"Ouch!" Theodore exclaimed as he was rudely awoken by the three-pronged tip of a large metal pitchfork.

The pitchfork immediately retreated before a man's voice reached Theodore's ears.

"Who's in there?" the man asked in a stern tone. "I swear if you don't show yourself, you'll be getting more than just a pitchfork in your guts!"

Theodore didn't need to be told twice, and raising his open hands through the hay that he'd covered himself with, he made his presence known.

"Please," Theodore said in a low tone. "I just slept in here… I drank some of the water and ate a handful of the food intended for the animals, but I mean you no harm… and I don't look to take anything from you."

There was a hesitation before any further response, a silence that Theodore wondered if he should fill with more of an explanation of how he arrived in this place, but before he could speak again, the man finally replied.

"Out you come," he said in a far softer voice this time, "Let's have a look at you."

Theodore carefully emerged from the haystack, his eyes adjusting to the new brightness of the room. He found himself face to face with a middle-aged man with dark hair and a short beard. His rugged features were etched with years of hard work and sun exposure, and the man's eyes bore into Theodore, assessing him with a mixture of suspicion and curiosity.

As Theodore stood before him, the man's stern expression softened slightly. He lowered the pitchfork, leaning it against the wall before extending a calloused hand towards Theodore.

"Let me help, God's what's happened to you?" the man asked solemnly. "You're lucky I didn't skewer you right then and there. What's your name? And where did you say you came from?"

Theodore hesitated for a moment, the weight of his forgotten memories pressing upon him. At least he could answer this line of questioning, though. "I... My name is Theodore," he said quietly. "I woke up in the desert with no recollection of who I am or how I got there. I walked for so long and simply ended up here…"

The man's eyebrows furrowed, his scepticism apparent. "You expect me to believe that? A convenient story, isn't it?"

Theodore's voice trembled with earnestness as he continued. "I understand it must be hard to trust a stranger, but it is the truth. I found this place whilst seeking shelter and sustenance. I have no ill intentions, and I'm grateful for the water and food I took." Then he added quickly, "I'll work off what I took if that is what you would like?"

The man studied Theodore for a few more moments, his gaze probing. Finally, he let out a gruff sigh and nodded. "Alright, stranger. For now, I'll take your word. But don't think for a second that I won't be keeping an eye on you. My name's Jack, by the way."

Relief washed over Theodore as he nodded in gratitude. "Thank you, Jack. I truly appreciate your understanding."

Jack gestured towards a wooden crate table in the centre of the room. "Sit. We'll talk more, but first I need to finish my chores. Don't you go anywhere."

Theodore obeyed, settling into a weathered wooden chair as he watched Jack tend to the animals, his movements efficient and practised. There was a sense of familiarity in the way he worked, a comfort born from years of routine and dedication.

As the moments passed, Theodore's mind began to drift, contemplating the events that had brought him to this moment. He wondered if Jack held some of the answers to his forgotten past or if this encounter was simply another chapter in his mysterious journey.

Eventually, Jack finished his tasks, disappeared for a few moments and then returned with a steaming pot and two cups. Sitting down across from Theodore at the table, he poured two helpings of steaming tea, sliding one towards Theodore.

"Drink up," Jack said gruffly. "I've heard tales of memory loss before. Some folks regain their recollections with time, while others are left to start all over again."

Theodore wrapped his hands around the warm cup, the fragrant steam rising to his face. He took a sip, savouring the comforting flavour that filled his mouth.

"I hope to find some answers," Theodore confessed, his voice tinged with a mixture of hope and uncertainty. "But for now, I'll be grateful for anything you can tell me about where I might've come from or what I was doing. Truly, I remember nothing up until the moment I awoke within that crater in the sand."

Jack regarded him thoughtfully, his eyes narrowing. "You're a peculiar one, that's for sure. But there's something about you, a certain spark that tells me there's more to your story than meets the eye. But I can see you've been through a lot. Suppose if you weren't wearing those robes, then I might've taken a different approach, but as it is."

Theodore's heart quickened at the possibility that Jack might hold some information about him, but then he remembered that these robes weren't his own. He looked down at the robes again, black with red flashings and tried to remember if he had indeed worn something similar in his past, but nothing came to him. Either way, he wasn't about to tell this man that he had stolen them from a dead man.

"And… what do these robes mean?" Theodore asked with wonder in his eyes.

"The robes are of the Brotherhood of the Flame," Jack replied. "I have heard reports…" Jack stopped and looked Theodore in the eyes. "If that's where you came from… then I'm sorry, but your home… it isn't there any more."

"The battle?" Theodore asked. It wasn't news to him, but at least it sounded like Jack knew something about the fight that had left Theodore without his memories and, even better, the people who were involved. He leaned in, eager for any shred of information that could help unravel the mysteries that plagued him.

"The Brotherhood, the ones who wear the robes as you do, they were found by the King's army in their fort, and I've heard that the place is no more. I'm sorry, Theodore, but if that's where you've come from, then I don't know how you survived."

Theodore's heart sank as Jack delivered the devastating news. The Brotherhood of the Flame, his supposed home, had been decimated by the King's army. The reality of the battle that had taken his memories and seemingly his identity crashed over him like a tidal wave. But then, was it his home? For all he knew, he could've been on the side of the King's army.

Surely that was the right side to be on, wasn't it? He tried to figure out if Jack was happy that the King's army had removed the Brotherhood from their home or not, but it seemed like the man was giving nothing away. He could only assume, from what Jack had said about the robe, that he was in favour of the Brotherhood and not the King.

Theodore struggled to process the information, his mind swirling with grief, confusion, and a lingering sense of guilt. The robes he wore, once symbols of his supposed belonging, now held a weight of sorrow and loss. He couldn't help but wonder if he had played a part in the destruction that befell his former comrades, whichever side they happened to be on.

"I... I don't remember anything," Theodore whispered, his voice heavy with emotion. "But I can't shake this feeling... this sense that I'm somehow responsible, that I had a role to play in what happened."

Jack's expression softened, a glimmer of empathy in his eyes. "It's natural to feel that way, especially when you're confronted with such devastation. But you can't blame yourself for things you can't remember. You have a chance now to start anew, to discover who you truly are."

Theodore nodded, gratitude and determination taking root within him. He couldn't change the past or reclaim his memories right now, but he could at least work to shape his future and strive to become someone worthy of the second chance he had been given.

"I... I appreciate your understanding and guidance, Jack," Theodore said, his voice steady despite the turmoil within. "I don't know where to go from here, but I'm willing to learn, to rebuild, and to find my place in this world."

Jack regarded Theodore with a newfound respect. "You've got a strength about you, Theodore. I'll do what I can to help you on your journey. But remember, the path ahead won't be easy. There are forces at play, secrets to uncover, and trials to face. Some people may blame you for the actions of the past, whatever they may be, but remain strong, and you'll find your way."

Theodore's gaze hardened, determination replacing his earlier doubt. "I'm ready to face whatever comes my way. I won't let my lost memories define me. I will forge my own path and discover the truth, no matter how difficult it may be."

Jack nodded approvingly, a hint of a smile touching his weathered face. "Then, Theodore, welcome to the journey of self-discovery. We'll start by learning the ways of this farm and the skills required to survive. And along the way, we might just find the answers you seek."

It took a moment for Theodore to realise that Jack was telling him that he was going to put him to work, but in truth, what other options did he have?

He had nowhere to go, no one to look out for or care for and in this entire world, he had no idea how he was even going to survive. Then there was Jack, a stranger who had simply decided to give him a chance.

"Dad, Dad!" a young boy's voice entered the storage building, and its small owner followed it. The young boy couldn't have been any older than seven or eight, and he looked identical to his father, only in a much smaller form and with no facial hair.

The boy came to a skidding halt as soon as his eyes fell upon Theodore, and as he did so, Jack spoke up.

"Don't worry, Malek," Jack said. "This is my new friend, Theodore. He will be helping us around the farm, OK?"

Malek looked back and forth between Theodore and his father but kept his lips tightly shut.

"Don't be scared, son," Jack encouraged in a soothing tone.

"How are you doing?" Theodore asked calmly and offered a warm smile along with his question.

"O… OK…," the boy replied eventually, still evidently unsure of what was happening. "Hello," he said, trying to steel himself.

"Theodore, this is Malek, my son," Jack said unnecessarily. "He knows he shouldn't be running around out here, and he knows he shouldn't be just bursting into places without making his presence known."

"But I called out," Malek replied. "I didn't just burst in."

"He has a point, you know," Theodore agreed with Malek. "He did call out."

Jack gave Theodore a harsh look as if to tell him not to get involved and then turned back to his son.

"OK then, running. You know you shouldn't run around here; it could be dangerous."

"But you said I could run if something's urgent," Malek said.

"That's true," Jack replied. "Is there something urgent happening?"

"Yes," Malek replied.

"And that is?"

"Oh, right! There are some people coming. They are almost here. They look shiny in all their armour and their swords and stuff." The words seemed to shock Jack, though Malek didn't seem to have any feelings about the approaching soldiers one way or another.

"Get back into the house, Malek," Jack ordered, and the boy did not even stop to question the order, dutifully obliging and leaving as quickly as he'd arrived.

"Theodore, you need to get out of those robes right now. If the guards catch you looking like that, it doesn't bear thinking about. Take them off now, quickly, quickly."

Theodore hesitated for a moment but watched as Jack turned his back and moved to the entrance of the storehouse to see where the soldiers were. Turning back to see Theodore entirely naked and covering himself with his hands, Jack looked slightly calmer.

"We have about five minutes," he said. "I'll get you something to wear, but you need to keep your mouth shut. Follow my lead, and if they ask you any questions, just look at me, right?"

Theodore nodded, and a second later, Jack was gone. He wondered if it would be a good idea to go and fish his sword out of the hay where he had been hiding, though he concluded that it probably wouldn't be a good idea to fight off well-armed, armoured and trained soldiers with a sword that very well may have come from one of them. Plus, regardless of how Jack was taking their arrival, he didn't know if he was actually one of them yet or not; perhaps they could be out here looking for him to try to help.

Jack then returned a moment later with a pair of brown trousers and a thin white shirt. Taking them and putting them on, Theodore couldn't help but feel that these clothes must've been uncomfortable, even for a farmer.

"Go and stand over there, at the back," Jack muttered, pointing to where Theodore had been hiding the night before. He dutifully moved into position and kept his head facing downwards.

"By the order of the King! We are here to search for survivors of the battle between the King's armies and the treacherous mages of the Brotherhood of the Flame. Do you have anything to declare?"

The shout sounded rehearsed and not specific to this location, but the voice sent shivers down Theodore's spine. It sounded very much like they were looking for survivors, but to him, it sounded like whenever they found any, they were to be punished, killed perhaps, rather than welcomed back into the fold with open arms.

Theodore didn't feel like a fire mage, though. Yes, he had awoken on a battlefield surrounded by people who looked as though they had been killed by fire magic, and yes, he had worn the cloak of a member of the Brotherhood – but he had stolen that anyway. Regardless, he still didn't have his memories, so there was nothing that he could do to be sure either way.

"We are in here," Jack announced loudly as he stepped out of the storehouse. Theodore still couldn't see the soldiers, but he could tell from the volume that they would no doubt be within in a second or two.

"Do you have anything to declare?" The soldier replied. "Open your eyes."

Theodore didn't know why, but as soon as he heard that phrase, along with it came the tiny feeling of sadness, perhaps even pain. But then it was gone. He didn't know what it was, but those words just seemed so familiar.

"Anyone else here?" the soldier said, apparently fine with whatever he had seen in Jack's eyes.

"There's my hand back there in the stable. Not really fit for a meeting with soldiers in such clean uniforms, though. Bit of a rough one is our Theo."

But the soldier didn't seem to care for Jack's attempt to keep the soldiers away, and within a second, they had entered the storehouse.

A group of five soldiers, one of them very clearly the superior of the group, all looked at Theodore, who did his best to keep his eyes fixed on the ground and his arms down by his sides.

Theodore could feel the soldiers' gaze upon him, their eyes scrutinising his every move. He could sense the tension in the air, their suspicion palpable. He tried to steady his racing heart, reminding himself to stay calm and follow Jack's lead.

One of the soldiers, the apparent leader, stepped forward, his armour gleaming in the dim light of the storehouse. He carried an air of authority, his eyes sharp and piercing. Theodore dared not meet his gaze, his head still bowed and eyes fixed on the ground.

"Who are you?" the soldier demanded, his voice laced with a mix of curiosity and authority. "And why are you here?"

Theodore stayed silent, his throat tightening with unease. He searched for strength in Jack's presence, hoping the man would intervene and provide some semblance of protection.

Jack, ever the quick thinker, stepped forward and answered, "This is Theodore, our farmhand who we pay in shelter. He's harmless, just trying to find his place in this world."

The leader of the soldiers studied Theodore for a moment longer before turning his attention back to Jack. "Very well," he said, a hint of scepticism in his tone. "But be warned, anyone associated with the Brotherhood of the Flame will face consequences. We won't hesitate to root out the traitors."

Then he began to turn away but stopped in the motion, turning back to face Theodore.

"Open your eyes," he ordered.

Chapter 3 - Magic

"What?" Theodore asked without looking up. "Why?" He didn't know what the order meant, but his instinct was to try to refuse right away. There was just something about it that seemed wrong, like it was a threat somehow.

"Because I want to look into them," the soldier said through gritted teeth, "to see if you have any magic within you. Now do what you're told, or I'll carve your eyes out myself and have a good look on the backs of them to see what you're hiding."

"Don't worry, Theo," Jack said from behind the soldiers. "Let them have a look, and they'll be on their way."

Theodore's heart raced as he weighed his options. The soldier's threat hung heavily in the air, and the consequences of resistance seemed dire. He thought about diving into the hay for his sword to try to defend himself, but again he knew it would be futile, and no matter the fact that he didn't really know Jack, he didn't want to put the man at risk.

Reluctantly, Theodore lifted his gaze, meeting the soldier's piercing eyes.

The soldier approached, his expression grim, and reached out to pry open Theodore's eyelids. Theodore's instincts again screamed at him to resist, to protect his secrets, but he fought against his own resistance and allowed the soldier to examine his eyes.

The soldier's scrutiny lasted only a moment before he released Theodore's eyelids and took a step back. His face showed a mix of surprise and confusion as if what he had witnessed had defied his expectations.

"There's no trace of magic," the soldier muttered, his voice heavy with disbelief.

Jack's voice cut through the tense silence. "I told you he's harmless. Now, if there's nothing else, we have work to do."

The soldier grumbled under his breath, clearly dissatisfied with the outcome. With a final suspicious glance towards Theodore, he turned and re-joined his comrades, leaving the farmstead behind.

As the soldiers departed, Theodore's mind swirled with a mix of relief and curiosity. He hadn't known what to expect, but the soldier's reaction suggested that he possessed no inherent magical abilities. This revelation only deepened the mystery surrounding his past and the Brotherhood of the Flame.

Jack approached Theodore, a comforting hand on his shoulder. "You handled yourself well," he said, his voice filled with admiration. "I didn't expect them to leave so easily. We're fortunate that you look and smell as bad as you do, I think they wanted to get out of here as soon as possible!"

Theodore nodded, but then something began to gnaw at him.

"My lack of magic? They can tell that by looking into my eyes. And tell me, what would've happened if they did detect magic within me?"

Jack let his hand fall away from Theodore before he spoke solemnly. "It's easy to forget how little you must know about this world," he said. "Some things that are just so normal… well, it doesn't really matter, I suppose. All you need to know is that King Roderick has outlawed all magic from this kingdom. Well, all except the air mages, I suppose it's because they're a part of his army, so I've heard. In any case, if you are found to have magic within you, or are found harbouring one that does, then that's the end of you." Jack gestured with a finger across his throat.

Theodore's mouth hung open in disbelief. "And you were so sure that I had no magic that you risked your life for me?"

"Nah, it wasn't much of a risk," Jack said. "I would've seen the mana within your eyes when we spoke earlier; I know you don't have anything to hide."

"But what if I do?" Theodore asked with wide eyes. "What if I'm hiding things that could get me and your entire family killed, but I just don't remember?"

"Then that's not your fault," Jack replied. "If you aren't doing it on purpose, then you can't be blamed. Besides, I see something in you, no not magic," he added quickly, "something else, like I should help you. I don't know why, but that's just the way I'm wired, I guess."

Theodore looked at Jack for a long moment, trying to detect if he was being sarcastic or sincere. In the end, he could only do one thing, and that was to thank the man.

"Thank you," Theodore said simply. "Thank you for taking a chance on me."

"Listen, friend," Jack said. "I know that we don't really know each other and all, but it seems to me that when somebody comes to you in need of a little help, it's the decent thing to do what you can to provide that help. If that person then turns that back against you, then that's on them, not you. I won't let anybody else change who I am." Then he lowered his voice to just above a whisper. "And between you and me, I think the mages have it tough enough already. What that King Roderick has done – and I don't just mean to the mages, but to the kingdom as a whole – I'm surprised there hasn't been a full-scale uprising already. I mean, we do well for ourselves here, and we can afford to pay our way, but I know some that don't, and each month they seem to want more and more from us. Eventually, there won't be anything left."

Theodore stared at Jack for a long while before he responded. He wasn't sure why Jack had just told him so much information, but the information was what he lacked, so he was grateful to hear it.

Theodore's gratitude for Jack's candidness mingled with a newfound sense of empathy for the plight of the mages and the kingdom as a whole. A few pieces of the puzzle began to fall into place, connecting the dots of the larger picture. His amnesia may have robbed him of his memories, but it also granted him the opportunity to approach the world with fresh eyes and an unbiased perspective.

"I understand," Theodore said, his voice filled with sincerity. "And I want to help in any way that I can. If there's a way to bring change and restore balance and fairness to this kingdom, then count me in."

Jack's eyes sparkled with a mixture of appreciation and hope. "I had a feeling you might say that," he replied, a smile tugging at the corners of his lips. "We may be just a small farmstead, but we have our own ways of making a difference. The first step is to work the land, provide for those who need it and share what we have. But I have a feeling that eventually there will come a time when we'll need to take a stand, to fight for what's right. And that's when you'll stand with us."

Theodore nodded in silent acceptance of his task. He would work, and he would do his best to make the lives of the people around him a little easier because that was the right thing to do.

"Oh!" Theodore suddenly exclaimed. "I forgot that I found something out there where I woke up on the battlefield." And moving over to the hay where he had hidden himself, he rummaged around for a moment before producing the beautiful silver sword that he had liberated from the battlefield. "It might come in handy at some point?"

Jack's eyes widened in surprise as he beheld the gleaming silver sword Theodore presented. He reached out and took the weapon, examining it closely. The craftsmanship was impeccable, and it radiated a sense of power and purpose.

"This is no ordinary weapon," Jack remarked, his voice filled with awe. "It's been forged with great skill and care. The fact that you found it on the battlefield suggests that it may have belonged to someone of importance."

Theodore nodded, a flicker of intrigue in his eyes. "It feels right in my hands like it's been perfectly balanced. Even if I can't remember who I was, this sword feels like it's a part of my new life."

Jack handed the sword back to Theodore. "Then it shall serve you well," he said. "Hold onto it, for it may hold the key to unlocking the mysteries of your past."

As Theodore gripped the sword, a surge of confidence coursed through him. He could sense the hours and days that had been put into forging it, and he knew that it would certainly aid him in any battles to come. With the sword in his possession and a newfound purpose burning within him, he felt ready to face whatever challenges lay ahead.

The problem was, though, that the challenges that lay ahead for the rest of the day all revolved around animals and farm work. Certainly nothing that involved an ornate-bladed weapon.

As the morning sun rose higher in the sky, Theodore and Jack set out to tend to the daily chores of the farm. It was something completely new to Theodore, much like everything was, but this seemed so alien to him like his body and muscles had no recollection of whatever it was that he was trying to get them to do.

Theodore tucked the silver sword into his makeshift belt, knowing that, for now, its purpose would have to wait. Today, his task was to learn the ways of a farmer, to understand the rhythms of the land and the needs of the animals. He was going to give it his all, no matter what.

They started with the livestock, beginning with the cows. Theodore watched intently as Jack demonstrated how to milk them, his hands moving with practised ease. As he worked, he explained how he shared the milk around with his neighbours so that they had something nutritious to drink, even if they had to give almost everything they had to the crown.

Then it was Theodore's turn to try. He approached the gentle cow cautiously, feeling a mix of nervousness and anticipation. Placing the bucket beneath the udders, he mimicked Jack's motions, his hands tentative at first.

Gradually, he gained confidence, finding a rhythm that elicited a steady stream of milk. To his surprise, the cow seemed not to give a single care, and eventually, their buckets were full.

Next, they moved on to the chickens, gathering eggs from the coop. Theodore carefully reached into the nests, feeling the warmth of the eggs against his palms. He marvelled at the intricate patterns and colours of the shells, each one a small treasure of life. As he placed the eggs gently into the basket, he couldn't help but feel a sense of fulfilment, a connection to the cycle of nature.

Theodore's education continued as they tended to the crops. Jack taught him how to prepare the soil, digging trenches and removing weeds that threatened to choke the young plants. Theodore's hands quickly grew cut and bruised as he worked the earth, his whining muscles straining with the effort. Sweat dripped down his brow, mingling with the dust and grime of the farm, but he persevered, driven by a determination to learn and contribute. It was clear to Theodore at this point that he hadn't been much of a worker in his past life. His body seemed to object to each and every strain, and his muscles seemed tiny in comparison to Jack's, who had clearly been tending to this farm for much, if not all, of his life.

Watering the crops became a rhythmic dance as Theodore carefully guided the flow of water from the nearby well. He watched as the thirsty plants soaked up the life-giving liquid, their leaves perking up with gratitude. It was a simple act, but one that brought Theodore a sense of satisfaction, knowing that he played a role in nourishing both the land and its inhabitants.

Throughout the day, Theodore learned about the intricacies of farm life. He witnessed the delicate balance between tending to the needs of the animals and the demands of the land. He discovered the importance of hard work, patience, and resilience in the face of unpredictable weather and the challenges of rural life.

By the time the sun began its descent, casting long shadows across the farm, Theodore felt a deep appreciation for the work that went into every aspect of farming. The simple routines offered him a glimpse into the interconnectedness of all living things, reminding him of the fragility and strength of the natural world.

As Theodore and Jack made their way back to the farmhouse, exhausted but content, a sense of belonging settled within Theodore's heart. The farm had become more than just a place of refuge; it was now a part of him, a symbol of growth and a community to nurture.

"You're welcome to sleep out here in the storehouse tonight. I'm sorry I don't have much room in the house, but it doesn't look like rain tonight, and the air is warm…"

"It's fine," Theodore replied with a smile. "Honestly, I think it will give me some time alone with my thoughts."

Jack offered Theodore a half-hearted smile and turned to leave. Theodore quickly moved over to the hay where he had slept previously and lay down to rest for the night. It was less comfortable this time as he was aware that the hay was prickling him from beneath, but nevertheless, a combination of satisfaction from a hard day's work and fatigue meant that again, he didn't keep his eyes open for very long.

Chapter 4 - Memories

High above the farm where Theodore had just spent his day working, his attention fell upon a single white feather that listed back and forth. He wasn't entirely sure how his consciousness had managed to climb so high that it could follow the path of the feather as it rose and fell, but he remained silent as he watched it, wondering which way it was going to go next.

Theodore watched as the feather rose high up into the air, gently turned and then began a nosedive down toward the storehouse where his physical body slept. He watched as it slowly and quietly gained speed as it accelerated down towards the roof of the storehouse. It fell and fell, and by the time it reached the roof of the building, it suddenly changed path, spinning and twirling through the open entranceway and down to just inches off the ground. The feather didn't slow in its pace, though.

Swirling about the animals, through the chicken coop and between the legs of the cows, the feather then sped back outside as though caught in some divine hurricane. It traversed the trenches that Theodore and Jack had dug themselves that very day through the growing plants and around the well that held the water. The feather was beautiful, but Theodore couldn't help but think that it held some purpose that he was yet to divine.

But then the feather began to rise again, up high into the sky above, and Theodore couldn't figure out what it was doing or why it was travelling so high.

Up, up and up it went, twirling all the way as though caught in an updraft, but now not once did it begin to fall again. The feather had a destination in mind, and nothing was going to force it to stray from its path.

Theodore's gaze followed the ascending feather, his mind captivated by its graceful dance through the vast expanse of the sky. As the feather soared higher, it carried Theodore's imagination along with it, transporting him to a place beyond the boundaries of his current reality.

As the feather continued its ascent, the world below transformed into a distant tapestry of colours and patterns. Theodore marvelled at the patchwork of arid desert sands, fields, rivers, and forests stretching out in all directions, forming a breathtaking landscape beneath him. The ordinary became extraordinary as he witnessed the beauty of nature from this elevated perspective.

But as the feather soared even higher, a new sight came into view. In the distance, Theodore spotted what looked like some ethereal city, suspended in the sky by an intricate network of gigantic balloons and colossal fans. The city seemed to defy gravity, floating with an air of enchantment and mystery. The architecture was unlike anything Theodore could ever imagine, a blend of elegance and innovation, whites and golds forming sharp points against the backdrop of the clear blue sky.

The buildings shimmered in hues of gold and white, their surfaces adorned with intricate carvings and delicate latticework. Towering structures reached towards the heavens, their spires disappearing into the clouds. Gleaming glass domes revealed gardens and parks, vibrant with life and colour. It was a city of wonder, a testament to its creator's ingenuity and the power of the air.

As the feather approached the city, Theodore could hear the faint hum of the giant fans propelling the city forward and keeping it up high in the sky. The air around him carried a distinct energy, a swirling mix of excitement and anticipation. This was a place where the Cyclonic Essence resided, where the air mages practised the power of wind and storms.

Suddenly, a flash of memory pierced through Theodore's mind. It was fleeting, like a whisper carried by the wind, but it held significance. He remembered stories of the Cyclonic Essence, the air mages who called this floating city their home. They possessed the ability to manipulate the very air itself, summoning storms, creating gusts of wind, and wielding the power of flight.

But no, it was more than that. He remembered this place. It was like it had once been his home, and he struggled to hold onto that memory.

The realisation sent a shiver down Theodore's spine. The feather, the city, the memory — it all converged, forming a connection to his forgotten past. He felt a surge of longing, a yearning to uncover more about his own connection to the air mages and the magic that he simply knew once flowed through his veins.

As the feather disappeared into the bustling streets of the floating city, Theodore knew that this encounter was no mere coincidence. It was a sign, a beckoning towards the truth that lay dormant within him.

He willed his mind to follow the feather, and the visions before him dutifully obliged. Theodore found himself now within a house, staring up at a man and a woman, who were positively beaming down at him.

Theodore stood in awe as he witnessed the memory unfolding before his eyes. And there was something more now; he recognised the man and woman standing over him, their faces radiating love and pride. They were his parents.

The memory flooded his senses, immersing him in a warmth and familiarity that he felt had been lost to him for so long.

His father, with his kind eyes and weathered hands, knelt down before the young Theodore, his voice gentle yet filled with excitement. "Do you feel it, son?" he asked, his words tinged with anticipation. "The power within you, waiting to be awakened?"

Theodore's younger self looked up at his father, his eyes shimmering with curiosity. "What power, father?" he asked, his voice filled with innocent wonder.

His mother, standing beside his father, smiled warmly. "You are special, my child," she said, her voice carrying a melody of love and reassurance. "You possess the Cyclonic Essence, the magic of the wind and storms!"

Theodore's heart swelled with a mixture of awe and longing as the memory continued to unfold. He remembered exactly how he had felt in this moment the first time he had experienced it, the moment he had made his parents so proud, and the moment that he knew that one day he would become a powerful air mage.

His father placed a hand on his shoulder, his touch grounding Theodore in the present moment. "Listen to the wind, my son," he said, his voice carrying the weight of ancient wisdom. "Feel its embrace, its power. Breathe it in and let it awaken the Cyclonic Essence within you."

Theodore closed his eyes, surrendering himself to the elements. He felt the air caress his skin, carrying with it a surge of energy. The wind responded to his presence, swirling and dancing around him in a delicate choreography.

With a deep breath, Theodore spread his arms wide, embracing the power that coursed through his veins. He called upon the Cyclonic Essence within him, and in that moment, he became one with the wind. His eyes shot open, and there Theodore knew, both the Theodore of the memory and the Theodore witnessing it now, that his eyes glowed with a bright golden hue, betraying to all who would look, that he was an air mage.

Theodore's golden eyes shimmered with the raw power of the Cyclonic Essence as he stood amidst the swirling winds. His younger self, filled with awe and wonder, marvelled at the spectacle before him. The winds danced in response to his presence, bending and swaying as if paying homage to their newfound master.

His parents watched with a mixture of pride and tenderness, their love for their son shining brightly in their eyes. They knew that this moment marked the beginning of Theodore's journey as an air mage, a guardian of the floating city.

The memory shifted, transporting Theodore to a grand workshop nestled within the heart of the city. The workshop buzzed with activity as air mages tended to the intricate mechanisms that kept the city afloat. Giant balloons, meticulously maintained and adorned with vibrant colours, bobbed overhead while massive fans whirred all around with a rhythmic hum.

Young Theodore eagerly joined his fellow air mages, his eyes brimming with excitement. He observed the skilled artisans meticulously inspecting the balloons, adjusting their buoyancy, and ensuring their structural integrity. They were responsible for maintaining the delicate balance between the city's weight and the lifting power of the balloons, and the only way to do so was for them all to call upon their Cyclonic Essence.

And again, Theodore could remember. With each passing day, he honed his skills, learning the delicate art of tending to the balloons. He meticulously checked for any signs of wear or tear, skilfully repaired the delicate fabric, and carefully adjusted the airflow within them to maintain the city's equilibrium.

His days had been filled with a sense of purpose and camaraderie. He worked alongside his fellow air mages, sharing laughter and stories as they collectively nurtured the lifeblood of their floating home. The bonds forged in the workshop ran deep, and the air mages were as a family.

As Theodore relived this memory, he couldn't help but feel a profound sense of belonging. The workshop had been a sanctuary, a place where he had discovered his true potential and found solace in the company of kindred spirits. He had embraced his role as a protector of the city, knowing that his efforts helped ensure the safety and prosperity of its inhabitants.

Theodore's heart swelled with gratitude for his parents, who had nurtured his gifts and guided him on this path. Their love and support had ignited the flame within him, and he vowed to honour their memory, but what had happened to them still evaded him.

Theodore willed his mind to return to action, to remember all the things that he had forgotten, but no matter how hard he tried to force it, the more it simply seemed out of reach. In the end, he resigned to the fact that he would be shown by the memories whatever they would, and he would have no say in the matter.

Theodore's reminiscences then brought him to another pivotal moment in his past — the memory of a dark alleyway, where he found himself confronted by three larger boys, their sneers filled with malice. The memory had a sharp edge to it, a tinge of fear mingling with determination.

Theodore, now a teenager, stood his ground, his golden eyes narrowing as he faced his assailants. They towered over him, their intimidating presence intended to provoke fear. But Theodore had been trained in the ways of air mana, and he knew that his abilities could be his greatest weapon.

The first bully lunged forward, his fist aimed at Theodore's face. But Theodore's reflexes were swift. He sidestepped the attack with grace, his body moving as though it had been carried on the wind. In response, he summoned a whirlwind, directing it towards his assailant, and the spell caught the bully off guard, knocking him off balance and sending him crashing into a nearby wall.

The second bully, undeterred, charged at Theodore, aiming to tackle him to the ground. Theodore evaded the assault again, using his agility to his advantage. This time he conjured a powerful gust of wind, propelling himself into the air and out of harm's way. As he soared above his attackers, he unleashed a torrent of air blades down towards the ground, slicing through the air with precision, and the blades struck their mark, leaving the bully momentarily disoriented and vulnerable, tiny cuts beginning to bleed all over his body.

Meanwhile, the third bully stepped forward cautiously, his eyes filled with a mix of fear and aggression. He attempted to cast a gust of wind of his own, hoping to disrupt Theodore's balance. But Theodore, drawing upon his inner strength, channelled his mana into a counter-spell. A pulsating wave of energy emanated from him, and through the look on the third boy's face, Theodore could tell that he could no longer cast his spell. Both Theodore and the memory of Theodore smiled a cocky smirk as they both realised that their spell had worked: he was able to prevent the others around him from using their own mana.

The bully's spell dissipated into nothingness, leaving him defenceless.

Seizing the opportunity, Theodore summoned a powerful cyclone, whipping the air around him into a swirling vortex. The cyclone acted as his ally, lashing out at the remaining bully. Gusts of wind buffeted the assailant, sending him sprawling to the ground. Helpless, he could only watch as Theodore's mastery over the Cyclonic Essence overwhelmed him.

With the fight now firmly in his control, Theodore focused his mana, directing a concentrated blast of air towards each bully in succession. The force of the blasts knocked them off their feet, leaving them battered and defeated.

Theodore stood triumphant amidst the aftermath, his chest heaving with exertion and adrenaline. His golden eyes blazed with a combination of resolve and self-discovery. In this moment, he had tapped into the essence of his power, emerging victorious against those who sought to intimidate and harm him.

As the memory finally began to fade, Theodore reflected on the significance of this encounter. It was a testament to his own strength and resilience, a reminder of the potential that lay dormant within him. The fight had unveiled a glimpse of his true capabilities, reaffirming his identity as an air mage and igniting a spark of purpose within him.

Then the memory faded once more, and Theodore was greeted with a new scene. He was back in his parent's house, though this time it was their bedroom. He remembered exactly how it looked and where everything was placed. But more than that, he remembered this moment.

His mother lay on the bed, her skin grey and her body frail. His father was in the other room; this was the time for Theodore to be alone with his mother. To say his goodbyes to her.

Theodore felt the weight of his sorrow pressing down upon him. He was in his mid-twenties at this point, he knew, but that did nothing to stave off the feeling of loss and despair because those were feelings that never left a person, and experiencing them never made the next time any easier.

"Mother, please don't leave us," Theodore heard himself begging through his tears. "Please... you don't have to. We haven't tried everything... surely..."

Theodore's mother weakly raised an arm from the bed and softly placed it upon her son's cheek.

"My time has come, my son. My beautiful son."

Theodore's voice wavered as he choked back sobs, his heart breaking at the sight of his mother's weakened state. He held her delicate hand in his, desperate for any sign of hope, any glimmer of a chance to keep her with him.

His mother's touch was feeble, but her eyes radiated love and reassurance. Her voice, though faint, carried a strength that resonated deep within Theodore's soul. "Listen to me, my brave son," she whispered, her words fragile yet filled with unwavering certainty. "Life is a journey, and sometimes our paths take unexpected turns. It is not for us to question why but to embrace the moments we are given and cherish the love we hold in our hearts. We will always be the people we are supposed to be. Be good, and lead a good life, my son, and I will be awaiting you in the afterworld."

Tears streamed down Theodore's face as he clung to his mother's every word. The weight of the impending loss bore down upon him, but he drew strength from her unwavering spirit.

"Promise me," she continued, her voice barely above a whisper, "that you will carry the essence of the wind within you. Let it guide you, protect you, and bring you solace in the face of adversity. Embrace your identity as an air mage, and let the Cyclonic Essence be your beacon of light."

Theodore nodded, his voice choked with emotion. "I promise, Mother,' he managed to utter, his voice quivering. "I will honour your memory, and I will strive to become the person you've always believed I could be."

A gentle smile graced his mother's lips as her eyelids began to flutter. "You have always been my greatest source of pride and joy," she murmured, her voice growing fainter. "Never forget that, my dear Theodore. I will always be with you, watching over you."

With those final words, Theodore's mother closed her eyes, her hand falling limp in his grasp. A profound silence settled over the room, mingling with Theodore's grief and pain.

And that was it. Theodore's vision faded to darkness, but deep down inside, he remembered that vow to his mother. He had promised to never forget, to honour her as well as the Cyclonic Essence within, and it was a promise that he once again intended to keep.

Chapter 5 - Life

A low mooing from the cows wanting their morning feed woke Theodore, though, in truth, his awakening had been supplemented by the warmth of the sunlight on his face as it broke through the gaps in the storehouse. Theodore didn't get up right away; he felt somehow comfortable in the warmth and the soft hay, and what was more, he remembered a big part of who he was now. It wasn't everything, but he remembered his life in the sky city, his parents, and his mana. He remembered how he had been a skilled mage who the sky city had relied upon to keep them floating high above the rest of civilisation, safe and flourishing.

Theodore slowly rose from his makeshift bed; the memories of his past swirled within him. He continued to probe his broken mind for more information within, but as usual, it proved stubborn and unhelpful. It was clear that whatever had allowed Theodore to remember his past was going to do so on its own terms.

The already familiar sights and sounds of the farm greeted him. The gentle mooing of the cows and the rustling of the wind through the fields outside reminded him of the simple beauty that existed in this grounded world. Yet, deep within him, Theodore yearned to return to the city that felt all too familiar to him – the city in the sky.

"Ah, you're finally awake," Jack said as he walked carefree into the storehouse. He offered Theodore a warm smile and rolled up his sleeves, ready to begin working for the day.

Theodore returned Jack's smile, gratitude shining in his eyes. He felt a kinship with Jack, a connection that went beyond the ordinary farmer-apprentice relationship - like they had already become brothers. Jack had taken him in, offered him shelter, and provided him with guidance and support when he needed it most. Theodore owed him a debt of gratitude that he couldn't easily repay.

"Good morning, Jack," Theodore greeted, his voice filled with both enthusiasm and determination. "I'm ready to work and make a difference today."

Jack chuckled, the sound resonating with warmth and familiarity. "That's the spirit, Theodore. We have much to do, but we'll make it happen together."

Theodore joined Jack as they made their way over to the cows, the scent of hay and livestock filling the air. The cows looked up expectantly, their large, gentle eyes meeting Theodore's gaze. He approached them with a sense of reverence, remembering his role in tending to these animals the day before.

But something felt different to Theodore as he worked. He knew who he was now, didn't he? He was an air mage, filled with the Cyclonic Essence, yet… he had nothing. He didn't feel the mana inside him even for one fleeting second. He tried to search for it by probing his own faculties, but even though he remembered using his mana in his past and in his dreams, it simply wasn't there.

"Jack… I need to tell you something," Theodore announced suddenly. He hadn't thought much about what he would say, but Jack deserved to hear the truth about Theodore.

Jack turned to Theodore, a curious expression on his face. "What is it?" he asked, his voice laced with concern. He could sense that something was weighing heavily on Theodore's mind.

Theodore took a deep breath, gathering his thoughts. "Jack, I've been remembering things," he began, his voice steady yet filled with a tinge of uncertainty. "I remember my life in the sky city, my parents, and my role as an air mage. But... something feels different from how I remember it. I can't feel the presence of my mana, the Cyclonic Essence, within me anymore."

A flicker of surprise crossed Jack's face, quickly replaced by fear, and he took three steps back away from Theodore.

"An… air mage?" he pushed his hands out in front of him as though in surrender. "You're an air mage?" he almost spat out the words.

Theodore was taken aback by Jack's sudden reaction. The fear in Jack's eyes and the way he distanced himself sent a wave of confusion through him. He hadn't expected this kind of response from someone he had come to trust and confide in.

"Jack, what's wrong?" Theodore asked, his voice laced with concern. "Why are you acting like this? I thought you would understand."

Jack took a deep breath, visibly composing himself. His voice trembled slightly as he spoke. "Theodore, you don't understand," he said, his words filled with a combination of fear and apprehension. "Air mages... they... you..." Jack managed to calm himself, sighing deeply. "The air mages are a part of King Roderick's army. They are the only magic users that he will allow, and I suspect only if they do his bidding. You have to understand, Theodore, that users of the Cyclonic Essence are not only the enemy of the free people but also of all other mages. I can't believe... I don't... are you sure that this is who you are, Theodore?"

Theodore's heart sank as he listened to Jack's words. The fear and apprehension in his friend's voice only deepened Theodore's own sense of uncertainty. He had expected Jack to be surprised, perhaps even sceptical, but he hadn't anticipated this level of fear and mistrust.

"I... I am certain of my memories, Jack," Theodore replied, his voice filled with a determination and a vulnerability he hadn't displayed before. "I remember my life in the city in the sky, my parents... but beyond that, it's still all blank. But listen to me, Jack. What you are saying, it can't be true. The place in my memories was high up in the clouds, far away from the kingdom and the King; the mages there didn't fight for or serve the King; all they wanted to do was lead their lives and keep them apart from everything else. I don't know what happened to change any of this, but I am sure that the air mages are not the monsters you have been led to believe."

Jack's eyes flickered between doubt and confusion, torn between the stories he had heard and Theodore's unwavering conviction. He sighed heavily, his shoulders slumping with the weight of the conflicting information.

"Theodore, I don't know what to believe anymore," Jack admitted, his voice tinged with vulnerability. "The world has changed so much. The kingdom has cracked down on magic, and those who possess it are either forced to serve the King or go into hiding. I know that in the King's armies, air mages are used as weapons, and not many can stand up to them. But I also trust my instincts. I don't see those mages within you. I know that we have only just met, but I see kindness and caring within you and not a desire to cause hurt and suffering."

Theodore's brow furrowed, his mind racing to make sense of the disparity between his memories and Jack's accounts of the current state of affairs. He couldn't deny the possibility that things had changed in the time he had lost, but he couldn't reconcile the image of the air mages he remembered with the stories of their oppression.

"But Jack, what about the essence of who we are?" Theodore pressed, his voice filled with frustration. "Can the Cyclonic Essence, the very magic that flows through the air mages, change so drastically? Can it turn something noble and pure into a tool of oppression? I don't believe it, Jack. I refuse to believe that the air mages I remember are now serving the King as pawns. My mother taught me to be a good man, to lead a life of worth and value, and that is a promise I made to her that I would never break, and I make that same promise to you right now."

Jack met Theodore's gaze, the conflict within him still evident. "Theodore, I wish I could see the world through your eyes to hold on to that hope and belief," he said, his voice heavy with a mix of regret and uncertainty. "But the reality is harsh, and the stories I've heard paint a different picture. I don't want to believe them either, but it's hard to ignore the suffering and the fear that plagues our land."

Theodore's shoulders slumped as he absorbed Jack's words. The disconnect between his memories and the present reality weighed heavily upon him. He felt a surge of frustration at his own limitations, unable to bridge the gap between the two versions of the world that existed within him.

"Jack, I understand your concerns, and I appreciate your honesty,' Theodore said. "But I cannot let go of who I remember myself to be and what I remember of the air mages and the people I once knew as my friends and family. I will seek the truth, Jack, and find a way to reconcile the past with the present. Even if it means challenging the narratives that surround us."

Jack looked at Theodore; his gaze softened though still uncertain. "Theodore, I want to trust you, and I want to believe in the goodness of the world," he said, his voice tinged with both hope and caution. "But promise me, promise me that you won't mindlessly dive into this without caution. There is so much at stake, not just for you but for all of us. My family…"

Theodore nodded before Jack could complete his question, understanding the weight of his words. "I promise, Jack," he replied, his voice steady with resolve. "I won't rush into this recklessly. I will seek the truth, but I will also be cautious and mindful of the consequences. I will fix this, I promise."

Theodore didn't know how exactly he was so sure that the air mages hadn't simply picked a side in this battle against the other magic users, but the people he remembered and the city high up in the sky were not warmongers. He knew it.

A few days passed, and not much changed on the farmstead. Each day,

Theodore worked until his body complained and ached, and each day nothing new came to pass. They didn't see another soldier since the time the group had asked Theodore to 'open his eyes', and he wondered if he'd ever see them again. Life did seem a little futile to him, though, knowing that he was surely destined for bigger and better things, but he'd made a promise to Jack to work the farm, and if he was anything, he was a man of his word.

Theodore had also seen Malek a few more times, doing his best to help on the farm where he could, but most of the time, he simply ended up playing with the animals when his attention finally wandered.

Jack also had a wife called Maia, though she had barely even looked at Theodore, let alone spoken to him. In fact, each time Theodore had attempted to catch her eye or send her a friendly smile, she quickly turned away or moved along to another task. Jack had told him that his wife was simply wary of strangers and to think nothing more upon it.

But he had no more dreams or floods of memories.

Days turned into weeks, and Theodore settled into the routine of farm life. He woke up each morning to the sounds of nature, the familiar mooing of cows and the rustling of leaves in the wind. There was a certain peace in the rhythm of the farm, a simplicity that allowed Theodore's mind to wander and reflect.

During breaks from the physical labour, Theodore would often find himself gazing up at the sky, yearning for the familiar sight of the city in the clouds. The memories of his past tugged at his heart, reminding him of the air mages and the sense of purpose they had embodied. Yet, the reality of his present circumstances grounded him in the fields, his hands in the dirt, and his feet firmly planted on the earth.

Theodore continued to work alongside Jack, the bond between them growing stronger with each passing day. They shared stories and laughter, their conversations a respite from the weight of uncertainty that surrounded Theodore's identity and purpose. Jack's trust and friendship became a steady anchor for Theodore, reminding him that he wasn't alone in his search for truth.

Malek, too, became a familiar presence on the farmstead. Although the young boy struggled to find his place, his enthusiasm and willingness to help brought a sense of joy to Theodore's heart. They would often spend time together, exploring the fields, feeding the animals, and occasionally engaging in playful competitions.

As the weeks went by, Theodore couldn't help but continue to notice the guardedness of Maia, Jack's wife. He respected Jack's explanation that she was wary of strangers, but a part of him couldn't shake the feeling that there was more to her aloofness. He wondered if there was a deeper reason behind her reluctance to engage with him, and he couldn't help but feel a sense of curiosity and longing to bridge the gap between them.

But for now, Theodore focused on the work at hand, finding solace in the simplicity of farm life. He knew that the journey to uncover the truth about his past and the current state of the air mages would require patience and careful planning. And so, he embraced the farm work with dedication, knowing that every day at least made a little difference to someone, somewhere.

Theodore's days were filled with the tasks of tending to the animals, nurturing the crops, and lending a helping hand wherever it was needed. The physical labour became a form of meditation, allowing his mind to wander and piece together the fragments of his memories. Each day, he hoped for a breakthrough, a clue that would guide him towards the truth he so desperately sought, and each day, he felt his body growing stronger and healthier, but unfortunately, his mind remained resolute.

But for now, the farmstead offered him a sense of purpose and belonging. It was a place where he could contribute, where he could make a difference in the lives of those around him. And as Theodore toiled under the sun, he held on to the promise he had made to Jack.

Chapter 6 - Power

"There's going to be a storm tonight," Jack said to Theodore as he looked out across the farmland. The sky had turned a deep purple-black, and the wind carried a cold that made Theodore shiver. He wondered how much warmth his makeshift bed was going to provide, with it not yet tested against anything more than a moderate warmth. He hoped that at least the roof was watertight when faced with a downpour. Otherwise, he might find himself waking in a very unpleasant, damp storehouse.

Theodore glanced up at the darkening sky, noting the impending storm that Jack had mentioned. The wind howled through the fields, carrying with it a sense of foreboding. He pulled the coat that Jack had brought for him to wear tighter around himself, seeking some semblance of warmth in the face of the approaching tempest.

"I hope the storm doesn't cause too much damage," Theodore remarked, his voice laced with concern. He had witnessed the power of storms in his memories as an air mage, and he knew first-hand the devastation they could bring. The farm and its livelihood were surely vulnerable to the whims of nature, and they relied on their hard work to protect their crops and animals.

Jack nodded, his eyes scanning the horizon. "We've weathered many storms before," he said, his voice filled with a mix of confidence and resilience. "We'll do what we can to minimise any damage, tie the animals down as well as anything that's loose, but sometimes we have to accept that nature just has its own plans."

Theodore nodded and stared out across the land for a long moment. Then he turned his attention back towards Jack, curious to know more about his life outside of the farmstead. "Jack, I know you said it's nothing… but Maia, she really despises me, doesn't she?" he asked, his tone gentle yet filled with genuine curiosity.

Jack didn't turn to face Theodore but answered as he looked straight forward.

A wistful smile played on Jack's lips as he spoke of his wife. "Maia, she's a strong and determined woman," he began, his voice tinged with fondness. "She has always been passionate about the farm and the well-being of our family. But there's a part of her that's wary, especially when it comes to magic."

Theodore's brow furrowed with curiosity. "Wary of magic? Is there a reason behind it?" he asked, his voice laced with intrigue. He had always felt the distance between Maia and himself, and he had always wondered if it was because of who he was, or what he was.

Jack sighed, his gaze fixed on the storm brewing in the distance. "Maia's past is a delicate subject," he admitted, his voice hesitant as though he wasn't sure if he should be sharing this information. "She has experienced things that have made her cautious, particularly when it comes to mages."

Theodore's eyes widened with curiosity, his desire to understand Maia's perspective growing stronger. "Jack, I want to know her story, to understand why she feels the way she does," he said earnestly. "I won't pry if she doesn't wish to share, but if there's a chance for me to bridge the gap, I would like to try."

Jack's expression softened, his eyes meeting Theodore's, and he did his best to seem caring. "Theodore, I appreciate your curiosity and your desire to connect," he said sincerely. "But Maia's story is hers to tell, and I can't speak for her. All I ask is that you approach her with patience and respect. If she chooses to share, it will be on her own terms."

Theodore nodded, a flicker of hope shining in his eyes. "I understand, Jack. I won't push, but I will be there, ready to listen and support her if she ever decides to open up," he vowed, his voice filled with sincerity.

Then Jack's tone switched back to one of a taskmaster: "But enough of this; we need to do what we can to storm-proof the farm before the wind picks up. Come, place ties on all the cows, and make sure the hens are locked in their coop. We can't do much about the crops, but they're hardy plants; they'll do what they can."

Theodore smiled at the fact that Jack had personified the crops in the fields, but he realised that there was nothing they could do for them anyway; either they would be damaged by the storm, or they wouldn't.

The pair then went about their work, doing what they could to minimise any damage that the storm would cause, but eventually, the rain started to fall, and they knew that their time would soon be up.

The raindrops began to fall gently at first as though they were nothing more than a light shower, but steadily they grew in size and intensity. The sound of each droplet hitting the earth merged with the new sound of the low rumble of thunder in the distance, creating an impending symphony of nature's might.

They worked swiftly, the rain-soaked ground making each step a challenge. Theodore's clothes clung to his body, and the wind tugged at him, but he pushed forward with determination. The cows, sensing the approaching storm, moved about their pen restlessly, their mooing adding to the cacophony of the storm's arrival.

With each new gust of wind, the once gentle rain intensified until it had turned into a torrential downpour. The droplets came down in sheets, drenching everything in their path and restricting the men's visions to half of what they were used to. Theodore could feel the wetness seeping through his clothes, the chill creeping into his bones. The storm had arrived with full force, unleashing its power upon the farmstead. The sound of the storm quickly became deafening, and Theodore almost had to cover his ears as the rain battered the roof of the storehouse and the wet ground.

Theodore and Jack nevertheless worked tirelessly to secure the animals, ensuring their safety amidst the chaos. The wind whipped around them, howling through the open storehouse like a wild beast, threatening to uproot trees and tear apart their fragile shelter. The thunder roared, punctuating the symphony of rain and wind with its deep, reverberating echoes and the sky filled with forked lightning. Theodore had never seen a storm like it, and it filled him with fear and foreboding for it to have arrived so suddenly.

As they finished doing what they could, the pair stood in the entranceway to the storehouse, looking out at the farmland. The wind pushed against them, making them both have to steady themselves, and they knew that they both were worried about what this storm would bring.

Theodore could feel the sheer force of nature pushing against him, testing his resolve. Yet, amidst the tempest, he felt a strange connection, a familiarity that stirred within him. The storm mirrored the turmoil within his own being, the clash between his memories and the present reality.

Theodore could hear the rain drumming relentlessly on the roof above him, its rhythm creating a soothing yet haunting melody. The storehouse creaked and groaned under the pressure of the storm as if it, too, struggled to withstand the onslaught.

The dim light of the burning torches cast flickering shadows on the walls, creating an atmosphere of both comfort and unease. The sound of rain against the wooden structure was a constant reminder of the battle being waged outside. Theodore and Jack took a moment to catch their breath, their eyes meeting, silently acknowledging the intensity of the storm surrounding them.

In that moment, Theodore couldn't help but feel a newfound appreciation for the raw power of nature. The storm reminded him of the forces he had once commanded as an air mage, the exhilaration and responsibility that came with harnessing the Cyclonic Essence. And yet, he couldn't shake the feeling that his connection to that power had somehow been severed.

But then, a deafening boom of thunder rang out, accompanied by a blinding flash of lightning. The sudden assault on their senses sent the cows into a frenzy; they mooed frantically in a tone that Theodore didn't know that cows could reach, and then one of them reared up, breaking its rope apart, and it darted for the exit.

Theodore shifted himself to chase after the cow, not wanting the animal to brave the storm alone, but before he could move, a blur of motion darted past him. It took him a moment to realise what it was, but before he could do anything to stop it, Jack was shouting above the sound of the storm.

"Malek, NO! Come back!" he shouted.

Malek had always been fond of the animals, and he had no doubt had the same thought as Theodore; to save the cow from the storm.

Malek was outside before either Theodore or Jack could stop him, and in an instant, he had been swallowed up by the storm, disappearing from view out into the farmstead.

"Quickly!" Jack ordered Theodore. "He can't stay out there!"

Theodore didn't need to be told twice, and he leapt into action immediately. The pair exited the storehouse together, and it only took them a moment to find Malek, his hands stretched out before his face as he attempted to force his body to move through the oppressive gale.

"Malek! Get back inside!" Jack screamed at the top of his voice, but it was barely a whisper above the storm.

The boy turned to see why he was being called when another flash of lightning lit up the sky, and a crash of thunder made him yelp. This time though, it wasn't the only sound that filled the air.

Theodore's heart pounded in his chest as he witnessed the horrifying scene unfolding before him. The intense flash of lightning illuminated the sky, revealing a massive tree standing tall in the distance. The storm's ferocity seemed to concentrate its fury upon that towering giant.

Suddenly, another blinding bolt of lightning struck the ancient tree, the crackling energy electrifying the air. Theodore and Jack watched in disbelief as the tree shook violently, its branches quivering with an otherworldly energy. The force of the strike reverberated through the ground, sending tremors beneath their feet.

The wind, now a tempestuous cyclone, seized hold of the tree, and with a deafening roar, it uprooted the mighty giant, tearing it from its earthly home. The tree then became a projectile, hurtling through the air with unimaginable force, propelled by the storm's wrath.

Theodore's eyes widened in terror as the massive tree hurtled toward them, its trajectory sending it on a path that ended exactly where Malek stood.

Time seemed to slow down, every second stretching into an eternity as he watched the tree's path intersect with the building.

The impact was devastating. The tree crashed into the storehouse, its branches splintering through the roof, sending debris flying in all directions. The walls groaned under the immense weight, threatening to collapse upon themselves. A cloud of dust and debris filled the air, obscuring Theodore's vision.

Driven by a surge of adrenaline and fear for his friend's safety, Theodore rushed forward, pushing against the debris to make his way inside the partially destroyed storehouse. Jack, equally determined, followed closely behind.

Coughing and sputtering amidst the thick dust, they called out for Malek, their voices strained with desperation. As the dust began to settle, they caught a glimpse of him, trapped beneath a fallen beam and some debris from the wall and roof, his face etched with pain and fear.

Everything was in chaos, and the battering rain just made everything worse.

Without hesitation, Theodore and Jack sprang into action, using every ounce of their strength to lift the heavy beam that pinned Malek down. But their efforts proved futile. The beam was too heavy, and their combined strength wasn't enough to free him.

Malek was crying in pain, but nobody could do anything to alleviate his suffering right now, and if his tears did anything at all, it was to enthuse his father and Theodore's efforts to free him.

"What's happ…" a new voice called out as Maia approached the entrance of the storehouse. And then she saw her son lying there trapped and crying.

Maia didn't say a word; she simply placed her hands on the beam that

Jack and Theodore were doing their best to prize up and away from the boy, but no matter how hard they tried, how loud they screamed with effort, there was nothing they could do to free Malek.

Tears streamed down Maia's face as she wept, still trying fruitlessly to do something, anything to free her son. But Jack had stopped trying to lift the beam, knowing that it was far, far beyond even their combined strength.

Theodore's heart sank as he witnessed the despair etched upon Maia's face. He couldn't bear to see her in such anguish, and he refused to accept the helplessness that consumed them all.

In that moment, a surge of determination welled up within Theodore, a flicker of the power he once held. He closed his eyes, focusing his thoughts, and reached deep within himself. He called upon the memories of his past, of the Cyclonic Essence that coursed through his veins. But this time, he wasn't searching for answers or asking questions of the power that once resided within him; he was telling.

As if in response to his unfaltering order, a slight gust of wind stirred around him, building in strength quickly and eventually picking up the loose debris surrounding it in its swirling vortex. Then Theodore's feet left the ground, and he hovered a few inches above the rain-soaked earth, and the rain itself seemed to bend around him as though he was within some bubble made of wind. Theodore was filled with both awe and disbelief at the sudden manifestation of his long-lost abilities. He could feel the power within him now, but he still couldn't remember exactly how he used to use it.

But it didn't really matter; the power that he needed right now didn't have to be wielded with precision. He needed to free Malek, and there was only one way that was going to happen.

Theodore directed his power toward the fallen beam and everything else on top of it. The gust of wind he commanded immediately grew in strength as though it knew exactly what Theodore needed, turning into a powerful vortex that gripped hold of the beam and the debris that trapped Malek. The force was clearly stronger than any hurricane, ripping apart the shattered remnants of the storehouse within a second.

The beam then lifted off Malek's body, freeing him from the weight that held him down, and Theodore immediately let his spell fail, dropping everything that it had carried along with it, everything that it had whisked up onto the back down to the ground. Then he gently set the boy on his feet, Malek's face beaming with relief and gratitude. The winds were now absent the debris, but the storm still raged on.

Malek was still in tears, but he could stand, so Theodore knew that nothing was broken, but he had a different emotion within him now, and all that he could do through the rain that cascaded down his head and fell to the ground from his chin was laugh.

Then he turned to see both Jack and Maia looking at him with their mouths open and their eyes wide. The pair stood in awe of what had just transpired. Maia, her tear-streaked face filled with a mix of astonishment and gratitude, embraced her son tightly. Jack looked at Theodore with wonder in his eyes, not wanting to ask the most obvious question. It didn't matter, though; by the brightness of the golden glow within Theodore's eyes, Jack had all the answers he needed.

"Theodore... you... you saved Malek," Jack said slowly, his voice filled with astonishment. "How...?"

Theodore took a deep breath, his eyes reflecting a newfound understanding. "I don't know yet," he replied honestly, his voice filled with a mix of wonder. "But I believe my connection to the Cyclonic Essence has been restored. Or at least a part of it. I don't know how it all works, to tell the truth… I knew there was only one way to save the boy, so I called upon the winds to save Malek, and they answered."

Maia's gaze shifted between Theodore and her son, her own expression filled with both awe and gratitude. "Thank you," she whispered, her voice trembling with emotion. "Thank you for saving my son."

Chapter 7 – A Broken Home

Theodore stood under the small amount of shelter that the remnants of the storehouse provided, his clothes soaked from the relentless downpour. Maia, her tear-streaked face now dried, approached him with a look that Theodore was sure he hadn't seen from the woman ever before: appreciation. The storm had unveiled a new facet of Theodore's abilities, and it was clear that Maia now felt compelled to share her story to explain the depth of her distrust and fear.

"Please, let's all go to the house and shelter there. It's made of stone and mortar, so it won't fall apart like the storehouse."

Theodore didn't need to be told twice - it was the first time Maia had invited him to do, well, anything, and so the group quickly braved the rain; Malek walked at his shoulders by his father until they reached the house a few moments later.

Thunder continue to boom overhead, each deafening clap a reminder of nature's power.

As they approached the house, Theodore couldn't help but notice the toll the storm had taken on the lands that he had tended with such dedication. The once serene surroundings were now transformed into a scene of chaos and destruction. The garden once filled with vibrant blooms, now lay trampled under the weight of the storm. Flower petals mingled with mud, scattered in disarray across the ground.

The house itself stood tall amidst the turmoil, its stone walls weathered and strong. The rain cascaded down its surface, forming rivulets that trickled off the eaves. The wooden door creaked as Jack pushed it open, revealing a still and dry sanctuary from the raging elements.

Stepping inside, the group found themselves in a small foyer, where coats and boots were hastily discarded, dripping water onto the tiled floor. The air inside was cool and damp, contrasting the warmth they had felt in the storehouse. Theodore's eyes scanned the room, taking in the familiar furniture and decorations that spoke of a simple and comfortable life.

But even within the shelter of the house, the storm's presence was still felt. The windows rattled in their frames, the occasional gust of wind finding its way through small cracks. The sound of rain drumming against the roof provided a constant backdrop, a reminder of the chaos outside.

As they moved deeper into the house, Theodore noticed signs of wear and tear. A shattered vase lay on the floor, its delicate pieces scattered across the wooden surface. The sound of dripping water resonated from a leak in the ceiling, creating a soft, rhythmic melody.

Theodore couldn't help but feel a pang of sadness as he surveyed the damage. It was a reflection of the storm that had swept through their lives, leaving behind scars and reminders of the pain they had endured.

Yet, despite the destruction, the house still offered a sense of solace. The walls provided a shield against the storm's relentless assault, offering a semblance of safety and stability, and together, they found their way to the living room, where a crackling fire in the hearth cast a warm orange glow upon their weary faces. The flickering flames danced with a resilience that mirrored their own spirits, defying the storm's attempt to extinguish their hope.

"Thank you again for saving Malek," Maia began as they all slumped into the chairs and the sofa in the room, not caring that they were still entirely soaked through. Her voice still trembled with a mixture of emotions that she clearly wasn't used to. "I… I want to explain something to you. Something that has shaped my view of the soldiers and the air mages... something that tore my family apart. This is the reason that I have not spoken with you and the cause for my apprehension."

Theodore's eyes focused on Maia, his expression a blend of curiosity and empathy. He knew that her words would carry a heavy weight, and he braced himself for the revelations that were about to unfold.

"Three years ago," Maia continued, her voice barely above a whisper, "my sister, Lina, had her mana awaken within her. Her eyes shone with a brilliant green, a sign of her affinity for earth magic. I don't know how it happened or even why, but it happened…"

She paused for a moment, the memories weighing heavily upon her. "The soldiers came to our village, claiming that Lina needed to 'open her eyes.' They said she had to be taken away to the city for execution. My parents... they tried to protect her, to run, but they were no match for the soldiers and the air mages that accompanied them."

Maia's voice quivered with anguish as she recounted the events of that fateful day. "The air mages, wielding their wind magic, stopped my parents in their tracks. They were helpless against the power of the Cyclonic Essence. And just like that, they were executed on the spot for trying to run; their lives cut short for merely trying to protect their daughter."

A profound sadness settled over Theodore as he listened to Maia's heartbreaking tale. He couldn't fathom the pain and loss she had endured, the depths of her hatred and mistrust.

"Then, a week later," Maia continued, her voice strained with grief, "Lina and a group of other mages were executed in the city. The soldiers, the air mages... they didn't see them as individuals with hopes and dreams. They saw them as threats, as enemies to be eradicated."

She paused, taking a shaky breath. "I've carried the weight of that tragedy ever since. The fear, the anger, the grief... it consumed me. I vowed to protect my family, to keep them safe from the soldiers and the air mages who had taken so much from us."

Theodore's heart ached for Maia, for the loss she had endured and the burden she had carried. He understood now the depth of her mistrust, the reason behind her initial reluctance to accept him.

"I am so sorry, Maia," Theodore said, his voice filled with genuine remorse. "I can't imagine the pain you've gone through, the loss you've experienced. But I want you to know that I am not like them. I want to bring about change, to challenge the prejudices and the violence that has torn us apart. I don't know what has caused these mages to act the way they have, but the memories I have of the air mages and of the place I grew up, it was peaceful and happy, not a place or a people to be feared."

Maia's gaze met Theodore's, her eyes searching his face for sincerity. She could see the earnestness in his eyes, the determination that burned within him. And in that moment, a flicker of hope sparked within her.

"I want to believe you, Theodore," Maia said, her voice softening. "I want to believe that there can be a different future for us, a future where mages and the non-magical citizens can coexist without fear. But trust is not something that can be given lightly, especially after everything I've experienced. I need to see your actions align with your words, Theodore. I need to see that you are willing to fight for the change you speak of."

Theodore nodded, understanding the gravity of Maia's request. "I am ready to prove myself, Maia. I will do everything in my power to challenge the oppressive regime that has caused so much pain and suffering. I will seek the truth, uncover the secrets that lie beneath the surface, and work towards a future where no more lives are lost needlessly."

Maia studied Theodore's face, searching for any signs of deception. The storm still raged outside, its relentless assault a reminder of the tumultuous path that lay ahead. But amidst the chaos, she found a glimmer of hope. She reached out, placing her hand on Theodore's, a gesture of tentative trust.

"I hope you are true to your words, Theodore," she said, her voice filled with caution and hope. "For the sake of my family and for all those who have suffered at the hands of the soldiers and air mages, I hope you can bring about the change we so desperately need."

Theodore turned his hand over beneath Maia's and grasped it tightly, his eyes filled with determination. "I promise, Maia. I will do everything in my power to bring about that change. We may face many challenges along the way, but together, we can build a better future."

In that moment, as the storm raged outside and the weight of their shared pain and hope hung in the air, Theodore and Maia found solace in each other's presence. They were united by a common goal, driven by the desire to create a world where fear and hatred were replaced with understanding and compassion.

As they sat in the dimly lit room, their hearts heavy with the weight of their past and the uncertainty of their future, Theodore couldn't help but feel a flicker of hope. After all, if he didn't have hope, what else would he have?

A long silence followed, at the end of which Maia announced: "Tea, anyone?"

Theodore smiled warmly. "I think that's a great idea "

Maia quickly stood up and left the room, and it gave Theodore and Jack the chance to talk again. It took a moment for Jack to put his thoughts together, and what eventually came out was simply a string of questions.

"What did it feel like… using mana, I mean… and did you know you could do that? And how long have you known?" then, after a pause, he quietly added: "And can you use them again?"

Theodore leaned back in his chair, contemplating Jack's questions with a crooked smile. It was clear that his display of power during the storm had sparked curiosity and intrigue. He took a moment to gather his thoughts before responding.

"It was... incredible, Jack," Theodore began a hint of awe in his voice. "Using mana felt like tapping into a wellspring of energy, a connection to the elements themselves. At that moment, when the storm was at its height, I felt a surge of power within me. I didn't know I could do that, not consciously, at least. It was as if something deep within me awakened, responding to the storm's call."

He paused, reflecting on the profound experience. "As for how long I've known... well, my memories have only recently returned, so I haven't had much time to explore my abilities fully. But I do remember being an air mage, skilled in harnessing the Cyclonic Essence. And if I could tap into that power once, there's a possibility that I can do it again."

Theodore looked at Jack, his eyes again filled with determination. "I believe that my connection to the elements is still there, waiting to be rediscovered. And with that power, I can help bring about the change we seek."

Jack nodded, absorbing Theodore's words. He had seen first-hand the strength and potential within his friend, and now he understood that there was much more to Theodore's identity than he had initially thought. There was a sense of purpose and destiny that lay ahead, intertwined with the mysteries of the past and the challenges of the present.

"I have faith in you, Theodore," Jack said, his voice filled with conviction. "I've seen what you're capable of, and I have faith that you can harness your mana once more. I know that the air mages aren't exactly the favourite kinds of people around here, but there's something different about you. I honestly don't believe you could be as cold-hearted as the ones we've had dealings with, and it begs the question: where are all the good air mages? Do they know what's happening here with the others? And if so, why aren't they stopping them?"

Theodore's brows furrowed as he considered Jack's questions. They were valid and echoed his own thoughts on the matter. If there were good air mages, ones who sought peace and harmony, why hadn't they intervened to stop the atrocities committed by their brethren? The mystery deepened, and Theodore realised that unravelling the truth would require more than just his personal journey of rediscovery.

"I've been wondering the same thing, Jack," Theodore replied, his voice tinged with concern. "There must be air mages out there who share our values, who believe in the power of unity and understanding. But perhaps they are also silenced, afraid to challenge the status quo or unwilling to confront the darkness within their own ranks. Or even perhaps they simply don't know what's happening down here, if they remain up in the city in the sky."

He leaned forward, his gaze focused intently on Jack. "That's why we need to find them, Jack. We need to seek out those who are willing to stand against injustice and violence, to join us in our quest for a better world. We can't do this alone. Together, we can be a beacon of hope, a force for change that even the most jaded among the air mages would have to acknowledge."

Jack nodded. "You're right, Theodore. We have to reach out, connect with others who share our vision. And if there are air mages out there who have turned their backs on the darkness, we need to find them and show them that they're not alone."

Theodore smiled, his conviction growing stronger. 'Exactly, Jack. We will seek out those who hold the same ideals as us, who believe in a future where fear and hatred are replaced with understanding and compassion. We will find a way to make a difference, to challenge the oppressive forces that have tainted the reputation of the air mages."

Maia's voice preceded her entry into the room, with a tray in hand holding four mugs.

"Do you know where they are or how to contact the rest of the air mages? At the very least, it would be good to know if they are even against this or not, right?" she asked.

Theodore turned his attention towards Maia, gratitude evident in his eyes as he saw her carrying the tray with mugs. The warm aroma of the tea filled the room, offering a momentary respite from the weight of their conversation.

"You raise a valid point, Maia," Theodore replied, accepting one of the mugs from her with a grateful nod. "It's important for us to understand where the rest of the air mages stand in all of this. If they share our vision for a better world, then they may be willing to join our cause."

He took a sip of the tea, allowing its warmth to soothe his senses before continuing. "But finding them... I won't lie, I remember my time in the sky city and all, but I don't know how I came to be down here in the kingdom… so I don't even know how I would go about finding them. The air mages I know and remember keep to themselves high above the world. They have intentionally distanced themselves from the conflicts and turmoil of the kingdom, seeking solace in their own domain… it might come back to me, but for now, I have no idea where to even start."

Maia listened intently, her gaze fixed on Theodore. She understood the challenges they would face in locating the elusive air mages and convincing them to join their cause. But the flicker of hope in her eyes remained, a testament to her belief in their mission.

Then she sighed. "I don't think we can go around asking people if they know anything about the air mages… and your eyes… there's no way that anyone around here is going to trust you; they'll never believe that you're simply a 'good' air mage. But wait, can't you just walk into the city and talk to some of the air mages at the palace?"

Theodore thought on that idea for a long time as he sipped at his tea, but there was just something that he couldn't be sure about. "But then what? They either recognise me and remind me of who I was before, feeding me their stories to turn me to their side, or they don't, and they take to me with suspicion. No, if these mages truly are a group that fly in the face of the rest of the air mages, we need to find this floating city, talk to the rest of the air mages and find out what's really happening here. I really don't think that walking into the lion's den is a good idea, not right now at least."

Maia nodded in understanding, recognising the validity of Theodore's concerns. She took a sip of her tea, contemplating their next course of action. After a moment of silence, a spark of realisation lit up her eyes.

"You're right, Theodore," Maia said, her voice filled with determination. "Walking into the heart of the city may not be the wisest move at this moment. We need to gather more information, find leads that can guide us towards this city above and the other air mages. There must be clues, hidden knowledge, or individuals who hold insights into their whereabouts."

She set her mug down on the table and turned to Jack, hoping to find some ideas there.

But it wasn't Jack who spoke; rather, it was the tiny voice of Malek, who had not yet said a single word since he'd been freed from the broken storehouse.

"Can't you just fly up there and have a look around?" he asked.

"I can't…" Theodore began to say reflexively, but then he stopped. He was about to say that he couldn't fly, but he had floated off the ground already, and he was an air mage; why couldn't he fly? And could it be as simple as that? Could he just fly high up above the clouds and 'have a look around'? He clicked his tongue, trying to decide if it was a good idea or not.

"You know, Malek, that might just be the breakthrough we need," Theodore said, a glimmer of excitement in his eyes. "If I can tap into my air magic fully, there's a possibility I could fly up and explore the skies. It won't be without risks, but it could offer valuable insights. That's a great idea!"

Jack and Maia exchanged intrigued glances, their interest piqued by the idea. They both saw the potential in Theodore's abilities and the unique advantages they could bring to their mission.

Maia leaned forward, her voice filled with anticipation. "Theodore, if you can harness your air magic and take flight, you may be able to scout the skies and search for any signs of the city, or perhaps even encounter other air mages along the way. It could be huge… but… is it really possible? A person can fly?"

Theodore took a deep breath, contemplating the risks and rewards. The memory of his recent display of wind manipulation during the storm served as a reminder of the power he possessed, waiting to be fully realised. The prospect of flying through the open skies, defying gravity with the Cyclonic Essence fuelled his determination.

"I believe it's worth a try," Theodore said, his voice steady with resolve. "But we must exercise caution and plan our approach carefully. I will need time to practice and refine my control over the air magic. Once I feel confident in my abilities, we can embark on this aerial exploration."

Jack nodded, his faith in Theodore's potential unwavering. "Take the time you need, Theodore. We will support you every step of the way.

The room was filled with a renewed sense of purpose and anticipation. As they finished their tea, the trio began discussing their next steps, trying to figure out how exactly a person was supposed to learn to fly.

Chapter 8 – Skyward Ascension

Theodore raised his arms to either side, preparing for his first attempt at flying. He hadn't yet made any attempts because he had been so busy with the rest of the family repairing the storehouse and rounding up all the animals that had fled during the storm. But the work had finally been completed, and he was about to try to call upon his mana so that he could perhaps make some sense of who he once was in this world, and what he was capable of.

Jack, Maia and Malek all stood a few metres away from Theodore as he prepared himself. They didn't want to get too close in case anything went wrong, but they wanted to do all they could to offer him some support in discovering who he was.

Theodore took a deep breath, his mind focused and his heart filled with determination. He closed his eyes and began to centre himself, letting go of any doubts or distractions that threatened to hinder his concentration. The memories of his time in the city above floated in his mind, reminding him of the freedom and power that awaited him in the skies.

He extended his senses, feeling the subtle currents of air swirling around him. It was as if he could hear the whispers of the wind urging him to embrace his true nature as an air mage. Drawing upon the deep reservoirs of his mana, he called forth the Cyclonic Essence that resided within him.

A gentle breeze caressed Theodore's skin, carrying a familiar energy that tingled through his veins. The feeling was not like it had always been though; this time, it was a connection to something greater that transcended the physical world's boundaries. With each passing moment, he felt his bond with the air strengthen as if the very fabric of existence responded to his call.

Slowly, Theodore raised his arms higher and his body began to feel lighter, as if he was being buoyed by an invisible force. Then his feet lifted off the ground, and he hovered a few inches above the earth, defying gravity with a newfound grace. A smile formed on his lips as he embraced the exhilarating sensation of flight.

Theodore's eyes opened, revealing to the rest of the group a glimmer of awe and wonder. He gazed down at his friends, who watched in amazement, their eyes reflecting a mixture of surprise and pride. It was a moment of triumph, a testament to Theodore's unwavering spirit and the limitless potential within him.

He adjusted his posture, finding balance in the air as he slowly ascended higher, guided by his intuition and the invisible currents that carried him. The wind whispered in his ears, assuring him that he was safe in its hands, and he instinctively felt that he could trust it. This was who he was. This was who he had always been.

But quickly, he found that the higher up he rose, the more difficult it was to remain balanced. The wind rushed around him, granting him this ethereal buoyancy, but he could feel the strain that his mana was under, just trying to keep him from spiralling out of control. Quickly, he began a descent, though when he reached within a metre of the ground, he lost his balance entirely and fell backwards as though he had slipped off a stone in a rushing river. His back hit the softened ground, and although it hurt, he could tell that it hadn't caused him too much damage.

Pain shot through Theodore's body as he landed on the ground, his breath momentarily taken away. He lay there for a moment, feeling the ache in his back and the sting of disappointment. He had hoped that his first attempt at flight would be flawless, a testament to his growing mastery over his air magic.

Slowly, Theodore sat up, rubbing his sore back. Jack and Maia rushed to his side; concern etched on their faces. They helped him to his feet, supporting him as he regained his balance.

"Are you alright, Theodore?" Jack asked, his voice filled with genuine worry.

Theodore nodded, his expression one of disappointment. "I'm fine, just a little bruised. It seems I still have much to learn and refine in order to fully harness my abilities."

Maia placed a comforting hand on Theodore's shoulder. "Don't be disheartened, Theodore. Surely you knew that mastering your air magic would take time and practice. But we're here to support you every step of the way."

Theodore appreciated their words of encouragement, their unwavering belief in him. He knew that setbacks were a natural part of the learning process, and he was determined to rise above them.

"I won't let this setback deter me. I will continue to train and hone my skills. Together, we will find a way to make this work. I have faith in our mission, and I have faith in us."

Jack and Maia exchanged nods, their spirits lifted by Theodore's determination. They understood the challenges that lay ahead, but they were united by a shared purpose and the belief that they could overcome any obstacle.

Theodore abruptly rose to his feet and raised his arms for a second time, ready to try again.

Focussing his energy and his eyes fixated on the open sky above, Theodore called upon the Cyclonic Essence within him, feeling the familiar surge of power coursing through his veins. The air around him seemed to respond, swirling gently as he channelled his mana.

This time, Theodore approached his flight with a calm focus. He concentrated on maintaining a steady balance and controlling the flow of the wind around him. Again, Slowly, his feet lifted off the ground, and he ascended into the air with a newfound grace.

He adjusted his posture, again finding stability in the currents that carried him. The wind whispered its secrets to him, guiding him up and into the vast expanse of the sky. Theodore's body swayed with the rhythm of the air, his control becoming more refined with each passing moment.

His friends watched in awe as he soared higher, his figure a silhouette against the backdrop of clouds high up in the sky. Theodore felt a surge of exhilaration and freedom as he moved through the open sky, his heart filled with a sense of purpose and wonder.

Theodore raised himself higher and higher, determined for this to be the time that he proved to himself that he could do this, that this was a part of him, and nothing would stand in his way.

Balancing was easier this time because he anticipated the need for it. He willed the air around him to press into him from all angles so that it created a kind of invisible bubble all around him, and to his amazement, it worked.

After a short pause to ensure that he was as safe as he could be, Theodore began to will the Cyclonic Essence to move him back and forward, side to side, and it all seemed so natural.

He willed the air to take him further and faster, moving laterally whilst all the time remaining upright. From his new vantage point high in the sky, he could see the rolling landscape below as it spanned across the world underneath him. The farmhouse standing beside the dense green forest, the desert sands where he'd walked from not many days ago and far, far away beyond the forest, he could see the outline of the central city of the kingdom of Avondale.

But then he saw the palace within the city walls, and something inside of him sparked with recognition.

Suddenly, his mind was transported back. It was like when he had dreamed of the floating city above, though this time, there was no excuse for his attention to change and for the vision to arrive. He could remember walking the halls of that palace in the centre of Avondale, other air mages watching him as he passed. Guards allowed him to make his way into a wide-open chamber. The King, awaiting his arrival.

He could see that the King was beyond angry, though whatever he was saying as his mouth moved, he couldn't hear it. Whatever it was, it seemed very, very bad.

Then Theodore's attention returned to him as the vision faded away into nothingness, and he realised that he was falling. His focus had gone from his mana and the air around him as he hadn't been tending to his spell, and he was hurtling towards the ground, sure to hit within the next few moments.

Theodore saw Jack and Maia trying their best to pull a haybale onto the patch of ground that was sure to be his end, but it was heavy and so far away. Everyone must have known that they wouldn't be able to place it into position in time, even if they were accurate with their placement.

He had just seconds to go before he would meet his end, and there was nothing that he could do about it.

But there was. Theodore was an air mage, a wielder of the Cyclonic Essence and at the last second, he willed everything within him to place a cushion of air between him and the ground and obediently, his mana activated, and he stopped no more than a single inch from the ground, facing down, his nose almost touching terra-firma.

Theodore's heart raced as he hung suspended just above the ground, his body inches away from a potentially disastrous impact. The rush of adrenaline coursed through his veins, and his mind quickly assessed the situation. With a surge of determination, he mustered his focus and control, gradually levitating himself back to a stable and upright position.

Jack and Maia rushed to Theodore's side, their faces filled with relief and concern. They could hardly believe what they had just witnessed - the narrow escape from a fatal fall.

"Are you alright, Theodore?" Jack asked, his voice filled with genuine worry.

Theodore nodded, his body trembling slightly from the shock of the near-miss. "I'm fine... just... caught off guard. I lost focus for a moment... but I managed to save myself with my mana."

Maia placed a hand on Theodore's shoulder again, her eyes filled with concern. "You must be more careful, Theodore. When you're up there, you're going to have to concentrate, or you're going to die. Just one moment of distraction can lead to disaster... and I don't want to have to clean that up."

Theodore took a deep breath, his hands still trembling with the remnants of the intense experience. He understood the gravity of the situation and the need for heightened caution.

"You're right, Maia," Theodore replied, his voice steadying. "I… I'm sorry. Thank you for being there, both of you. And thank you for trying to save me."

"Fat lot of good it would've done," Jack said with a smile. "But we didn't know what to do… don't think a single haybale would've saved you, falling from that height."

"I… I won't let it happen again," Theodore replied gingerly."

Jack nodded in understanding, his own worry gradually easing as he saw Theodore regain his composure. They knew that this was a learning experience, a reminder of the challenges and perils that Theodore could eventually face.

"We're in this together, Theodore," Jack said, his voice now strong. "But maybe… just tell us if you plan to fall from the sky again?"

Theodore's determination was reignited, and he took a moment to gather himself, reaffirming his commitment to mastering his air magic and remembering his past. The vision he had experienced during flight lingered in his mind, stirring a mixture of curiosity and concern.

"I saw something," Theodore said abruptly, his voice tinged with uncertainty. "During my flight, I had a vision of the palace in the central city. The King... he was angry, and I was there for some reason. I couldn't hear the words, but it was intense."

Maia and Jack exchanged nervous glances, their interest piqued by the revelation. The significance of Theodore's vision was not lost on them, and they both worried about what it could have meant.

"We should try to forget it," Maia said firmly. "There's nothing good in the city for any of us; we'll be much better off sticking to the original plan:

find the sky city where you came from, and try to find answers there. Besides, if the King was angry with you, maybe you did something he didn't like, and that's why you were thrown out and ended up here?"

Theodore frowned, his gaze now focused. He didn't get the impression from the vision that the King had meant him harm, although he couldn't be sure. It seemed more like the King was angry about something else, and Theodore had been sent in there to try to fix it. It didn't matter either way; Maia was right. He needed to find out more about his past before he could poke his nose into the city, where the dangers could be very real.

So Theodore allowed the air beneath him to dissipate, dropping his feet softly to the ground. The sensation felt strange as his legs and knees again took his weight where a moment before he had been effectively weightless, but after a moment, he regained his balance, and his legs began to behave as they should.

"OK," Theodore announced to the group. "I think I've got this. This time I'm going to go as high as I possibly can and see if there is any trace of that city. But please, if I start to fall, try to get something softer than just the one haybale."

Then he gave them a warm smile and pushed off the ground and began to float upwards, buoyed once more by his bubble of air.

As Theodore ascended into the sky once again, Jack and Maia watched with a mixture of awe and concern.

With each passing moment, Theodore grew smaller and smaller in their sight until he became a mere speck against the vast expanse of the sky and clouds above. The wind carried him higher, his body moving with an ethereal grace. He surveyed the sky all around him, searching for any sign of the city, or even the balloons he knew floated above it, the place that held the key to his past and perhaps even the future of the air mages.

Theodore's eyes scanned the horizon, his gaze piercing through the layers of clouds that drifted across the sky. He strained his senses, listening to the whispers of the wind and feeling its subtle currents guiding him. But no matter how high he soared, there was no trace of the city, no sign of the place he once called home.

Frustration tugged at Theodore's heart, but he refused to let it consume him. He understood that his journey would be filled with challenges and uncertainties. This was just the beginning, and he knew he had to remain patient and persistent.

But then he realised what the problem was. The clouds were surely obscuring his vision, so with an almighty pressure of will, he forced his mana to drive him higher, breaking through the clouds and into the bright clear skies above.

It took a few seconds for Theodore to look all about himself, and then he saw it. Unmistakably it was the floating city, a fair distance away, kept afloat by its colossal balloons and great spinning fans.

Theodore didn't waste any time. He floated towards the city, gazing in wonder at its sheer size. Dozens of balloons the size of buildings floated high above the chunk of earth that seemed all too happy to sit in the sky, away from its rightful place below.

Atop the earth that floated suspended in the air, a beautiful city stood. Stone buildings, walls and other structures paired with vibrant grasslands, trees and other greenery to create what most would call a paradise. And it was this place that Theodore knew was his home.

Fighting against his own eagerness, Theodore took his time to approach the city. He wanted the air mages within to know that he posed no threat to them, ensuring that in his slow approach, he would telegraph to them all that he was there and he was making no effort to hide from any of them.

Eventually, the finer details of the city came into view, and he could already see people beginning to arrive at the flat, open section where he was about to land. Something felt familiar about this exact place, though Theodore couldn't place it. It was a cobblestone clearing with a large tree that seemed to sprout from the ground as though in defiance of the man-made courtyard, and by the time he arrived there, he could see a veritable stream of air mages making their way forward through the city to meet him.

Theodore willed the pocket of air surrounding him to lower him gently to the ground before dismissing it completely. He barely felt the pressure this time as his knees bent slightly, and he returned to the normal gravity that the world beneath him provided.

Chapter 9 – Grandmaster

To his surprise, the group of air mages that now surrounded Theodore quickly began falling to a single knee and placing a single clenched fist across their chests. All of them turned their gaze to the ground, and within a few moments and before Theodore could even ask what was happening, there were hundreds of people before him, kneeling as though he was some sort of god.

Most of the people wore simple plain clothes of light linen or similar flowing fabrics, and every single one of them wore some flashes of golden yellow to betray their status as users of the Cyclonic Essence. Theodore didn't need the clothes to tell him what these people were, though; he could feel the power in the air.

"Grandmaster..." an older man with long white hair stepped forward, though he kept his eyes on the ground. "We did not expect you to return..."

"What?" Theodore asked, not entirely sure if this man knew who he was talking to, or perhaps there was someone far more important standing behind Theodore that he didn't know about. He looked behind him quickly, just in case that's what was happening, but there was no one there.

"Grandmaster?" Theodore asked. "What do you mean?"

"Forgive me, Grandmaster, is this some kind of test?' he asked. "Only... we thought that you were dead."

"I was almost dead. I think," Theodore replied. "But whatever happened didn't manage to kill me, rather, I awoke in a crater in the desert, and here I am." He decided not to correct his title for now, just in case he was being mistaken for someone else.

"But… that is not what I meant," the man said, his voice clearly strained. "We thought you had been dead for years. This was why we assumed you had not returned with any news or any of the others…"

"Others?" Theodore parroted. "You mean the other air mages? We all left together?"

The man winced as though the conversation pained him, and honestly, Theodore could relate.

"Please," Theodore said before the man could reply again. Let me explain what has happened to me so that you can understand why I am asking these questions."

Nobody said anything, so Theodore started talking.

"Recently, I awoke in the aftermath of a great battle. This battle took the lives of many, many soldiers and mages of the Eternal Flame. But when I awoke, I was alone, and I had no memories of where or who I was. Just my name and not even any clothes to call my own. But I had a dream about this place, and it told me that this was once my home. So I have returned to seek answers. I hope that you can help me."

Theodore could see that some of the crowd had begun to look up at him now, though none of them seemed brave enough to raise themselves from their knees.

"Grandmaster I… I do not know what to say," the man said. "You truly remember nothing of your past?"

Theodore shook his head solemnly. "I remembered some things, flashes of my time here, my parents, but nothing more."

"Then… you know none of us? Our names or our families?" the man asked.

Looking at the man intently, Theodore shook his head slowly. The man didn't even seem familiar to him in the slightest.

"And please," Theodore said to the crowd of mages. "Do not kneel before me; stand, and we can talk as equals."

"But Grandmaster… you taught us…" the man started.

"Let me stop you right there," Theodore said. "I am nothing more than a man, no better than any of you here now. So please, make no assumptions of what I desire or how I expect to be treated. Treat me as an equal so that we may speak clearly."

The man seemed to stammer for a second, not entirely sure what to do next; then eventually, he straightened his back and held out his hand for Theodore to shake.

"My name is Volnus, and I have been tending to the needs of the Sky City in your absence."

Theodore grasped the man's hand and shook it firmly. He offered Volnus a wide smile before letting go of the handshake, and as soon as he did so, he could feel the tension in the crowd begin to fall. Then the rest of the mages began to rise to their feet and stand facing Theodore, a little apprehensive but certainly less submissive. One thought that did occur to him, though, was the fact that he had mentally called this place a sky city when this Volnus had called it The Sky City.

"Was I… was I a leader here?" Theodore asked as he surveyed the faces that, when they looked at him, were filled with foreboding.

"Oh yes," Volnus said. "But please, why don't you come with me, away from this place and we can speak properly about, well, everything."

Theodore took another look at the crowds around them and decided that it probably was a good idea to find out what was happening before he did or said anything stupid.

Volnus then led Theodore away and down a few side streets without saying a word. It all felt so familiar to Theodore, but rather than the detailed memories he'd already experienced, it was more like he kind of just knew the place.

The high stone buildings spanned upwards overhead, and the streets were lined with triangular cloths and rags suspended on ropes above, apparently there to provide some cover when the sun shone. Above the clouds, there was no reprieve from the burning light above, and the more Theodore thought about it, the more he realised that he was hot and very glad for the shade above.

Eventually, Volnus led Theodore through a small store archway into an open courtyard, again covered by large triangles of cloth and sat down on a wooden bench.

Theodore took the man's lead and sat opposite him, still not entirely sure what had happened and why they needed to speak in private.

"I have to ask, Grandmaster, is this a test?" Volnus asked.

Theodore stared at the man, again shocked at what he was being asked. Eventually, he shook his head.

"Is that something that you think I would do?" He managed to ask, inwardly wondering what kind of person these people thought he was. And 'Grandmaster'? That wasn't something that he remembered being called before arriving at the Sky City.

Volnus looked visibly relieved as Theodore denied the notion of a test. He leaned back on the bench, his expression contemplative. "Forgive me, Grandmaster. It's just... we simply assumed that you had perished. The Sky City mourned your loss. The news of your return, alive and well, has come as a shock to us all."

"Perished? But why? You have to understand Volnus," Theodore chose his words very carefully, "that I do not remember a thing. I know that I hail from this place but beyond that, I do not remember who I was or why I ever left this place to begin with. Please, you must tell me everything… it may help me to understand better what happened to me and why."

"Grandmaster," Volnus said, nodding his head slightly. "You were a skilled air mage from a very young age. You seemed to have far more control over the Cyclonic Essence than many of your peers, and as you grew, so did your power. You skipped through the ranks of Apprentice, Journeyman and even Master in your teenage years, becoming the youngest-ever Archmage in the history of our city. It was not until your mother perished, though, that you took on the title of Grandmaster…"

Theodore listened intently, trying his best to remember, though nothing came.

"It was with this new title and the passing of your mother that we all began to see changes within you," Volnus said and winced slightly as though he was expecting to be reprimanded for his words.

"Please… go on," Theodore said. "I promise you, I have no ill will towards you, and you can speak freely with me."

"Very well," Volnus replied apprehensively. "As I said, you, uh, changed. Where once you were a caring person, eager to help – someone who worked to maintain our beautiful city and its residents tirelessly, day in and day out – now those things seemed beneath you. You offered no help to anyone who asked, and you made examples of those who you thought were not becoming of the title of 'mage'. Grandmaster, forgive me for speaking frankly, but it seemed that overnight, you had become a tyrant. And nobody was powerful enough to stand up to you."

Theodore's brows furrowed as he absorbed the weight of Volnus' words. The revelations about his past self painted a picture vastly different from the person he believed himself to be. It was disconcerting to hear of his transformation into a tyrant, a stark contrast to the compassionate and just leader he aspired to become.

"I... I find it hard to believe," Theodore started, his voice laced with confusion and self-doubt. "I cannot recall any of this, and it goes against everything I feel in my heart now. I want to make amends and bring unity to our people, not perpetuate division and tyranny. Are you sure that I am the person that you believe me to be?"

Volnus nodded sympathetically, his gaze filled with understanding. "Grandmaster, You are most certainly this person, but it is clear to me that you have changed. Whether it was a result of your memory loss or some other factor, I cannot say. But the fact that you seek to make amends and restore balance speaks volumes of the person you are now and the person I knew in our distant past. Perhaps the past can be reconciled with the present, and we can find a way to heal the wounds inflicted upon our community."

Theodore took a deep breath, grappling with the complexity of his situation. The memories of his time as Grandmaster were still shrouded in darkness, but he couldn't dismiss the possibility that they held truths he needed to confront. If he truly wished to unite the air mages and reunite the Sky City with the surface, he had to face his past head-on.

"Volnus, I appreciate your honesty and your willingness to speak openly with me," Theodore said earnestly. "I want to know more about the actions I took, the decisions I made. Only then can I truly understand the consequences of my past actions and work towards redemption."

Volnus nodded, his expression filled with both uncertainty and hope. "I will share what I can, Grandmaster. But some of the things that I have to say will not be easy to hear."

Theodore nodded in understanding and added: "Please, I need to hear this."

"Well, as mages failed to live up to your expectations, and as they failed to grow at the rate you had in your time with the Cyclonic Essence, you began to punish people. At first, it seemed harsh but overall harmless. Then it began to grow worse and worse, and with news that the King on the surface below had begun to wipe magic from the face of the earth, it escalated further. It seemed clear to everybody that you wanted to raise an army."

"An army?" Theodore asked with wide eyes. "I wanted to overthrow the King?"

Volnus nodded. "That is what we all had assumed. But things got so bad here that the people began to fear you. People would stay in their homes, fearing that you may conscript them to your army or punish them for their weakness. It was only when your father confronted you that we all saw the changes that truly had occurred within you."

"My father?" Theodore asked slowly.

"He was a good man," Volnus replied, and Theodore's heart sank. Surely he hadn't…

"You did not take his life," Volnus said quickly before Theodore came to the wrong conclusion. "But he questioned your decisions, your leadership and told you in no uncertain terms and in front of the entire city that he believed you to be in the wrong. To make an example of the lengths that you were willing to go to, you exiled him, never to return to this place."

Theodore's heart sank as he processed the devastating truth. The weight of his actions bore down on him, and he felt the pain of regret coursing through his veins. The realisation that he had exiled his own father, someone he had once loved and respected, was a bitter pill to swallow.

Tears welled up in Theodore's eyes, a mixture of grief, guilt, and a profound sense of loss. "I... I didn't know," he whispered, his voice filled with anguish. "How could I have done such a thing? How could I have become so blind to the consequences of my actions?"

Volnus reached out a hand and placed it gently on Theodore's shoulder, offering a comforting presence. "Grandmaster, it is clear to me that you are deeply remorseful for what has transpired. You cannot change the past, but you have the opportunity to make amends and strive for a better future. The fact that you are willing to confront these truths is a testament to the person you are now."

Theodore nodded, his voice choked with emotion. "I want to make things right, Volnus. I want to bring my father back, but tell me, what happened next?"

"It was not long after that you decided to round up all of the Archmages with the Cyclonic Essence. And then you all left. Off to wage war against the King and his oppression. To fight back on behalf of mages of all elements and paths. But you never returned, and neither did any of the other mages, or even any word of what transpired. Before you left, though, you ordered the Sky City to lock down and await your return, to stay away from the surface at all times, for the safety of us all. That is why we have remained, and that is why we are so shocked to see you now."

Theodore's eyes widened with each word he heard, his mind grappling with the enormity of what Volnus was revealing. The decision he had made to lead the Archmages in a rebellion against the oppressive King had far-reaching consequences that he had never anticipated, but what had happened to them all?

"I... I led the Archmages to war?" Theodore's voice trembled with a mixture of disbelief and sadness. "And I ordered the Sky City to remain locked down, to isolate ourselves from the world... for our safety?"

Volnus nodded solemnly. "Yes, Grandmaster. The city has remained hidden from the surface for years, cut off from the outside world, waiting for your return. The people have lived in fear and uncertainty, holding onto the hope that one day you and the other mages would come back victorious, that you would restore balance and freedom to our kind. We had all but lost that hope, but not the last order you had given us."

Theodore's heart ached as he absorbed the weight of the responsibility he had unknowingly carried. The consequences of his past actions had reverberated through time, affecting the lives of all those who had remained above the surface in the Sky City.

"I never meant for things to turn out this way," Theodore whispered, his voice filled with regret. "I wanted to protect our people, to stand against oppression, but I failed to foresee the consequences of my choices. I failed to consider the impact it would have on the Sky City and its residents."

Volnus placed a hand on Theodore's arm, offering reassurance. "Grandmaster, we understand the challenges and complexities of leadership. Mistakes are inevitable, especially in times of turmoil and uncertainty. What matters now is how we move forward, how we learn from the past and work towards a better future."

Theodore nodded, determination shining in his eyes. "You're right, Volnus. We cannot change the choices we've made, but we can learn from them. We can seek forgiveness, make amends, and strive to build a stronger and more united Sky City."

Volnus smiled, a glimmer of hope returning to his gaze. "Grandmaster, our people have longed for your return. They have waited patiently, hoping that one day you would come back to lead us. Now that you are here, ready to confront the truths of the past and embrace a path of redemption, we will stand by your side. Together, we will face the challenges ahead and forge a new destiny for the Sky City. But tell me, what becomes of the surface below? Is the tyrant King now overthrown? Is the surface safe for the mages?"

Theodore shook his head slowly.

"The King yet lives. And magic is still outlawed. I can only assume that whatever it was that we tried, it was unsuccessful. The surface below is unsafe for all mages except..." then his eyes bulged. "Except for the air mages that work within the King's guard! They must have infiltrated the palace with a plan to eventually kill the tyrant King!"

"The air mages work for the King? How can this be?" Volnus asked with wide eyes.

"I do not know how it came to pass," Theodore said quickly, "but I have had visions of being inside the palace and speaking with the King… it must be what they are doing. I do not know why they haven t acted yet, but it is the only explanation!"

Volnus scratched his chin in thought before saying: "Yes, I can see that it would make sense. But how can we be sure? And how could we contact them if it is still not safe on the surface?"

Theodore practically beamed. "It may not be safe for you on the surface. But by all accounts, I am the Grandmaster that worked with the Archmages within the palace. I am a part of their group, and that means…"

"That means that you alone are the one person who could actually walk right in through the front door," Volnus announced with a wide smile. "Surely it could not be so easy?"

"I expect not," Theodore agreed. "But this will go one of two ways, either I will be accepted back into the palace and find out what has been happening all this time, try to remember our plan to overthrow the King… or they will try to capture or kill me. If that is the case, I will simply fly from their grasp and return here and we will figure something else out."

Volnus hummed thoughtfully. It was a strange sound, but it was also kind of soothing.

"It is a very dangerous plan," Volnus eventually replied. "And there are dangers that we cannot rightly foretell. But I do not see an alternative. The best course of action is, therefore, to rest upon the thought for a day, and if it is still a good plan tomorrow, then we shall act upon it. Besides, you have an entire city to convince that you are not a tyrant yourself, Grandmaster."

Chapter 10 – Welcome Home

"My friends, my family," Theodore said as he stood on the stone platform in the centre of the Sky City. Hundreds of air mages had gathered on his behest so that he could speak to them all en-masse, not wishing to have to repeat his statement over and over.

"I know that many of you see me as someone to be feared. As someone who once wielded power over you all with an iron fist. Who kicked you when you were down..." he took a deep breath as he heard one or two mutterings of agreement from the crowd. He couldn't single anyone out, though, not that he wanted to.

"This is not the man that I am any longer, and I am here, standing before you right now to apologise. To beg for your forgiveness for the wrongs that I have done to you. For the pain and the suffering that I have caused." Theodore spoke with genuine emotion, and let his head hang in shame.

"This is no trick, no test or subterfuge, just a simple apology and perhaps an explanation of what has passed."

"Can we go down to the surface?" a woman's voice rang out amidst the otherwise silent crowd. Again Theodore couldn't see where it had come from, but rather a general area within the people amassed before him.

"It uh," he stuttered. "It is not yet safe for mages on the surface. But we have a plan, and soon I believe that we will all be welcomed there with open arms."

"So the tyrant King still lives?" a man's voice asked this time, and this time Theodore saw where it came from.

"Yes, I am afraid that the King still lives and that magic users are still banned on pain of death, from the kingdom of Avondale.

A silence fell over the crowd. It lasted for almost a minute and was broken when another question rang out.

"And what of the Archmages? Are they to return?"

Theodore sighed. "I am afraid that I do not know. It would seem that I am yet to regain my memories of what has occurred so far, but I know that with time, everything will become clear. It is with this in mind that I plan to return to the city and speak with the Archmages, who I know still live and have successfully infiltrated the King's palace. I know it may sound odd, and I know that I do not have all the answers that you seek, but I promise you that I am a changed man and I will do everything to bring peace to all people."

The crowd didn't erupt into cheers or jeers; rather, a wave of mumbling spread through the citizens of the Sky City.

Theodore patiently waited for the murmurs to subside, understanding the uncertainty and scepticism that lingered among the air mages. He knew that his words alone would not be enough to convince them of his transformation and the path of redemption he sought.

"I understand your doubts and concerns," Theodore spoke up, his voice projecting a sense of sincerity. "Trust is not easily earned, especially after the pain and fear and pain I have caused. But I stand here today, not as a tyrant seeking power, but as someone who wishes to make amends and lead us all towards a brighter future."

He scanned the faces before him, meeting the eyes of those who looked both hopeful and cautious. Their silent gazes reflected a collective longing for change, for a leader who would guide them with compassion and wisdom. A leader that would deliver them the freedom to live their lives as they wished.

"I do not expect your forgiveness or trust to come easily," Theodore continued, his voice steady. "It will take time for me to prove myself, to show through my actions that I am committed to a path of unity and justice. I am willing to face the consequences of my past and work to earn back your respect and faith."

He paused, allowing his words to sink in, aware of the weight they carried. The air mages listened attentively, their expressions shifting from scepticism to a glimmer of hope.

"And this is why I am willing to offer to you all this pledge right now. I will go into the city below. I will speak with the Archmages of the Cyclonic Essence who have inserted themselves into the palace, and together, we will do what is right and what is best for our people. I want you all to understand, though, that there has already been too much fighting, too much war and too many deaths. I will strive to do everything that I can to come to a peaceful solution. I swear to you all."

A short pause followed.

"We stand with you, Grandmaster," a voice rang out, followed by pockets of others joining in. The air mages echoed their commitment to Theodore's vision, their voices strong and united.

Tears welled up in Theodore's eyes as he looked out at the crowd, feeling a surge of hope and gratitude. He had been given a chance to make things right to redefine his legacy, and he was determined to seize it with unwavering resolve.

"Thank you," Theodore said, his voice filled with emotion. "Thank you for your trust, your understanding, and your willingness to believe in a better future. Let us begin this journey together, step by step, and create a Sky City where justice, unity, and the power of the Cyclonic Essence shine brightly!"

As the crowd erupted into applause and cheers, Theodore's heart swelled with renewed purpose.

With tears streaming down his face, Theodore raised his hand, signalling for the crowd to quiet down. Gradually, the cheers subsided, and a hushed silence fell over the gathering. He took a moment to compose himself, his emotions still raw but his determination unwavering.

"Thank you for your support, for entrusting me with the responsibility to lead us towards a better future," Theodore spoke, his voice steady despite the lingering traces of emotion. "But let us not forget that true change begins with each and every one of us. It is not solely my burden to bear, but a collective effort to heal the wounds that have divided us "

"We will build bridges, not walls. We will foster understanding, not animosity. And we will extend our hand in friendship, not in conquest," Theodore declared, his voice carrying a conviction that resonated through the hearts of those who listened. "The power of the Cyclonic Essence flows within each of us, and with that power, we have the opportunity to shape a future where all mages can live freely, without fear or oppression. Let us begin this journey together, not just as air mages, but as brothers and sisters bound by a common goal," Theodore proclaimed, his voice ringing with conviction. "We will confront the darkness that threatens our world, and in doing so, we will illuminate the path to a future filled with hope, equality, and the freedom to express our true selves!"

The air mages erupted into applause once more, their cheers resounding throughout the Sky City. Theodore stood at the centre of it all, his heart filled with gratitude and determination.

He stepped down off of his stone platform and walked towards the crowd of air mages surrounding him. They tentatively backed away from him at first, though when it became clear that he offered nothing but friendly smiles all around, the people of the Sky City seemed to place their apprehension to the backs of their minds.

"It is so nice to have you back," a man said as Theodore made his way through the people. He was by no means their leader and had no thoughts of becoming such, but these people seemed to place him like he was one, and so he would do whatever he could to give them all a sense of purpose and direction.

The man who had spoken was not familiar to Theodore, but he seemed to be of a similar age. He smiled warmly, and Theodore returned it genuinely.

"I must admit, it feels good to be home," Theodore replied. "Honestly, it feels like this is a big part of me, but still, the memory evades me. I hope that it'll come back soon. Tell me, though, are we friends? Maybe if you tell me your name, it'll jog my memory? Forgive me if that sounds rude."

The man seemed to deflate slightly, though he didn't let his smile fall.

"My name is Sorin," he said, "does that mean anything to you?"

Theodore thought hard for a moment, but it was futile; the name meant nothing to him. Eventually, he shook his head, not wanting to disappoint Sorin further.

"We grew up together," he said. "We first met when I had fallen in with a bad group. You showed me how wrong I was… but then, as we aged, we became friends. You were always so strong, so willing to help people and to work to keep the Sky City afloat. There was always something so different about you, and I don't just mean the power you were able to cultivate. When I was still an Apprentice, you were already a Master. But that never seemed to be an issue to you. Of course…" he trailed off as though he wanted to say more but was afraid of what the response would be.

"Please, go on," Theodore urged.

"I uh…" Sorin said, then visibly steeled himself. "I'm sorry to say, but after your mother died… you changed. You were already an Archmage, and shortly after, you proved yourself even more powerful than the title. But with your newfound power, you seemed to shun everyone that was below you, and believe me, with your power, everyone was below you. It pains me to say, Theodore, that at the time you left the Sky City, we were no longer friends. In fact, I don't believe you had any friends after the way you treated people – they were either useful to you, or they were an annoyance. I hope that this is no longer the case."

Theodore's heart fell. He was being told repeatedly that he was, in his own eyes, a terrible person. It seemed like he had no time for anyone else, and anyone who had cared for him in the past, he had shunned.

Theodore listened to Sorin's words, his heart heavy with the weight of his past actions. The revelations painted a picture of a person he struggled to recognise — a person consumed by power and blinded by his own ambition. The pain in Sorin's voice echoed the pain Theodore felt within himself as he grappled with the consequences of his past behaviour.

"I... I am deeply sorry, Sorin," Theodore said, his voice filled with remorse. "I cannot change what has already transpired, but I promise you that I am not the same person I was back then. I have learned the value of compassion, empathy and the importance of true friendship. If you are willing, I would like to make amends and rebuild our friendship, starting anew."

Sorin's eyes softened, and he nodded slowly. "I want to believe you, Theodore. I truly do. But rebuilding trust takes time, and it will require consistent actions on your part. I am willing to give it a chance, but know that forgiveness is not immediate, nor should it be expected."

Theodore nodded, his heart filled with determination. "I understand, Sorin. Trust is earned, and I am committed to proving myself worthy of it. Please hold me accountable, challenge me when necessary, and help me become the person I aspire to be."

Sorin offered a small smile, the first genuine one since their conversation began. "I will, Theodore. Let us take this opportunity to start anew and forge a friendship built on mutual respect, understanding, and growth."

Then for the first time since he had been back in the Sky City, recognition flashed in Theodore's eyes. He did recognise Sorin's face, but not as a person from his past, but rather from the vision he'd had of his own childhood; Sorin was one of the three bullies that he had fought back against and overcome in his teenage years.

The memory was strange. Theodore knew that in youth, people did things they regretted, and the man that he saw before him gave him no reason to feel angry or threatened, but he wondered what their history would have truly been like, if one of his most prominent visions had been of him fighting against this very person. He decided not to bring the subject up; after all, it would do no good to do so right now. As time went by, and if the opportunity arose, then he might revisit the past.

"Thank you for giving me the opportunity to redeem myself, Sorin," Theodore said genuinely. "I have a plan that I will need to enact, but I hope that when I return to this city, it is with good news and the ability to rekindle old friendships." He then held out his hand, and he and Sorin grasped each other's wrists in the formation and bond of friendship.

Chapter 11 – A Royal Welcome

Just as Theodore had arrived at the Sky City, the crowds of air mages watched as he took a single step off the courtyard where he had first landed and began his descent back to the surface below. For a few moments as he fell, all that he could see were the clouds below him, so effectively shielding the Sky City from anyone below.

Theodore felt both excitement and trepidation as he descended through the thick layer of clouds, not because he was worried about his descent, but rather because of what he had learnt about himself in the Sky City. The memories of his past experiences on the surface were still out of reach, but he knew that the world below had changed significantly since the Sky City had known it. The oppressive rule of the King had not been ended, and the struggles faced by the magic users weighed heavily on his heart.

As he emerged from the clouds, Theodore's gaze was met with the sprawling landscape, and he knew where he wanted to go first. He needed to visit Jack and Maia so that he could update them with his plans and retrieve the sword that he had left hidden in their storehouse. He felt that if he was going to go to the palace, then he was at least going to have to take something sharp along with him.

"Theodore! You're back!" Jack exclaimed, rushing forward to embrace him as he walked through their door like he hadn't missed a beat. Maia followed suit, her eyes filled with concern. "Did you learn anything up there? And what was it like? Did anyone remember you?" the questions came all at once, and they took Theodore off guard. He took a moment to compose himself before he spoke.

Theodore returned Jack's embrace with a warm smile, feeling the genuine joy of their reunion. He then turned to Maia, taking her hands in his and looking into her eyes. "I have learned much, my dear friends, and there is still much to discover. The Sky City is a place filled with power and history, and its people have known a different version of me than the person I am now."

He released Maia's hands and took a step back. "But let us not dwell on the past. I am here to make amends, seek a path of redemption and bring about change for all magic users. The world below is still under the oppressive rule of the tyrant King, and I cannot stand idle. I have a plan, and I think it could work."

Jack and Maia exchanged glances, their expressions betraying their concern, but also their determination. It was clear that they were ready to stand by Theodore's side once again. Jack spoke up first, his voice filled with unwavering loyalty. "You know we're with you, Theodore. Whatever you need, we're here to help. But what is your plan? How do they plan to overthrow the King? And how can we help?"

Theodore took a deep breath, gathering his thoughts before answering. "First, I need to gather the remaining Archmages who have infiltrated the palace. It seems that this was the plan all along, but somewhere along the way, things have been put on hold. I believe that the Archmages that are working for the King are there for a dual purpose, and I need to speak to them to see if they plan to turn on the King."

Maia stepped forward, her eyes burning with determination. "We've faced hardships before, Theodore. We've stood against adversity and fought for what we believe in. Let us help you. Tell us what we can do."

Theodore nodded, grateful for their unwavering support. "Thank you, both of you. I know I can count on you. But this is something that I must do alone. I alone should be able to walk through the palace doors without any threat to my life. But it is what comes next that could cause issue…"

Jack's voice carried a resolute tone. "Consider it done, Theodore, whatever it is before you ask. You saved our son, and you are a brother to this family. We will do whatever you need, and we won't rest until justice is served."

Theodore looked at his two friends and knew that they meant what they said. They would follow him. Do what they could to help and without question, but he knew that right now, they couldn't follow him into the city.

"I need you to spread the word amongst everyone who opposes the King. I need them to know that hope is coming and, along with it, change. I need the people to understand that when the next big things come to pass within this kingdom, that they will be ready and willing to accept whatever will happen next. Can you do this for me? Can you give the people hope?"

Jack smiled weakly. "It is all we have known for so long," he said almost deflated. It was clear that he was hoping for a more active role in all of this, but he knew that whatever Theodore needed, he would be happy to do. "The people of Avondale, everyone who has suffered under the rule of King Roderick, has done so because they believe that one-day things will change. That things will get better. I don't think finding people who are ready to embrace change will be an issue, brother."

Theodore couldn't help but smile in return. "Thank you, brother," he said. "But there is one more thing that I must do. I left something in your storehouse." He looked rather sheepish, and Jack gave him a confused look.

The three of them left the house and entered the rebuilt storehouse where Malek was tending to his cows. Theodore greeted the boy warmly but then walked to the very back and to the haybales where he'd spent his first night. It only took him a moment of searching before he produced the wonderous silver sword that he had taken from the battlefield and had kept hidden ever since.

Jack's eyes widened as they fell upon the masterwork blade.

"The Gods," he breathed. "Such a fine sword… in ten lifetimes, I'd never be able to afford such a weapon…" he held his hand outstretched as though he was going to touch it, then pulled it away. "And you kept this in my storehouse all this time? I could've been killed for theft!"

"I did hide it pretty well," Theodore replied. "Besides, you could always have told them you knew nothing about it; after all, it's the truth, is it not?"

"Well, yes, but…" Jack cut his sentence short, again captivated by the shining blade as the light danced off it.

"What will you do with it?" Maia asked. "Surely this is something that is recognisable to the soldiers, or even the King himself… if they catch you with it…"

"I don't think it will be a problem," Theodore replied happily. "It is my thought that I will be allowed to walk right into the palace myself. If that is not the case, then I will offer the sword as tribute, telling the guards that I found it on the battlefield and sought to bring it back. But as I said, I think that the sword either belonged to someone close to me or perhaps even myself."

Jack and Maia both looked at Theodore as though he'd grown an extra head. How could something so valuable have possibly belonged to him?

"After all," Theodore said. "I am the Grandmaster of the air mages."

"Grand…" Jack stuttered and took a small step away from Theodore, and this time, it was less in shock and more in petrification. Theodore held up his hands defensively.

"Don't worry," he said. "There are just some things that I have learnt that I will need to explain to you."

Theodore then spent the next fifteen minutes explaining everything he had learnt about himself, his past, his power, and the reason that he and the Archmages had given for coming down to the surface. By the time he had finished speaking, Jack and Maia had to pick their jaws up from the floor and close their mouths.

"But…" Maia finally said. "But… why haven't they done anything? And why didn't you kill the King in all the time you were all working for him? It just doesn't make sense."

"I know," Theodore replied. "Perhaps they wouldn't do it without me. I understand that part, but there must have been a reason that we did not kill him the moment we had infiltrated his guard, or even the first time we stood man to man. Whatever it is, I need to know, and the only way to find out is to get back in there – thus, the reason for my plan."

"And then you will kill him?" Jack asked in a low tone. "You will leap into action and kill the King, ending his tyranny and making the lives of everyone within the kingdom better?"

Theodore nodded. "That is what I plan to do. I cannot think of a single reason why I would not do so, and that is the part that has me hesitant. If the air mages are in a position to bring harm to the King, even if it means the end of their own lives, the trade would be worth it. I will discover the truth, though, even if it is the last thing I ever do."

Both Jack and Maia clearly had an issue with the air mages. It was difficult for them to think of them as anything other than monsters, but Theodore was telling them that they were really there to help. But they had done nothing but the King's bidding ever since they'd arrived in the public eye, and that was something that they simply couldn't overlook.

"Are you sure that what you have been told is the truth?" Maia asked. "Are you sure this isn't all a plot to entrap you or to throw another mage to the palace and the King?"

Theodore rubbed his chin at the question. Truthfully, it wasn't something that he had thought about, but he supposed that it was possible.

"What if the King has the families of some of the air mages and is forcing them to do what he says?" Malek said from behind the three adults. "If the King had me, you'd do whatever he said, wouldn't you?"

All three turned to face Malek, who had evidently been listening to their conversation.

"That is a very good point, actually," Jack said softly. "What if the King is holding people who you all care about… would the cost then be too high to take him away? If it was your son or daughter, your mother or father… would you be able to sacrifice their lives to end his reign?"

Theodore bit his lip. "In truth, I do not know. But I have no memories of these things, and it is nothing more than speculation. I need more information, and the only way for me to find out the truth is to go back there. If the King does hold something over all of our heads, then it will be something that needs to be dealt with. But I will say that the Sky City said nothing of families being taken or having gone missing. I do not think that this is the case. But I promise that once I find the truth. I will tell you, no matter what happens. I will find a way."

Jack and Maia exchanged a glance, their expressions filled with concern and uncertainty. They understood the gravity of the situation and the potential risks involved. But they also trusted Theodore and his commitment to uncovering the truth. They knew that he wouldn't make a decision lightly and that he would prioritise the well-being of their loved ones.

After a moment of contemplation, Maia spoke up, her voice filled with determination. "Theodore, we may not fully understand everything that has transpired, but even though you are an air mage… we trust you. We believe in your intentions and your desire to bring about change. We will support you in whatever path you choose, but we also want you to consider all possibilities carefully. If there are lives at stake, we must also find a way to protect them."

Jack nodded, his gaze steady. "We will stand by your side, Theodore. We will do what we can to gather information, uncover the truth, and ensure the safety of our loved ones. Together, we can navigate the challenges that lie ahead and bring about the justice and freedom that the kingdom deserves."

Theodore felt a surge of gratitude for his friends' unwavering support. They were his pillars of strength, grounding him in moments of uncertainty. He knew that they would be there for him every step of the way, offering guidance, loyalty, and a listening ear.

"Thank you, both of you," Theodore said, his voice filled with sincerity. "Your trust and support mean the world to me. But I must leave this place, and I must do this right now. I know that I cannot stand by and watch innocent people hurt any longer – especially if there is anything that I can do about it."

Jack and Maia exchanged a concerned look, but they understood the urgency in Theodore's voice. They had seen the determination in his eyes and knew that he was ready to take action. They had always admired his courage and his unwavering sense of justice.

"We understand, Theodore," Maia said, her voice still filled with worry, But still determination edged her words. "We will continue gathering information, spreading the word, and doing everything we can to support your cause from here. Just promise us that you'll be careful and that you won't take unnecessary risks."

Theodore nodded. "I promise, Maia. I will do everything in my power to protect myself and to ensure the safety of those who are dear to me. But we cannot let fear hold us back from seeking the truth and fighting for what is right. The people of this kingdom deserve a better future, and I won't rest until we achieve it."

Jack stepped forward, placing a hand on Theodore's shoulder. "We're behind you, brother," he said, his voice steady. "Go and do what you must. We will be here, ready to support you in any way we can. Just remember that whatever happens, you're not alone in this."

Theodore nodded, a sense of gratitude washing over him. He knew that he was fortunate to have such loyal friends by his side. With their support and the knowledge that they would continue their efforts to gather support and uncover the truth, he felt a renewed sense of purpose and determination.

"Thank you, both of you," Theodore said, his voice filled with gratitude. "I will keep you updated on my progress, and I won't hesitate to reach out if I need your help. Together, we will bring about the change that this kingdom so desperately needs."

As he turned to leave, Theodore felt a mixture of emotions. There was still much to uncover, many challenges to face, and a kingdom to free from the clutches of an oppressive ruler. But he knew that with the support of his friends, the determination in his heart, and the power of the Cyclonic Essence within him, he had a chance to make a difference.

With each step he took, Theodore's resolve grew stronger. He was ready to face whatever awaited him in the palace, to confront the King, and to uncover the truth behind the air mages' role in the kingdom.

Inevitably, Theodore took off into the sky, once again calling upon his Cyclonic Essence to carry him to where he wanted to go. He knew where the central city was from the farm, having already seen it from the air a number of times, so he willed his mana to carry him towards the palace that stood proud in the centre.

Theodore thought about simply dropping down at the gates and walking into the city, though he didn't feel as though the person he had been told he was in his past would do things by halves and with that in mind, he floated high above the city walls, then moved inwards to above the palace. Finally, he dropped down within the palace grounds. It was clear from the fact that no guards ran up to him shouting, and, in fact, not a single person saw him land that they simply weren't accustomed to expecting people to arrive from above. Theodore walked forwards, pushed open the great wooden doors of the palace and confidently stepped inside.

Of course, he wasn't dressed as a person entering a brilliant palace should be – still wearing the light, thin clothing that Jack had gifted him what felt like a lifetime ago, but he had nothing better, and he wasn't there to show off.

Theodore stepped into the grand palace, his eyes taking in the opulence and grandeur of the surroundings. The marble floors gleamed under the soft glow of the chandeliers, and the intricately designed tapestries adorned the walls. The air was filled with formality and power, a stark contrast to the struggles faced by the people outside the palace walls.

And there, standing before him as though he had been awaiting Theodore's arrival this entire time, was the King. The golden crown atop his head and deep red robes draped around him.

"Good afternoon, Captain Ren. I trust that your absence from the palace has not been too painful?"

Chapter 12 – Oh Captain (Past)

Theodore's eyes glazed over as every single memory that had eluded him in the last few days and weeks came flooding back all in one go. It was as though he had been hit by a lightning bolt; his head hurt, his vision blurred, and he tried to make sense of the images and thoughts he was experiencing.

Theodore's mind raced as the flood of memories crashed over him like it was a tidal wave. He remembered his past life as Captain Ren, a loyal servant of the King. The weight of his previous actions and the realisation of his role in the kingdom's oppression hit him with full force.

His gaze locked with the King's, and for a moment, the room seemed to fade away, leaving only the two of them in an unspoken confrontation. The King's expression was unreadable, his eyes holding curiosity, but also something else that Theodore couldn't quite decipher.

Regaining his composure and knowing that he was very much in danger of losing his disguise, Theodore straightened his posture, his voice steady despite the whirlwind of emotions within him. "Your Majesty," he greeted, his tone respectful. "I apologise for my absence. I was injured in the battle against the rebellious fire mages and have only just returned to my senses. Tell me, has everything been in order in my absence?"

The King nodded nonchalantly and waved his hand non committaly. "Yes, I don't believe that there has been much difference, actually," he said.

Theodore nodded slightly. "Well, I will go to see to the rest of the men; no doubt they have been lacking leadership in my absence. I will return later."

It was not normal for a soldier, even a captain, to speak to the King this way, but Theodore remembered. He remembered everything.

Back when he had been up in the Sky City, Theodore had been distraught at the passing of his mother. He had never before experienced such loss, never had felt the pain and suffering of losing one so close, and had never felt so helpless. No matter what task or obstacle he had ever faced in his early years, no matter how high the odds were stacked against him, he always, always had a way around it.

But not this time.

His mother had fallen sick and had died. It was as simple as that. But Theodore would not accept the frailty of the human condition; he knew better. He was better. And there was one group of people who he knew could make a difference. Who he knew could bring his mother back to the land of the living, even though she had already begun her journey onward into the afterwards. The mages who called upon the Arcani Soul. The death mages.

These mages had promised Theodore that they would be able to bring his mother back to him, though Theodore already knew what they had done to the previous King, and the very same promise that they had made to him.

When he had sought them out and asked them for their explanation, the death mages assured Theodore that their magic would not be able to harm him like the accident that befouled King Cedric, and the very thought that there was a small chance, no matter how tiny, that he could get his mother back, led Theodore to accept their aid.

It was, after all, a new spell and a terrible accident that had led to the death of the King and the death mages rightly pointed out that they had been persecuted as much as any other magic users within the kingdom since. They told Theodore of how they simply wanted to use their mana to help, to put families back together, just like his.

He knew it was too good to be true, but that was exactly why he agreed.

Theodore took his mother's body in the dead of night to a graveyard on the outskirts of the kingdom and met with nine death mages, who each stood ready to combine their powers to enact their spell.

Theodore stood beside his mother's body, who lay still on the stone crypt as the mages began to chant, and Theodore remembered how his entire body filled with hope, even through the tears that streamed down his face and wet his cheeks at the sight of his mother's lifeless body.

As the mages chanted their spell, it was clear that they were keeping their promise; the dark purple mana that began to swirl all around the mages, flowing back and forth, spiralling as though it was some ethereal smoke, began to grow larger and become denser and denser. Theodore watched with wide eyes as everything that he had hoped for was coming to fruition.

Then, without warning, the leader of the mages of the Arcani Soul threw his hands towards Theodore, and the purple mist accosted him within a second. Through his nose, mouth, ears and even his eyes, the mist flowed into him, and as he tried to scream, to keep it from his body, he knew in that moment that it was futile. He, like King Cedric, had been betrayed.

But then it was over.

Theodore now looked out from behind his own two eyes as though he was a passenger within his own body because something else was in control. Something powerful, far more powerful than he was. And he knew that all it wanted to do was cause death wherever it went.

The entity that controlled Theodore from within seemed to be able to share in Theodore's own memories from the moment he had taken control because it immediately sought to send Theodore back to the Sky City in order to raise his army. The entity was disappointed, though, when there were only a handful of Archmages within the flying city, and they seemed all too content with staying far above the kingdom below, where their magic would see them killed.

Theodore had tried screaming at first. He had tried forcing his body to move through his will. He had even tried begging the entity to stop whatever this was. But Theodore never received a response. He simply had to watch and listen as his body mocked people for being too weak, and punished mages when their magic or spells weren't as powerful or as accurate as they should have been. He even had to watch as the entity banished his own father from the Sky City when he had questioned Theodore's actions and the change he seemed to have gone through.

Theodore had become a monster. He had become hated, and there was nothing that he could do about it.

Eventually, Theodore had proven to the rest of the Sky City that he was far beyond them in his power and that he would be their leader either by their own allowance or by force if it so required. Not a single person stood up to Theodore's power. After all, as the Grandmaster, not even the Archmages would have been able to defeat him. Together, perhaps, but the risks of a confrontation were far too high and if there was a battle, it was likely that many of them wouldve perished.

The entity within Theodore then decided that it was time to return to the surface, though this time with a company of Archmages in tow.

The real Theodore did not know if the entity truly knew what was happening on the surface or if the plan that it had relayed to the Sky City was the truth or not, though this was the first time that the entity and

Theodore had similar feelings towards what was happening. The entity had told the rest of the Sky City that they were going to go down to the surface to kill the King, to bring an end to his oppression and hatred for all magic users, and at least this seemed to resonate with most of the people who had stood to listen. The Archmages, though, weren't given a choice in the matter.

Theodore remembered how he had felt as he had been a passenger within his own body as they had descended towards the surface. As they had seen the grand palace and made their way towards it from above, where the guards would not have been able to stop them. He remembered as, one by one, the wielders of the Cyclonic Essence entered the palace through a high, open window and stood awaiting the arrival of King Roderick within a small chamber.

"Do not speak," Theodore heard himself order the rest of the air mages as they stood on either side of the door. It was an odd experience; Theodore stood facing the door with the Archmages forming a sort of corridor through which the King would have no choice but to walk. "Whatever comes to pass here, whatever I say, it is all a part of our plan. If any one of you speaks out of turn, there will be dire consequences. And that goes for your friends and family too. Do not speak. Not one word."

It was the first time that Theodore had heard the entity threaten these Archmages directly, but it would not be the last.

Then the door opened as though it had been pushed without a care in the world, and King Roderick stepped into the room, walking forward as nonchalantly as Theodore had ever seen anyone walk.

He took three steps and then stopped as his eyes met Theodore. Within a moment, hatred had filled the King's gaze.

The wooden door slammed shut behind him, thrown closed by a powerful gust of wind.

"Your majesty," Theodore heard his voice seep out. "How nice of you to join us. We were all just talking about how we would like to show this all-powerful King how powerless he can truly be."

Theodore smiled wickedly.

"What is this?" Roderick replied, clearly forcing himself to appear strong and unfazed. It didn't seem to be working. "Guards!" he began to call for his guards, though quick as a flash, one of the Archmages had placed a hand over the King's mouth and silenced him.

"It is very rude of me to speak without first introducing myself, no?" Theodore asked. "My name is Renfrey, though you may call me Ren if you would prefer. I feel that a shorter name fits better with my short temper, you see?" Ren nodded to the Archmage who was covering the King's mouth, and he abruptly let go.

"Guards, GUARDS!" the King immediately screamed. "I am under attack! Come to me, NOW! Protect your King!"

Ren tutted and held a finger up mockingly.

"Do not think me a fool, my King," he said with a grin. "Did you honestly think that we would allow you to call for help? No, this room has been shielded from all sound getting in or, indeed, out. I am afraid that you may scream and shout for help all you like, but your words, much like your father's pleas for the return of his wife, will fall upon deaf ears."

Theodore's voice dripped with a chilling menace as he continued to taunt the King. Roderick's face twisted with anger and frustration, but he was powerless, surrounded by the formidable air mages who had infiltrated his palace.

Renfrey revelled in his newfound control, relishing the moment he had been waiting for. This was his opportunity to exact revenge on the King, who had oppressed and hunted down the magic users for years.

"Tell me, King Roderick, do you remember the countless lives you have shattered? The families that have been torn apart, the innocent blood spilt?'

The King did not respond to the question, sensing that whatever he said would not change the course of the conversation.

"What do you want," he growled. "Do you want me to beg? To tell you that I have seen the errors in my ways? Ha! I stand by my actions, and whatever you plan to do, you better do it quickly because I grow tired of this foolishness."

"Foolishness?" Renfrey asked in a mocking tone. "You misunderstand me, King Roderick. "I do not wish to stop you in your crusade against magic. No, I sense a power in you, a certainty in your actions that displays no fear or second-guessing. It is a rare thing, sir. No, I do not wish to stop you. I wish to join you."

Roderick's eyes widened in surprise, his expression shifting from defiance to confusion. The notion that one of the very mages he had hunted down and oppressed would willingly offer their allegiance was beyond comprehension.

"You... wish to join me?" Roderick repeated, his voice laced with scepticism. "Why would I ever trust the words of a mage? You are all the same…"

"WE ARE NOT ALL THE SAME!" Theodore bellowed, then lowered his voice to a more acceptable level. "And I wish to join you so that together, we can eradicate the weakness that is all of the other mages within the kingdom. My friends here and I," Ren gestured to the other mages in the room, who all looked very confused, though remained silent, "deserve to be the only mages in existence, without challenge or competition. And to answer your question of trust: know that we could have broken you the moment you stepped into this room. Even now, with the snap of my fingers, I could send you to your death, and the kingdom would be left absent its King." Ren held his fingers up threateningly, though the King did not reccil nor cower from them.

Theodore's consciousness struggled against the grip of Renfrey's control, alarmed at the direction the conversation was taking. He had thought that Ren's primary goal was to bring justice and freedom to the kingdom, not to align himself with the very source of its oppression.

"Renfrey, please stop this," Theodore's voice pleaded from within. "You cannot ally yourself with Roderick! He is a Tyrant!"

But Renfrey either pushed aside Theodore's objections or did not hear them at all.

"Think about it, King Roderick," he continued, his voice laced with persuasion. "Together, with our combined forces, we could reshape this kingdom, restore order, and bring an end to the chaos that plagues it. Imagine the power we could wield."

Roderick's expression softened for a moment as he considered the proposal. The prospect of having the very mages he had sought to eliminate as his allies must have appealed to his desire for absolute control.

"You speak of power, Renfrey," Roderick mused, his voice contemplative. "But how can I trust that you won't turn against me, that this isn't some ploy to deceive and destroy me? And if you are so able to kill me, why have you not done so already?"

Renfrey's smile grew wider, his voice dripping with false sincerity. "My loyalty, dear King, is unmatched. I am a servant of power, and I recognise the power that lies within you. Together, we could create a kingdom that will be forever remembered in history. But make no mistake. I can kill you whenever I so choose. But the kingdom… the people are conditioned to follow your rule, so that is what we shall present to them."

Theodore fought desperately to regain control, to remind Roderick of the suffering he had inflicted, but his pleas fell on deaf ears. Renfrey's manipulations were overpowering, clouding Roderick's judgment and exploiting his desire for dominion.

Roderick's gaze hardened once again, his earlier defiance returning. "Very well, Renfrey," he said, a cruel smile curling his lips. "If you are truly willing to pledge your loyalty and assist me in my pursuit of power, then perhaps there is a place for you by my side. But make no mistake; any betrayal will be met with swift and merciless retribution. I will place your mages as an elite unit within my army and bestow upon you the title of Captain Renfrey if that is what you so wish?"

"Captain Ren," Ren replied with a devious smile. And I look forward to working with you to rid the world of any who oppose us."

Theodore's heart sank as he witnessed the depths of Renfrey's deception. The path he had chosen, the alliance with Roderick, was a dark and treacherous one. He could no longer recognise the person he had become, and the weight of his actions bore heavily upon him.

As Roderick extended his hand, offering the title of Captain Ren, Theodore felt a surge of conflicting emotions. The desire to bring justice to the kingdom warred with the knowledge that he had become a puppet, controlled by an entity that sought power and domination.

"Very well, King Roderick," Ren said, his voice filled with a mix of resignation and determination. "I accept your offer. I shall serve as Captain Ren and lead your elite unit of mages to ensure the eradication of those who oppose us."

"Then let me bestow upon you this one gift," Roderick said with a smile. "To cement your new position within the palace, and a way of saying thanks for what you have done in my service today…" The King then unbuckled his own sword from his waist, and Theodore immediately recognised it. He recognised it because it was the very sword that he now carried. The sword that he had removed from the battlefield and had hidden when he had found Jack's farmstead.

Chapter 13 – Mutiny (Past)

"What is this?" one of the air mages finally spoke up, and when Ren's eyes fell upon the man, he could now see the looks of sheer disbelief from all of the others staring back at him.

Ren's gaze hardened as he turned to face the dissenting air mage. He could sense the unrest and confusion spreading amongst the group, threatening to undermine the facade he had carefully constructed and presented to the King.

"This is the path we have chosen," Ren declared, his voice cold and commanding. "We have seen the futility of resistance and the power that lies within our grasp. It is time to cast aside doubt and embrace the opportunities that an alliance of this magnitude presents. The time for change has come."

The air mage who had already spoken, unwilling to accept Ren's words at face value, stepped forward with a defiant glare. "You speak of change, Captain Ren, but this alliance with Roderick goes against everything we've fought for. We sought justice and freedom, not to become some pawns in his game."

Ren's grip on his power tightened, and the air around him shimmered and shifted, a warning to the air mage and the others who might question his authority. "Do not mistake my actions for weakness," he replied, his voice laced with a dangerous edge. "You will fall in line and act as you are ordered, or you will die."

The dissenting air mage, his resolve unbroken, met Ren's gaze with unwavering determination. "I will not be a part of whatever this game is, Captain Ren. I refuse to abandon the cause we once believed in."

Ren's patience waned, and with a wave of his hand, he summoned a powerful gust of wind that slammed the air mage against the wall, rendering him temporarily incapacitated. The other mages gasped in shock, their loyalty wavering in the face of such brutal force against one of their own.

"This is your only warning," Ren said, his voice seething with anger. "Any further objections will be met with severe consequences. Do any of the rest of you have anything to say?"

Ren's display of power silenced the remaining air mages, their fear and uncertainty now palpable.

"I… will… not… allow… this," the mage who had been slammed into the wall spluttered out, blood already dripping from his mouth.

Ren's expression twisted into a malicious grin as he approached the wounded air mage. He loomed over the fallen man, revelling in the fear and defiance that still burned within him.

"Your loyalty to the cause is admirable," Ren said, his voice dripping with sadistic satisfaction. "But loyalty without power is meaningless. You will learn that lesson, one way or another."

Ren raised his hand, preparing to deliver a final blow to the helpless air mage when suddenly, a gust of wind slammed into him so hard it was as though it was a brick wall. Ren shifted slightly, though he was apparently otherwise unaffected by the attack that had come from another of the Archmages.

Turning to see who had dared to attack him, Ren saw another of the Archmages step forward, ready to defend what he thought was right.

Ren smiled deviously.

"When you die, I will order your parents killed, your children killed, your friends and your families killed. This is the price for your actions and the price for your disobedience. So before another of you condemn all those you love to suffering and death, I implore you to think very carefully."

The mages all froze, finally feeling the weight of their situation.

Then the mage who had hit the wall let out a guttural scream, pulled a button free from his shirt and launched it towards the King with an immense explosion of air mana.

The button travelled like it was a deadly projectile towards the King, who had been stunned into silence and petrification and in that moment, he saw his life flash before his eyes.

But Captain Ren was there to protect him now.

As the button hurtled towards the King, Ren moved swiftly, intercepting it with a barrier of swirling wind. The explosive impact dispersed harmlessly against the shield, leaving the King unscathed and shocked.

Ren's eyes blazed with anger as he turned his attention back to the rebellious air mage. "You dare to challenge me, to threaten the life of the King?" he snarled, his voice laced with fury. "Your defiance will be your undoing."

With a flick of his wrist, Ren summoned a powerful spell that lifted the air mage off his feet, suspending him in mid-air. The mage struggled against the invisible force, his expression a mixture of pain and determination.

"You will pay for your insolence," Ren declared, his voice resonating with an unnatural authority. He tightened his grip on the wind, increasing the pressure around the mage, cutting off his breath.

The second Archmage, who had escaped the attention of Captain Ren, then began a spell of his own. But Ren could feel what was coming. He didn't even have to turn to will his mana into a second spell that generated a bubble of Cyclonic Essence all around him, and within that moment, no magic existed within the room. That was, of course, except for Captain Ren's own.

"Do you not see that there is nothing that you can do to stop me?" he growled. "Do you not realise that your power is nothing compared to what I can do? I am your leader, and you will do as commanded."

And with that, the Archmage, who had been gasping, struggling for breath, fell limply to the ground and the room went silent.

"Are there any more who would challenge me?" he asked in a low tone.

Nobody replied.

"Good. Then take that one away and make sure I never see him alive again. He pointed to the Archmage who had tried to attack him with a gust of wind, and almost immediately, two of the remaining Archmages took their comrade by the arms and pulled him out through the door.

Theodore remembered all of this as though it was happening all over again. He had been so helpless, trapped behind his own eyes, watching these heinous things occur. And he felt guilty. Like all of this was his fault.

Theodore's heart ached with guilt and regret as he watched the air mage being dragged away, his fate sealed by Ren's merciless command. The weight of his inaction pressed upon him, and he knew that he had to find a way to regain control, to stop Ren's reign of tyranny.

But then Theodore's memory fast-forwarded to years later. Past the conflicts he had fought in. Past countless murders of mages from all schools of magic, past parents begging for their children to be spared. Theodore remembered it all.

But then he remembered the academy that was hidden deep within the forest.

He remembered how the King had learnt that a skilled earth mage had founded a place deep within the forest for a group of young mages to use as their sanctuary. How most of these mages were no older than eighteen, and how Ren had felt an overwhelming delight at the fact that he had the chance to take so many down in one go.

Theodore had to watch again as Captain Ren and his Archmages began to clear the forest of the magical creatures so that they could effectively sweep the area in search of this academy.

Captain Ren's magic swept the forest clean of everything that he encountered, and when he eventually came across a group of young mages, his internal voice grew hoarse as he tried over and over to scream at the Arcani Soul who had taken over his body.

"Please, Renfrey…" he begged, but again it had fallen on deaf ears.

Theodore heard his own voice again, controlled by Captain Ren, spewing hatred and threats towards people who he had never known and who simply wanted to exist in peace.

"I want you to know your place, earth mage," Ren said, the voice low and threatening. "Magic is an abomination. Outlawed by our King, and as such, it carries the highest penalty of all. You should know that by now, shouldn't you?" then a pause, in which Theodore could see that this young girl was doing her best to will her mana into action so that she could protect herself and her friends.

"Pathetic," Captain Ren had scoffed.

Then a shout came from away to the side, and before Theodore had even noticed, a young man appeared, shouting whilst holding a wooden sword high above his head. Theodore, in that moment, simply wished for the attack to land, for all of this to be over. He simply couldn't take any more.

"Ah, a little stronger, this one," the Captain said loudly. "But not strong enough."

Then the sword within the boy's hands abruptly shrunk down into nothing before disappearing entirely, and two soldiers appeared between him and Ren, taking hold of the boy's arms before he could reach his target.

"Get your hands off me!" The boy had shouted as he struggled against the guards. It was no use, though; he was fighting a losing battle.

Then Captain Ren took a step forward towards the boy.

"What did you really think was going to happen here?" He asked with a sly grin on his face. "Surely you did not expect to disrupt an entire camp of the kingdom's soldiers?"

"I expected to do what was right," the boy said through gritted teeth.

Captain Ren chuckled darkly. "What's right is following the law, boy. Magic is forbidden in our kingdom, and those who practice it must be punished."

At that moment, a large Grimscale appeared seemingly out of nowhere. It was a huge beast, and Theodore again harboured the hope that this creature would bring about the end for him and Captain Ren. He had never seen one so large and so threatening before.

The soldiers all around, caught off guard by the beast's sudden appearance, hesitated for a moment before regaining their composure and raising their weapons.

But the Grimscale was too quick for them. It had charged forward with incredible speed, its claws and beak tearing through the soldiers without reply. The battle was short but deadly for most of the soldiers in the clearing.

Captain Ren, though, had been watching and hadn't made a single move.

"Come on, we have to go," the young girl said to the boy who had wielded the wooden sword, the soldiers who had held him now gone.

"I don't think so," Captain Ren announced loudly without turning his head. "Let me just deal with this, and I'll be back with you in a second."

The Captain then shut his eyes, and even though it darkened the world for Theodore, he knew what was happening.

But something amazing had happened. Theodore's body was swept off the ground, flying through the air and he impacted a very solid tree trunk, winding Captain Ren. It took him a few moments to regain his senses, but when he had done so, the young mages had made their escape.

Theodore remembered this scene fondly; it had been the very first time that someone had stood up to Captain Ren and got away with it. He could feel the anger within the Arcani Soul, but it wasn't blind rage or the need to rush after the mages and tear them apart. It was far scarier than that; this anger was contemplative, planned, and it made Theodore feel cold.

Then Theodore remembered the execution of the headmaster of the earth mage academy. Captain Ren had caught the man within the city himself and had even allowed the mage to send out a letter of explanation to his students. He knew they wouldn't be able to resist mounting a rescue operation for their beloved master.

But he hadn't counted on there being so many rebels within the city and that they would make their stand right there at the execution.

The fight had seemed all so one-sided for the most part, and the rebels were falling in waves. But when Ren had entered the battle, he finally discovered his limits. There was just so much happening, so many spells flying back and forth, so much mana filling the air. He had tried to control it, casting his spells as he usually had, but he had been hit, momentarily ripped from the fight, and in that moment, Theodore had again wished for death to take him.

Captain Ren, though, would again not be felled so easily.

He had redoubled his efforts, focussing his mana on single targets or smaller groups as he moved through the battle rather than the entire conflict all at once. Theodore again had to watch in horror as this new tactic became so effective that within minutes the few remaining mages were fleeing from the city, the rest lying dead in the palace grounds.

If Theodore could have been sick, then he would have.

But there was one more memory that stood out to Theodore. One shining beacon of hope that came back to him once he had finished reliving everything that he had done whilst under the control of Ren, the Arcani Soul. The great battle that had robbed him of his memories and almost left him dead, along with so many fire mages.

Captain Ren had been told to take a veritable army to the place that had been called 'The Pit'. It was another stronghold that housed and taught mages how to fight, though this time, it was wielders of the Eternal Flame. The reports that Captain Ren and the King had received were about the power that this place contained, the skill of its fighters and their resolve to be the strongest mages in the kingdom. Theodore felt, though, that Captain Ren did not fear these mages in the slightest. He could tell that Captain Ren saw them as nothing more than another annoyance, a stain on the kingdom that he would be the one to wash away.

They had attacked without warning and without mercy. They had bombarded the ancient fortress with magic and projectiles until the soldiers could enter inside and flush out the frightened mages within. The plan had been successful. Too successful.

The fire mages had exited their fortress and faced the soldiers and Captain Ren's Archmages on an open battlefield, undeterred and willing to give their lives for what they believed in.

But this place held something that Ren hadn't been expecting. Leading the rebel fire mages who he sought to overthrow, was a Grandmaster. Both Ren and Theodore could feel the man's power radiating from his body, and if Theodore could have smiled, he would have.

Both this new Grandmaster and Captain Ren exchanged a flurry of powerful spells, each one more potent than the last, as the rest of the soldiers and mages watched, allowing them to face off against each other in single combat. It was as though everyone else felt like whatever the outcome of this battle was, it would decide which side would come out the victor, and which would lose. In effect, though, that was what it was because with a Grandmaster fighting on either side, that side was sure to be unmatched.

A searing torrent of flames roared towards Ren, and he countered by creating a whirling vortex of air that snuffed out the fire before it could reach him.

Ren then retaliated with a series of lightning-fast air blades, slicing through the air towards the opposing Grandmaster, who in turn managed to deflect most of them with a barrier of flame, but a few slipped through, leaving shallow cuts on the man's arms and chest.

Theodore wondered how exactly some of the spells had managed to get through to Ren's opponent when the pair seemed so evenly matched, but then he had felt it. Captain Ren was enacting a subtler, hidden spell that this fire mage hadn't accounted for. It was so subtle, in fact, that had Theodore not felt his Cyclonic Essence ever so slightly diverted to fuel the spell, he might not have noticed it himself. It was certainly there, though, the spell that dampened the Eternal Flame within the opposing Grandmaster by a hundredth of a degree. Nothing extreme, but in a battle like this, it was enough.

A young boy had shouted something. A word of warning to his master, but Ren hadn't cared. He knew that this battle was all but over.

Captain Ren then moved to enact his killing blow. Again, Theodore felt his Cyclonic essence called into being to feed the spell that would take the life of this Grandmaster. This weakened man who was simply trying to protect those who looked up to him.

But then, before he cast his spell, a dark smoke had swept across the battlefield. Ren had hesitated, only for a second once he saw the smoke, and then everything was hidden from his view.

Ren froze for just a second, wondering if when the smoke dissipated that he would be greeted with an empty battlefield – the fire mages using the cover to make their escape. But then, a small, fist-sized fireball tore through the smoke directly at him. He could tell before it even got close, though, that this was not a spell launched by the Grandmaster.

Ren smiled. The students had come to their master's aid, and how futile it was. He flicked the fireball away with a snap of his wrist, as well as the poorly aimed string that followed.

But then Theodore felt something change, and he knew that Ren had felt it too. Like a burning culmination of power, a merging of Eternal Flames hidden, bending the smokescreen covering the battle. And it made Ren afraid. For the first time that Theodore had ever felt it from his unwanted puppetmaster, but it was there: genuine fear. Ren knew that this power, whatever it was, would rival his own. Perhaps even surpass it.

Ren leapt into action, summoning a colossal whirlwind that swept the battlefield clean to reveal three younger mages, his Grandmaster opponent on the ground and a young boy floating in the air above his fallen master.

Then after a few seconds passed, Captain Ren simply laughed.

"Well, well, well," he taunted, a wicked grin spreading across his face. "It seems our little friend here has bitten off more than he can chew. What a shame."

But Theodore could see through the bravado the Captain was portraying. It didn't matter how calm his tone was or how assured of his victory he seemed; he was still worried. Worried that he could lose this fight.

The young mages had been the first to act. One of them looked to aid the boy who floated there, seemingly in immense pain, whilst the other two began launching fireball after fireball at Ren. Ren, though, didn't stop laughing for a moment as the fireballs pinged away from his open hands. Some of them he even let hit him so that he could prove just how powerful he was in comparison to these annoying gnats.

"I am sorry," Ren finally said with a sneer in the lull of battle. "But your time has finally come to an end. I would say that you fought valiantly, though as the annoying insect, your lives, too, must come to their early conclusions.

Captain Ren then finally released his stored mana.

At first, a small cyclone wafted into existence before Captain Ren, but as it was fed by his mana, it quickly grew and grew until it reached high up into the sky before him. The sound that it gave off became deafening as it carried the very atmosphere around them with it.

There was no time for these young mages to escape any more.

Captain Ren clapped his hands together once, and the cyclone fell to the ground as though it had been detonated from its base.

Everyone and everything flew high into the air and far away from the battlefield within a second, the spell overwhelming everything it touched; that was, of course, except for the air mages still standing behind Ren.

"Well, I guess that put an end to all of that," Ren said with a smile, turning to his Archmages. "I doubt that any would survive when they do eventually land, but if they do… then they won't be any fit state to fight, wouldn't you agree?"

Again Theodore felt sickened. How could this person call himself a mage when all he wanted to do was kill and harm, and his own kind nonetheless? Again he wanted to shut his eyes, to look away, to forget… but again, he was unable, forced to watch as Ren carried out his unforgivable acts.

But the silence that returned from the Archmages gave Ren cause to pause. He slowly turned back around, and Theodore's heart leapt as he saw the still-floating form of the young mage, still in exactly the same place he'd been, only higher in the air now. He must've been in some pain, as even Theodore could see that his skin was burnt and blistered. But now, the boy was glowing.

Then the boy opened his eyes, and within them, Theodore saw only red anger and hatred.

The boy's voice dissected the battlefield between him and the air mages. "You think you've won? You think you can just destroy everything we've built and walk away?"

Captain Ren looked at him with a forced amusement but now also a hint of unease. "You're still here? You should be grateful you're alive, boy. Now, know your place and stay down."

Theodore could feel the Cyclonic Essence swirling about his body. Ren was trying to bring the boy back down to the ground and make him kneel, but the boy wouldn't budge, and no matter how much mana Ren attempted to funnel into the spell that pushed down on his opponent, the boy remained in place.

Then the boy spoke again, and the words shook Ren. "No. You've taken too much from us, and now it's time for you to pay."

The red glow surrounding the boy intensified, and the air around him crackled with energy.

With a deafening roar, a bright beam of pure red light shot high into the sky, and when it touched the clouds, the sky turned instantly black. Red tendrils of mana forked through the sky, and after a short pause, the first meteor fell, accompanied by the smash of red lightning.

Behind it came countless more. Each meteor was the size of ten men and burning with white-hot flames that trailed behind each before they slammed into the ground in a cacophony of explosions.

They slammed into Captain Ren and his air mages, who all tried to run or cast protective shells around themselves, but the sheer power of this attack was too much for them to handle, and within a moment, the devastation was evident.

The air mages were sent flying, their bodies battered and broken by the force of the spell.

Captain Ren, however, was not so easily defeated. With a grunt of effort, he managed to hold his ground. Just before the first meteors had impacted the ground, Ren had managed to construct a dome of protective mana around himself.

Theodore tried everything he could to will his mana back away from the dome, to allow just a single piece of this spell through to impact his stolen body, but again, it was no use.

Theodore's body was bleeding, and he had cuts all over his body, blood staining his royal white robes. But it still wasn't enough. It was close, but this wasn't going to be enough to kill him and the Captain.

But to Theodore's absolute delight, the boy wasn't done. The red glow around him grew brighter and more intense, and he let out another guttural scream as he launched a second, even more powerful attack.

Captain Ren's eyes widened in horror as the wave of heat bore down on him, causing the entire world to turn wavy as it approached. He knew that now he could do nothing to avoid the attack, and so he held his arms out wide and welcomed his end. Theodore mentally followed suit. This boy, this young man who he hadn't given hope in hell's chance of besting Ren in battle, had finally done it. He had ended Theodore's imprisonment and put a stop to the vile tirade that Ren had embarked upon.

When the spell hit Ren's barrier, it shattered like glass under the immense force, and Theodore's body was engulfed in the heat before he fell to the ground with a sickening thud.

In the moments before Ren had fallen, though, he felt something. It was hard to place at first because of the immense pain that he had been in, mostly due to the flames that engulfed him, though no, it wasn't because of that. This pain was different. It was almost as though someone was reaching into his soul, had taken a hold of Captain Ren and was wrenching him from Theodore's body.

He screamed louder than he had ever thought possible. His body was ripped apart from the inside, but he could hear no sound coming from his physical mouth. But then, he realised that he could hear himself. He was screaming. He was back in control, and the Arcani Soul that had taken over had finally been removed. Whoever this boy was, whatever he had done, he had saved Theodore's life.

Chapter 14 – Regicide (Present)

Theodore stumbled slightly as the memories pushed him off-balance, but he regained his composure and quickly made his way through the palace to the small room where he knew the rest of the Archmages would be, as they had been given a place of their own to rest and recover by the King.

Theodore knew there had only been fifteen Archmages at the point when the young fire mage had beaten him, but he had to do something to make amends; these were his people, his friends, and they needed to know that they didn't have to fear him any more.

As soon as he reached the Archmage's chambers, Theodore pushed the door open and stood face to face with fifteen Archmages of the Cyclonic Essence.

"C… Captain Ren," the closest of the mages, stuttered when his eyes fell upon Theodore, still dressed in his less-than-royal clothes and still carrying the majestic shining sword at his hip.

Theodore didn't respond but quietly closed the door behind him so that what he had to say next would not be overheard.

"Where have you been? We all thought you had perished in the…" the mage trailed off as though he remembered who it was he was speaking to.

"Who do you think you are talking to?" Theodore forced his expression to one of twisted anger. "How dare you presume that I, the mighty Captain Ren, would be felled by such weaklings!"

The room fell silent for a long pause, and then Theodore laughed heartily. It was strange. He could tell that the Archmages were certainly scared of him because of what Captain Ren had portrayed him as, but these people had once been his friends, his equals, and above anything else, he was pleased to see them all.

Theodore's laughter echoed in the room, a mix of relief and genuine joy. He saw the confusion and fear in the eyes of the Archmages, but he knew he had to dispel their concerns and let them see the truth.

As the laughter died down, Theodore took a step forward; his voice filled with sincerity. "My friends, it is me, Theodore," he said, his voice steady and calm. "Captain Ren is no more. But there is so much I have to explain to you all."

The Archmages exchanged glances, unsure of whether or not to believe Theodore's words. But as they looked into his eyes, they saw a flicker of the person they had once known, the person they had fought alongside and trusted.

"It's really me," Theodore pressed, his voice filled with emotion. "I cannot express how sorry I am for the pain I have caused, for the fear and confusion I have brought upon all of you. But I want you to know that I am here to make amends, to right the wrongs that were done under the influence of Captain Ren."

He paused, allowing his words to sink in. The room remained silent, the Archmages grappling with the conflicting emotions within them.

One of the mages, a woman with a determined expression, stepped forward. "If it truly is you, Theodore," she said, her voice cautious yet hopeful, "then prove it. Prove that Captain Ren is gone, that we can trust you once more. Or is this all some test? Something to see if we truly are loyal to your cause?"

"I am still the same person I have always been," Theodore said, his voice filled with conviction. "I will never again allow myself to be controlled by darkness. My purpose now is to right the wrongs, to bring justice and freedom to our kingdom. And I need your help to do so. But know that you are not the first to ask if this is a test; I have visited the Sky City, told them of my plans to come here and overthrow this oppressive and murderous regime, but I will need your help, for I cannot do this alone."

The Archmages exchanged glances once more, their expressions betraying uncertainty and cautious hope. They had witnessed the transformation of Theodore from the feared Captain Ren to the familiar face before them, but trust needed to be earned, especially after the atrocities committed under Captain Ren's control.

The woman who had spoken earlier stepped forward again, her voice firm but tinged with a glimmer of belief. "Theodore, if what you say is true, if Captain Ren truly no longer controls you, then we stand with you," she declared. "But we need proof, something to show that you are committed to the cause of justice and that our trust in you is not misplaced."

Theodore nodded, understanding their need for reassurance. He reached for the silver sword at his hip, the very weapon that had become synonymous with Captain Ren's terrifying presence.

"This sword," Theodore said, his voice resolute, "it has been a symbol of fear and tyranny. But now, it represents a new beginning, a symbol of redemption and the fight for freedom. I pledge to you all that I will use this sword to protect, not to harm. I will wield it in the name of justice and bring down the oppressive regime that has plagued our kingdom. I not only give you this pledge willingly, but I swear to you upon the very Cyclonic Essence that enriches my soul that I speak the truth and again beg you for your forgiveness."

The woman, still peering into Theodore's eyes as though she would be able to see a response from his Cyclonic Essence deep within, eventually sighed.

"Then Theodore," she made the effort to again speak his name. "Tell us what happened to you. Tell us who Captain Ren was and how you have broken free of his control. Tell us everything so that we can all make our own minds up as to whether you deserve our forgiveness or not."

The very fact that the woman had made this statement told Theodore a lot more than her words could; if she had said such a thing to Captain Ren, she would've been killed on the spot.

Theodore sighed, ready to tell his story for the very first time. "Captain Ren was not a person, but an entity of the Arcane Soul, the death mana that took control of my body and manipulated my actions," Theodore began, his voice filled with sincerity. "When my mother died… I mourned; I tried to tell myself that her passing was inevitable, just even. That she had gone to a better place, and perhaps one day I would see her again." He closed his eyes as he remembered his mother as she had lain before him, weak and dying. "But I fell into a dark place. A place where I convinced myself that there was something I could do to bring her back even. So I reached out to the masters of death and begged them to perform a spell to give her a renewed life. But some things are simply not meant to be, are they?"

The room fell silent, heavy with Theodore's heartache, but nobody interrupted him.

"I was trapped within my own mind, unable to control my own actions. I tried to stop him; I tried everything. I screamed from within myself until I grew hoarse from the effort, but it was no use. Ren used me as a vessel to carry out his dark desires, to sow chaos and fear in the name of power. He used my powers to kill and oppress in the name of the King, and where we all sought to fight for what is right in this world, Ren only wanted war and death. I do not truly know the reasons behind his actions."

He paused, his hands clenching into fists as he relived the memories. "Under Ren's influence, I committed terrible acts, acts that I will forever carry the weight of. But I want you to know that I fought against his control with every ounce of my being. I resisted his influence, and it was through the bravery and unexpected skill of a young fire mage that I was finally freed."

Theodore's voice trembled with emotion as he continued. "This fire mage, whose name I do not yet know, unleashed a power that surpassed even Ren's. He challenged Ren's authority and brought forth a devastating attack that shattered the hold Ren had over me, banishing him from my body and soul. It was in that moment that I regained control that I became Theodore once more."

He took a step closer to the Archmages; his voice filled with sincerity. "I stand before you today, not as Captain Ren, but as Theodore, a man burdened by guilt and remorse. I am here to atone for my actions, to fight for justice and freedom. I cannot undo the past, but I can work towards a better future, a future where the atrocities committed under Ren's command are never repeated."

The room remained silent, the Archmages absorbing Theodore's words. The woman who had questioned him earlier spoke again, her voice softer this time. "Theodore, if what you say is true, then you have endured a great deal. We cannot ignore the pain and suffering you have been through, nor can we deny the courage it takes to confront your past and seek redemption."

She paused, her gaze unwavering. "But forgiveness is not given easily, nor should it be. It is earned through actions, through demonstrating your commitment to the cause of justice and through proving that you are indeed free from Ren's influence. We will watch you closely, Theodore, and we will judge you by your deeds. Show us that you are worthy of our trust, and we will stand by your side."

Theodore nodded, his expression resolute. "I understand," he said. "I will do everything in my power to right the wrongs, to bring down the oppressive regime that has plagued our kingdom. I will prove to you, through my actions, that I am no longer controlled by darkness. Thank you for your consideration, Julia," he said honestly. "You have always been fair to me."

The room fell into a contemplative silence, the Archmages considering

Theodore's words, though the Archmage named Julia gave Theodore a warm smile at his use of her name. The road to redemption would not be an easy one, but Theodore was determined to walk it. He had been given a second chance, a chance to make amends and to fight for the freedom and justice that had been stolen from their kingdom.

As the silence lingered, Julia stepped forward, extending her hand once again. "Theodore, for now, we will stand with you," she said, her voice carrying the weight of their collective decision. "But remember, trust is fragile. It will be your actions that will truly determine whether you are deserving of our loyalty. Do not let us down." Then finally, she smiled and added in a far less dire tone: "Besides, we've been following you all this time already anyway, so if worse comes to the worst, nothing's changed, right?" a few of the other mages chuckled.

Theodore clasped her hand firmly, gratitude and determination shining in his eyes. "I will not let you down," he promised. "Together, we will forge a path to a brighter future, one where our kingdom can flourish once more."

A few of the other Archmages also voiced their pledges, and it made Theodore feel happy. Though a part of him wondered if some of them actually did think this was a test and they were simply doing what they thought would get them in the least amount of trouble.

"But we don't have any time to spare. With each moment that passes, the people of this kingdom and not just the mages, inch closer and closer to their demise. The King has sewn a rotten seed, and we must do whatever we can to stop him. I am afraid to have to say this," Theodore lowered his voice, "but we have no choice but to kill King Roderick, and soon. And I think we are going to have to do it in a big, public way if we are going to redeem ourselves, as well as the rest of the air mages, once this is all over."

Theodore's words hung in the air, the weight of their significance sinking in. The Archmages exchanged glances, their expressions some determined and some concerned. Killing the King was a grave decision, one that they all knew would carry immense consequences. But they understood the urgency and the necessity of their actions.

Julia stepped forward, her voice steady. "Theodore, your words ring true. King Roderick's tyranny has caused immeasurable suffering, not just to the mages but to all the people of our kingdom. If we are to bring about true change, we must confront him and put an end to his reign."

She turned to the other Archmages, addressing them as well. "We have witnessed first-hand the horrors inflicted upon our people, and it is our duty as users of the Cyclonic Essence to protect them. We cannot stand idly by while the King continues to oppress and destroy. It is time for us to rise up and reclaim our kingdom."

Theodore nodded, his gaze firm. "But we must plan our actions carefully, ensuring that we have the support of the people before we make our move. This is not just about removing the King from power; it is about restoring hope and justice to our land. We need to show the people that there is a better future awaiting them, free from the shackles of oppression. But we also need to ensure that once this reign has passed, that the Sky City and the air mages are not held accountable as allies of the King."

The other Archmages murmured their agreement, a shared determination filling the room.

Julia turned to Theodore, her eyes filled with resolve. "Theodore, lead us. Guide us in this fight for freedom and justice. We will follow your lead and support you every step of the way."

Theodore's heart swelled with gratitude and a renewed sense of purpose. He had once again found allies in the Archmages, companions who believed in his cause and were willing to stand beside him. Together, they would forge a path towards a brighter future.

"But… if we are going to do this, then let us do it publicly. Let us repay the torment and spectacle that the King brought to so many others; let the kingdom see that we are on their side. Tell me, do any of you have any ideas of how we can do this?" Theodore asked. He knew they looked to him for leadership, but that wasn't how he needed this to work. He needed a team, not a band of followers, and if he could gain insights from any of them, he was going to use that to his advantage.

The Archmages exchanged glances, their minds racing with possibilities. After a moment, one of them, a mage named Samuel, spoke up. "Theodore, what if we used the upcoming festivities?" his eyes were wide and practically bulging at the idea. "Most of the kingdom will be there, I am sure of it!"

"Festivities?" Theodore repeated slowly. "Is there…" and then it hit him. It could only be a few weeks away now, couldn't it? King Roderick had a birthday approaching, and as he did every year, he was throwing a huge party in the city for the rest of the kingdom. It was always a bit of a gloat, letting the rest of the citizens know that he was so well off that he could waste food and drink as he wished, but some had no choice but to attend, what with it being one of the few chances they ever got to have a proper meal. What was better, though, was the fact that the royal guard, the soldiers, and of course, the air mages themselves were always present to ensure a peaceful event.

The King's birthday celebration would gather not only the nobility but also a significant portion of the kingdom's population, making it the perfect stage to convey their message and garner support.

"You're right, Samuel," Theodore replied, a glimmer of excitement in his voice. "The King's birthday celebration is just around the corner. It's a public event where many eyes will be upon us. We can use this occasion to showcase our intentions and rally the people to our cause. Let the kingdom witness that we stand with them, that we fight for their freedom."

Julia stepped forward, her gaze focused. "We must ensure that our message reaches every corner of the kingdom. We'll need allies among the people, individuals who can spread the truth and rally support. Let's spread the word to people who can help us sow the seeds of change, ensuring that the people understand the injustices they've suffered and the hope we offer."

"Yes," Theodore practically hissed. "I think that we need just three to do what needs to be done, so I ask that twelve of you conceal your identities, spread out into the city and as far beyond as you can go. Spread the word of hope and invite all those you find to come and witness the change that is to come. I will tell the King that we are searching for traitors and doing what we can to root out any plans to cause nuisances at the festivities while working to undermine this tyranny."

Theodore's plan to have twelve Archmages conceal their identities and spread throughout the kingdom resonated with the rest of the group. They understood the significance of reaching out to the people directly and building a network of supporters who believed in their cause.

Julia nodded in agreement. "It's crucial that we have a presence in every corner of the kingdom. By concealing our identities, we can move freely and reach those who may be hesitant or fearful of openly supporting us. We will invite them to witness the change we are working towards, giving them hope and a glimpse of a brighter future."

The other Archmages began to discuss the logistics of their roles and how they could effectively spread the message without drawing unwanted attention. It was agreed that each Archmage would focus on a specific region or community, employing their unique abilities and talents to connect with the people and gain their trust.

Theodore spoke up, adding an important detail to the plan. "While the twelve Archmages work to rally support and spread hope, we must also remember to play our part in the palace so that the King does not grow suspicious. It will be difficult, I am sure, but not a word of this can reach ears sympathetic to the King. We must prevail for everyone."

Julia nodded enthusiastically. "We must be careful in our actions. The King's spies and informants are everywhere, and any misstep could jeopardise our cause. Each of us must prioritise discretion and secrecy, ensuring that our true intentions remain hidden until the right moment and that the right people are contacted. It should be easy when dealing with mages because none of them would stand with the King, but when dealing with the regular citizens... we must all be careful."

The Archmages began to finalise the details of their plan, assigning regions and communities to each of the twelve concealed Archmages. They discussed strategies to engage with the people, how to identify potential allies, and how to spread their message effectively without raising suspicions.

Theodore looked around the room, his gaze filled with determination. "Remember, we are not just fighting for ourselves or for the mages. We are fighting for the people of this kingdom, for their freedom and their right to a better life. Let us work tirelessly to undermine the King's regime and build a movement that cannot be ignored."

The Archmages were all in agreement, their resolve unwavering. They understood the risks involved, but they also recognised the importance of their mission. They were prepared to do whatever it took to bring about change and restore justice to their land.

As they dispersed to carry out their respective tasks, Theodore couldn't help but feel a mixture of excitement and anxiety. He took a deep breath, ready to face the challenges that lay ahead. It was time to set their plan in motion, to spread the message of hope and ignite the flames of change throughout the kingdom. The King's birthday celebration would mark the beginning of a new era, one where freedom and justice would prevail over tyranny and oppression.

Chapter 15 – A Feast Fit for a King

"My lord," Theodore said in a tone that was almost mocking. It was how Ren had always spoken to the King, so he knew that he needed to do his best to emulate that in his plans to remain undetected. "The preparations for your party are going well, I trust?"

Theodore's voice carried a tinge of false deference as he addressed King Roderick. He needed to maintain his disguise as Captain Ren, the persona he had used when dealing with the King all this time.

The King glanced up from his desk, a mix of irritation and satisfaction evident on his face. "Ah, Captain Ren," he responded, his tone arrogant. "Yes, the preparations for my birthday celebration are proceeding as expected. The finest food and entertainment have been arranged, ensuring a grand spectacle for the nobility and the commoners alike."

Theodore kept his expression neutral, hiding his true intentions behind a facade of loyalty. "Very good, my lord," he replied, nodding subtly. "However, I must caution you about potential threats to the event. Rumours have reached my ears that there may be traitors among us, planning to disrupt the festivities and cause chaos. I assure you, I am doing everything in my power to uncover their identities and prevent any such occurrences."

The King's eyes narrowed, suspicion evident in his gaze. "Traitors, you say?" he questioned, his voice laced with anger. "I will not tolerate any interference with my celebration. Find those responsible, Captain Ren, and bring them to justice swiftly. We cannot have any disruptions tarnishing this momentous occasion."

Theodore bowed slightly, maintaining his facade of loyalty. "Of course, my lord," he replied, his tone laced with a deceptive humility. "I will spare no effort in ensuring the safety and success of your celebration. You can rely on me."

The King returned to his work, dismissing Theodore with a wave of his hand. As Theodore left the room, he couldn't help but feel a sense of satisfaction; his plan was in motion, and the King's false sense of security would work to their advantage.

He had never been a particularly good liar, but Theodore had spent long enough watching Captain Ren, and that had taught him everything he needed to know about deceit, manipulation, and using your power to get what you wanted.

And, of course, Theodore's allies, the twelve Archmages who he had sent away to find allies and witnesses, were already making their way out of the palace, some keeping within the high stone walls of the kingdom and some venturing further out. They all knew that after the last rebellion, when the mages within the city had struck back at the execution of the high-ranked earth mage, almost all of the mages within the city had fled, but they were still sure that some remained and finding the resistance members was going to be a good place to start.

"And that just leaves us three," Theodore said to Samuel and Julia, the pair of Archmages who had remained by his side to act as the King's guards. He had his Royal Guard scattered about the palace, of course, but even the King knew that if a powerful mage decided to cause him some harm, then the only thing that could truly stand in their way was an equally powerful mage.

Theodore, Samuel, and Julia stood together, hidden behind their disguises as the King's guards and truthfully, Theodore was the only member of the three who had to make any kind of show that things were carrying on as usual. They all knew that their role in protecting the King had to remain intact to avoid suspicion. They were the closest to the King, and their position granted them access and influence within the palace.

"I trust our allies have set off on their mission," Samuel whispered, his voice barely audible. "They will spread the word and gather support. We must ensure that the people are aware of our cause and the injustices they have suffered under this reign."

Julia nodded, her eyes filled with determination. "Indeed, our comrades are skilled and resourceful. They will do what they can to gather allies and inform any of the resistance who still remain. But it is up to us to create the right circumstances for change. We need to be prepared for any eventuality.'

Theodore took a deep breath; his mind focused on the task at hand. "Our first priority is to maintain our cover," he whispered, his voice steady. "We cannot let the King suspect our true intentions. We will continue to serve as his loyal guards, but behind the scenes, we must work towards a better future."

Samuel nodded, his gaze fixed on Theodore. "And what of the King's birthday celebration?" he asked. "Do we proceed as planned?"

Theodore's eyes gleamed with a glimmer of mischief. "Oh, indeed we do," he replied, a hint of excitement in his voice. "The festivities will provide us with the perfect opportunity to make our move. We will use the grand spectacle to our advantage, capturing the attention of the kingdom and showing them that there is hope for change."

Julia's lips curled into a sly smile. "Let the people witness the true face of their ruler," she said, her voice filled with determination. "We will expose the King's true weakness and offer them a glimpse of the justice and freedom that awaits."

Theodore's heart swelled with a renewed sense of purpose. They were playing a dangerous game, but the stakes were too high to turn back now. The time had come to seize control and fight for the better future they all desired.

"We will need to coordinate our actions carefully," Theodore said, his voice steady. "Every move must be precise, every decision calculated. Our unity and trust in one another will be crucial. Together, we will bring about the downfall of King Roderick and reclaim our kingdom."

Samuel and Julia nodded, their determination matching Theodore's own. They knew the risks, but they were prepared to face them head-on.

Theodore's mind raced with the hope he had for the future, a future without the oppressive rule of the tyrant King. The pieces were falling into place, and the stage was set for their grand act of rebellion. The time had come to end this reign, rally the people, and fight for justice.

"We need to create a moment that will resonate with the people," he suggested. "A powerful display of unity and resistance that will inspire them to join our cause."

Julia chimed in, her voice steady and resolute. "We must coordinate our actions during the celebration," she said. "Our allies can be strategically placed to assist us. Together, we will ensure that the King has no way out of this."

Theodore agreed, his mind already working on the details. "We will need to rally the people," he said. "Through carefully planned speeches and actions, we will show them that there is an alternative to the King's oppressive rule. We will offer them hope and a vision of a brighter future."

Samuel glanced around cautiously, making sure no one was listening in on their conversation. "We should also consider a symbol," he suggested. "Something that represents our cause and can be displayed during the celebration. It will serve as a rallying point for the people."

Theodore's eyes lit up with a spark of inspiration. "Yes," he said. "A symbol that embodies our fight for freedom and justice. It will unite the people and give them a sense of purpose."

Julia nodded, her determination unwavering. "Together, we will create a spectacle that the kingdom will never forget."

Theodore's heart swelled with determination and resolve. They were a small group against a powerful ruler, but they possessed the strength of purpose and the support of their allies. They were ready to face whatever challenges lay ahead.

"Let us prepare, my friends," Theodore said, his voice filled with conviction. "The time for change is upon us. The King's reign of tyranny will end, and a new era of freedom will begin. We shall reclaim our kingdom and deliver justice to those who have suffered."

"Right," Julia replied. "But… I have to ask… once the King has been killed and the kingdom has been freed from his iron grasp… then what?" It was clear to Theodore that Julia had been wanting to ask this question for a while but had been afraid in fear of what the answer may be. He wondered if she thought that he planned to take control of the kingdom himself.

Theodore met Julia's gaze, his expression sincere. "Julia, I understand your concerns," he began, his voice filled with reassurance. "Our goal is not to replace one form of tyranny with another. We are fighting for a just and free kingdom where power is not concentrated in the hands of a single ruler. Our purpose is to create a system that upholds justice, equality, and the will of the people."

He paused for a moment, collecting his thoughts. "Once the King has been removed from power, we will need to establish a fair and true council that represents the interests of all the people. It will be a collective effort involving the participation of not just the mages but also the people of the kingdom without an essence within them. We will work towards a system that ensures accountability, transparency, and the protection of individual rights."

Theodore's voice carried the weight of his convictions. "Our fight is not just against the King, but against the system that allowed his tyranny to persist. We must address the underlying issues that have plagued our kingdom for far too long. It will require careful planning, dialogue, and compromise."

He looked at Julia directly, his gaze steady. "I have no desire for personal power or control. My purpose is to serve the people, to restore justice and create a better future for all. Together, we will forge a path towards a truly democratic and inclusive society."

Julia's expression softened, a glimmer of trust shining in her eyes. "Thank you for addressing my concerns, Theodore," she said, her voice filled with gratitude. "I believe in your vision and the principles we fight for. Let us work together to bring about the change we seek and ensure that the kingdom thrives under a new era of governance."

Theodore nodded, a sense of unity settling among them. "Yes, Julia," he replied, a determined smile playing on his lips. "We will walk this path together, guiding the kingdom towards a future that upholds the values of justice, freedom, and the well-being of all its inhabitants. Our journey begins now, and I am grateful to have you by my side."

As the day of King Roderick's birthday celebration approached, the kingdom buzzed with anticipation and activity. The preparations for the grand event were in full swing, showcasing the opulence and extravagance that the King revelled in. It was a stark contrast to the hardships faced by the common people, who suffered under heavy taxes and scarcity of even the most basic resources.

In the heart of the capital city, the Royal Plaza was transformed into a magnificent venue. Elaborate decorations adorned the streets and buildings, drawing gasps of awe from the onlookers. Vibrant banners fluttered in the wind, displaying the King's heraldry, though they were met with mixed feelings by the citizens.

A team of skilled artisans and craftsmen worked tirelessly to create magnificent sculptures and intricate designs, adorning the city squares and streets with symbols of the King's power and grandeur. Towering statues of marble and gold were erected, capturing the King in poses of authority and superiority, his face etched with an arrogant smile. The sheer size and grandeur of these structures were meant to impress and awe, serving as a reminder of the King's wealth and ostentation.

Food vendors and market stalls lined the streets, offering a variety of delicacies and treats. The scent of freshly baked bread, roasted meats, and sweet pastries filled the air, tempting passers by and providing a stark contrast to the hunger faced by many in the kingdom. The food was meant to showcase the abundance that the King enjoyed while the people struggled to make ends meet.

The city's elite, dressed in their finest attire, paraded through the streets, flaunting their wealth and privilege. Carriages adorned with ornate decorations carried nobles and dignitaries, their occupants revelling in the pomp and ceremony of the occasion. It was a display of the stark class divide, where the wealthy revelled in luxury while the common folk observed from the sidelines, their faces a mix of fascination and resentment.

Musicians, dancers, and performers entertained the crowds with their captivating displays. Bands played lively tunes, their melodies echoing through the streets and enticing people to dance and celebrate. Acrobats and jugglers showcased their skills, drawing gasps of amazement and momentarily diverting attention from the reality of everyday life.

The highlight of the celebration was the grand feast held in the King's honour. The banquet hall was adorned with lavish decorations, and the tables groaned under the weight of sumptuous dishes and delicacies from far-off lands. Fine wines and spirits flowed freely, adding to the atmosphere of decadence and excess.

Throughout the day, the King always made appearances, surveying the festivities with a self-satisfied smile. He basked in the adulation of the nobility, enjoying the spectacle and revelling in his own perceived greatness. However, beneath the facade of splendour, there would be an underlying tension and discontent among the common people, who were being constantly reminded of their suffering and deprivation.

While the celebration showcased the King's wealth and power, it also served as a poignant reminder of his detachment from the plight of his subjects. The grandeur of the event only deepened the divide between the ruling class and the struggling masses, fuelling the growing dissatisfaction and resentment towards the King's rule.

It was against this backdrop of excess and inequality that Theodore, Julia, and Samuel planned to make their move. They aimed to use the very spectacle of the celebration to expose the King's true nature and rally the people to their cause. The stark contrast between the extravagant display and the suffering of the kingdom's inhabitants would serve as a powerful catalyst for change, igniting a spark of rebellion that would shake the very foundations of the kingdom.

The day of the King's birthday had finally arrived, and the palace was abuzz with activity. As Theodore, still in the guise of the loyal Captain Ren, entered the King's chamber, he found King Roderick sitting at his ornate desk, surrounded by stacks of parchment and piles of gifts. The King's face was lit up with excitement, a childlike giddiness shining in his eyes.

"Ah, Captain Ren!" the King exclaimed, a broad grin spreading across his face. "Do come in! Look at all these gifts! It's simply marvellous, isn't it? My birthday celebration is going to be the grandest event this kingdom has ever seen!"

Theodore maintained his disguise, bowing respectfully. "Indeed, my lord," he replied, his voice laced with false enthusiasm. "The preparations have been impeccable. The whole kingdom eagerly awaits this momentous occasion."

The King chuckled gleefully, twirling a jewelled ring on his finger. "I can hardly contain my excitement, Captain Ren. The food, the music, the entertainment. It will be a celebration fit for a king! The people will adore me even more after this!"

Theodore nodded, concealing his disdain behind a mask of loyalty. "Of course, my lord," he said, forcing a smile. "The celebration will be a testament to your greatness and benevolence. It will surely solidify your position as the beloved ruler of this kingdom."

The King's eyes sparkled with delight as he leaned back in his chair. "Oh, Captain Ren, you understand me so well!" he exclaimed. "I've worked tirelessly to ensure that this celebration surpasses all previous ones. The people will be in awe of my magnificence!"

As Theodore listened to the King's self-absorbed ramblings, he felt a mixture of anger and determination. The King's obliviousness to the suffering of his people, and his callous disregard for their hardships only fuelled Theodore's resolve to bring about justice and freedom.

"Indeed, my lord," Theodore replied, keeping his tone respectful. "Your commitment to this celebration is truly admirable. The kingdom will be captivated by your grandeur."

The King beamed with satisfaction, completely oblivious to the true intentions behind Theodore's words. "I have even arranged for a special fireworks display," he said, clapping his hands in excitement. "It will light up the sky, a symbol of my power and dominance. The people will marvel at my greatness!"

Theodore fought to maintain his composure, his true intentions hidden behind a facade of loyalty. "That sounds truly awe-inspiring, my lord," he responded, his voice carefully modulated. "The fireworks will surely leave a lasting impression on all who witness them."

The King nodded eagerly, his attention already shifting to the next item on his agenda. "Thank you, Captain Ren, for your unwavering dedication to my cause; I will make you a Lord for your service!"

Theodore did not reply, simply smiling as though the offer actually meant something to him, but before he even had the chance to reply, Roderick dismissed Theodore with a wave of his hand, his demeanour darkening.

"Make sure everything is in order for today. I want nothing to mar this celebration. Now, leave me. I have important matters to attend to."

Chapter 16 – The Forest

Elara watched from the cover of her settlement within the Forbidden Forest that she had spent a very long time, along with her parents, the former students of the Hidden Academy, and all those who had followed her parents out of the city gates and away from the grasp of the tyrant King had created as their sanctuary.

Of course, not all of her people had a magical essence within them, but since entering into the forest, many had quickly found that a magical affinity for earth – Gaia's Grace – had awoken within them as though their proximity to the mystical location somehow amplified the mana dormant within them.

She watched as the hooded figure in dark robes approached, knowing that this would either spell danger or another individual searching for salvation from the city once their mana had awakened.

Elara's heart quickened with anticipation as she observed the hooded figure making their way towards her settlement in the heart of the Forbidden Forest. It had been a long time since she had encountered someone from outside their community, and every interaction carried the weight of uncertainty.

The settlement, hidden deep within the dense foliage and protected by the forest's enchantments, had become a refuge for those who sought to escape the grasp of the tyrant King and his oppressive rule. Elara's parents and the former students of the Hidden Academy, had led the way, and many had followed, seeking a life free from persecution.

As the figure drew closer, Elara's trained senses picked up on subtle magical vibrations emanating from them. It was a telltale sign that their mana, their magical essence, had awakened, just like many others who had found solace within the forest.

Keeping herself concealed, Elara observed the figure's movements, assessing their demeanour and intentions. The forest provided protection, but caution was still warranted. Not everyone who sought refuge could be trusted, and danger lurked beyond their safe haven.

The figure approached the settlement's entrance, their steps measured and deliberate. Elara's parents, standing guard at the entrance, watched with equal vigilance, their expressions masked by the shadows of the forest.

As the figure reached the settlement's boundary, Elara emerged from her hiding spot, stepping forward to meet them. Her presence alone conveyed authority and a sense of leadership in their community.

"Welcome," Elara greeted, her voice carrying caution, but also a small amount of curiosity. "I am Elara. What brings you to our humble settlement?"

The hooded figure looked up, revealing a face that she did not recognise, but his eyes shone a bright gold, revealing to her the fact that this man was an air mage. And the only air mages she had ever met had been working for the King, fighting the other mages and doing their best to eradicate any magic except their own from the kingdom.

Elara's initial caution deepened as she noticed this golden gleam in the hooded figure's eyes. The presence of an air mage, especially one not known to her, raised alarm bells in her mind. She remained composed, though, determined to assess the situation and protect her community from any potential threats.

Her parents, sensing the tension in the air, tightened their grip on the makeshift wooden staffs they'd become accustomed to carrying, prepared to defend their settlement if necessary. Their eyes remained fixed on the figure.

The hooded figure seemed to sense the tension as well, pausing for a moment before slowly lowering his hood.

Elara still did not recognise the man, but she could sense his power.

"Please," the man said. "My name is Zephyr, and I come from the palace at the centre of this kingdom. I know you have reason to distrust, perhaps even hate me and my kind. But I come to you now with a message of hope and a request for aid."

Elara's gaze remained steady as Zephyr revealed his identity and spoke of hope and his request. Her initial wariness tempered with a glimmer of curiosity. The Forbidden Forest had become a sanctuary for those seeking refuge from the oppressive rule of the tyrant King, and every interaction held the potential to shape their future.

"Zephyr," Elara replied, her voice measured yet she tried to remain as unbiased as she could. "Your presence is, frankly, kind of an insult. I don't know how you found this place, but you must understand that coming here… the consequences for all of us. Speak now before we take action to remove you as a threat to our people."

As Elara spoke, two large creatures that Zephyr knew to be Grimscales, with deep red eyes and danger in their expressions, walked into view and stood beside Elara as though they were ready to act upon her next command.

The massive creatures, covered in fur and black scales with razor-sharp claws and menacing beaks, gave Zephyr pause before he spoke. But he had a mission, and it was more important than his own safety.

Zephyr took a deep breath, the weight of his words evident in his voice. "The kingdom is in turmoil," he began. "The King's rule has only grown more oppressive, and the mages who once fought alongside him are now being turned against. The King seeks to eradicate any form of magic except the air mages, believing it will secure his dominance."

Elara's expression hardened, her memories of the King's tyranny still fresh in her mind. She had seen the destruction caused by his obsession with power, and she knew the suffering it had brought upon their kind.

"I know all about the King and his fight against magic," she practically spat. "But unless you have something new to tell me, then I have no choice but to assume you are here for some other reason, and we will have to detain you so that you cannot reveal our location to the King and his army."

The Grimscales each lowered their heads as though they were seconds away from launching themselves at Zephyr, but he held out his hands placatingly.

"Please, Elara," Zephyr implored, his voice tinged with urgency. "I understand your mistrust and the weight of the risks we face. But I bring news that could change everything. The King's grip on power is weakening, and there is a growing resistance against him."

Elara's expression softened slightly, a flicker of curiosity mingling with her wariness. The mention of a resistance against the King sparked a glimmer of hope, but caution still held sway.

"You speak of resistance," Elara replied, her voice laced with scepticism. "How can we be certain this isn't a ploy? The consequences of betrayal are too dire for us to take such risks."

Zephyr's gaze met Elara's, his eyes filled with earnestness. "I understand your concerns," he acknowledged. "But I am not alone in this. There are others like me who have witnessed the King's cruelty and wish to see an end to his reign. We have information, resources, and a plan to dismantle his power and restore justice to the kingdom."

Elara regarded Zephyr carefully, assessing his words and the sincerity etched upon his face. The choice she faced was fraught with uncertainty, but the possibility of uniting against the King and achieving true freedom tugged at her heart.

"Tell me," Elara said, her voice steady yet tinged with a hint of desperation. "Tell me of this resistance, of your plan. Convince me that your intentions align with ours, that you are not merely seeking to exploit our sanctuary or to have us all killed."

Zephyr nodded, acknowledging the weight of her request. "I will share everything I know," he vowed. "But in return, I ask for your trust, your consideration. Together, we can overcome the King's tyranny and forge a brighter future for all who suffer under his rule."

The Grimscales, sensing the shifting dynamics of the encounter, maintained their vigilant stance but eased back slightly, still awaiting Elara's next command.

Elara's gaze flickered between Zephyr and the creatures at her side. The decision she faced was not hers alone; it would affect the lives and safety of everyone within the settlement. But the yearning for freedom and the possibility of a united front against the King tugged at her spirit.

"Very well, Zephyr," Elara said, her voice firm yet filled with a cautious hope. "I will listen to what you have to say. But know this: trust will not come easily, and actions must align with your words. Prove yourself, and we may consider joining forces in this resistance against the King, if that truly is your goal."

A flicker of relief crossed Zephyr's face, his resolve strengthening. "Thank you, Elara," he said, gratitude lacing his words. "I will share everything I know, and together, we shall forge a path towards liberation."

"Follow me," Elara said and beckoned everyone to enter into the place that the earth mages had created as their home.

Nestled deep within the heart of the Forbidden Forest, the settlement of the earth mages stood as a testament to resilience, creativity, and the harmonious coexistence of nature and magic. A sanctuary for those seeking refuge from the tyrant King's oppressive rule, the forest home thrived with life, mystery, and an enchanting blend of natural beauty and magical craftsmanship.

As Elara led Zephyr through the bright green undergrowth, a vibrant tapestry of colours greeted their eyes. Sunlight filtered through a dense canopy of towering trees, casting ethereal rays that danced upon the forest floor. The air was alive with the chorus of rustling leaves, chirping birds, and the gentle murmur of flowing streams somewhere in the distance.

Amidst this breathtaking backdrop, the settlement emerged, seamlessly integrated within the forest's embrace. The earth mages had harnessed their magical affinity for the natural elements to create a haven that mirrored their connection with Gaia's Grace. Every structure was a testament to their deep bond with the earth and their commitment to living in harmony with their surroundings.

The settlement sprawled across a vast expanse, accommodating the needs of its inhabitants. Canopies, woven from vines and foliage, stretched high above, forming intricate lattices that filtered the sunlight and provided shade. Beneath these canopies, an assortment of dwellings blossomed, each uniquely crafted to blend with the forest's organic grandeur.

Elara paused to admire the sight. Tree houses, supported by sturdy branches and intricately woven with natural materials, perched like guardians among the towering trunks. Their design mirrored the surrounding trees, becoming an extension of the forest itself. Some tree houses were connected by rope bridges, swaying gently with the forest's rhythm, their sturdy construction a testament to the earth mages' craftsmanship.

The settlement was alive with activity. Paths, meticulously carved through the undergrowth, crisscrossed the settlement, leading to various communal areas. Lush gardens burst with vibrant flora, nurtured by the earth mages' caring touch. Colourful flowers bloomed in harmony with climbing vines, creating a picturesque backdrop to the settlement's organic charm.

A central gathering area served as the heart of the community. Here, a spacious clearing provided a place for communal gatherings, celebrations, and critical discussions. Large white stones encircled a crackling fire pit, imbuing the area with a sense of mysticism and ancient wisdom.

At the outskirts of the settlement, smaller enclaves offered solitude and reflection. Meditation groves, nestled in circles of towering trees, provided tranquil spaces for introspection and spiritual connection. Here, one could rest upon moss-covered stones, their surfaces smooth so that the mages could sit and commune with the essence of the forest, or to meditate and concentrate on Gaia's Grace.

The settlement's infrastructure reflected the resourcefulness of its inhabitants. Rainwater collection systems harnessed the forest's bounty, providing a sustainable water source. Elaborate root networks served as natural conduits, ensuring the distribution of essential resources throughout the settlement. The mages had even crafted natural composting systems, returning organic matter to the earth in a continuous cycle of growth and nourishment.

Within the settlement, the inhabitants thrived in harmony with nature. The couple hundred people who called this place home were bound together by a shared purpose and the desire for a life free from persecution. Each member contributed their unique skills, whether it be herbology, growing the world around them, shaping it into their home, or cooking meals for the inhabitants. It didn't matter if a person commanded Gaia's Grace or not; in this place, everyone was equal. Knowledge was shared freely, fostering a sense of unity and collective growth.

Children laughed and played amidst the embrace of the forest. Their youthful curiosity nurtured by elders who imparted wisdom through storytelling, passing down the ancient traditions and knowledge that had sustained the earth mages for generations.

Elara sat on a collection of roots that had been formed into a smooth bench, and a moment later, an older man and woman appeared at her sides. Behind them, the Grimscales took their position, and to Zephyr, this very much looked like he was being interrogated by the leader of these people.

"Zephyr," Elara said flatly. "This is our home. These are my parents, Serena and Marcus, and these are our friends," she gestured to the Grimscales, who did not move in reply. "Now, please, explain what you are doing here and why we should allow you to leave, given that you are a Master of the Cyclonic Essence and in my mind, an enemy of all mages."

"Archmage, actually," Zephyr responded almost automatically. "But that doesn't matter. I have come to seek your aid, to invite you to an event that could very well change the face of this kingdom and those who rule it. The Grandmaster of the Cyclonic Essence essence… his name is Theodore, but you may know him better as Captain Ren."

Zephyr was interrupted by one of the Grimscales rearing up at the name, and it was clear from that reaction that everyone knew who the mage was talking about.

"Theodore… he is not who you think he is," Zephyr started to explain before anyone could speak again. "He was my friend. Before we came down to the surface. His soul had been taken over, and he was being controlled this whole time by an entity who called himself Captain Ren. None of this was his choice… but he has become free now, and we look to return to the plan that we had in our minds when we arrived here: to remove the tyrant

King from his seat of power and return prosperity to the people of Avondale."

Elara's head lopped from side to side as she thought for a long moment. It was strange to see such a young girl and one who clearly didn't have full mastery over her mana yet, in a position of such power, but Zephyr knew that it would be best to keep his thoughts to himself.

Eventually, Elara spoke. "The choice to commit the acts of your friend may not have been his own – given that I believe you in this – but the choice to follow was yours, was it not? Have you not been a part of the capture, murder and torment of the people that have suffered at the hand of Captain Ren and even the King himself? Are you to tell us that you, too, were forced to do the things you did?"

Zephyr's expression morphed into one of sorrow as Elara's words hit him. It was something that he had already wrestled with, and he could only give one answer.

"I will answer for my crimes. But know this: the Archmages that reside within the palace, all of them… we had to do the things we were told, else Captain Ren would not only kill us in the most painful way, but he would find our friends, our families and exact his revenge onto those. We had no choice, but do not misunderstand me; I know that this fact does not make us, does not make me innocent."

Elara's eyes narrowed as she listened to Zephyr's remorseful words. The weight of his confession hung heavy in the air, and she couldn't help but feel a glimmer of empathy amidst her anger. She had witnessed the destruction caused by Captain Ren and his control over the mages, but now, faced with Zephyr's plea for redemption, she grappled with the complexity of their shared past.

Her parents, Serena and Marcus, exchanged a knowing glance, their expressions softening with understanding and consideration. They had seen first-hand the atrocities committed by the mages under Captain Ren's influence, and the wounds of those memories still lingered.

Serena, her voice filled with a blend of compassion and wariness, spoke up, her words directed at Zephyr. "You claim to seek redemption, to rid this kingdom of the tyrant King and restore prosperity. But forgiveness is not granted easily, nor is trust. Your past actions have brought immense pain and suffering. What assurances can you offer that this is not just another ploy, another manipulation?"

Zephyr's gaze dropped, the weight of his guilt evident in his lowered shoulders. He knew he had no easy answers, no immediate means of erasing the dark stains of his past. All he had was his unwavering determination to right the wrongs he had been a part of.

"I have no grand assurances to offer," Zephyr admitted, his voice tinged with remorse. "But I stand before you now, stripped of the control that bound me to Captain Ren's will. I pledge myself to the cause of liberation and the defeat of the King. I am willing to submit to whatever tests, whatever scrutiny you deem necessary to earn your trust."

Elara regarded him with scepticism, but also a hint of curiosity.

"Actions will speak louder than words," Elara finally responded, her voice carrying a sense of guarded hope. "If you are sincere in your desire to make amends and join our cause, then you will have to prove it. You will have to earn the trust of our community, showing through your deeds that you are committed to the liberation of this kingdom. Only then can we consider fully uniting our forces."

Zephyr nodded, his expression a mix of determination and gratitude. "I understand," he said earnestly. "I am prepared to face the consequences of my past, to earn your trust and the trust of all those who have suffered. I will do whatever it takes to right the wrongs I have committed."

Elara nodded once and then loudly exhaled. "Now then. Tell us what you plan to do about the King and why you are here now to seek our help."

Chapter 17 – A Young Man Named Kai

The scorching sun beat down upon the desolate landscape as Ethan, the lone air mage, trudged along the weary road. Dust swirled around his worn boots, carried by a warm breeze that offered little respite from the oppressive heat. He wiped the sweat from his brow and drank thirstily from his water bottle.

Ethan had been tasked with travelling to the dry north, where the hope was that he would find any remnants of the Brotherhood of the Flame and ask them, too, to bear witness to the plan that the air mages had to kill the tyrant King.

The land was barren, the once-thriving landscape reduced to ash and rubble by the King's relentless onslaught, then baked in the hot sun over years of neglect. Crumbling structures and scattered abandoned homes were all that remained, remnants of lives long extinguished. The absence of fellow mages was palpable, the air heavy with a sense of loss and despair.

Ethan's steps grew slower, weighed down by doubt. How could he convince others to join their cause if he couldn't even find them? His heart ached with each empty building he encountered, the silence echoing in his ears as a testament to the desolation that had befallen the land. He feared that the King's oppressive reign had already gone too far, and whatever they did next would do nothing to undo the pain, suffering and destruction that had been caused.

As the sun descended for another day, casting long shadows across the barren landscape, Ethan's weary legs carried him to a small grove of withered trees. Their skeletal branches reached out like pleading arms, their leaves long gone, victims of a world ravaged by fire and conflict. He sank down beneath the light shade they offered, seeking respite from the sweltering heat.

With a sigh, Ethan again pulled out his canteen from his satchel and took a sip of the lukewarm water. It offered temporary relief to his parched throat, but it couldn't quench the thirst for hope that burned within him. He gazed out into the distance, his eyes scanning the horizon in a desperate search for any signs of life, for a flicker of magic that might signal the presence of a fellow mage.

But the land remained barren as if it had been scorched not only by the flames of war, but by the very hope that had once flourished there. Ethan felt a heavy weight settle upon his shoulders, threatening to crush his spirit. Was he alone in this desolate world, the last remnants of a dying order?

Eventually, Ethan had no choice but to let his heavy eyes close and to drift off to sleep, knowing that in the morning, his journey would begin anew again.

The morning came all too quickly for Ethan, who felt as though he hadn't had a moment's rest. He was sure that he should have found some hidden settlement by now, some remnant of the home that the fire mages had resided within for so long. He remembered the battle, of course, but had this place been so truly devastated? And without a single other person to be seen for miles and miles?

Ethan had no choice but to return to the road once more and again hope that, eventually, he would find what he was looking for.

It had not been long, but eventually, something caught Ethan's gaze that caused his heart to leap; people were walking the road ahead, and they were coming straight towards him.

Ethan quickened his pace, a smile already on his face. This was finally it; he had found people. He could finally relay his message of hope.

He squinted to see who it was that was approaching and all of a sudden he realised that he had no idea what he was going to say to these people. He knew what he needed to tell them, what he needed to ask them, but the first words that would come out of his mouth were suddenly out of reach to him.

As the people drew closer, Ethan could see that they all wore long black robes with red flashing. It was strange that they seemed happy to pronounce the fact that they were all mages, given that their kind was outlawed and if he had indeed been there as a member of the actual army, then he would have to fight them and possibly even arrest them.

But there were too many for that. At least fifty too many.

And as they continued their slow approach, the glint of firelight reflected in their eyes, and Ethan could see the deep red that betrayed the Eternal Flame within them all.

Ethan raised his arms to his sides as a gesture of surrender, and to show these mages that he was no threat to them.

The fire mages closed in; their expressions, he could now see, were filled with anger and suspicion. Ethan came to a halt, his palms clammy with sweat, uncertainty gripping his every movement.

"Open your eyes!" a shout came from the fire mages before they had reached within touching distance of Ethan, and although he wasn't sure if this was an order or a joke, he opened his eyes wide and allowed his mana to flow freely. He knew what came next. His eyes shone with a bright golden hue that would be entirely unmistakable to this group. Each and every one of them would know that Ethan was a user of the Cyclonic Essence. They would all know that he was a threat to them.

The group of fire mages, upon seeing Ethan's eyes, abruptly halted in their tracks. That was, of course, except for the four mages at the front of the group, who leapt forward and raised their hands to call forth their mana and the spells that would no doubt be designed to end Ethan's life.

"Wait!" he shouted before any of the mages could act. "I am not here to fight!"

But his words had arrived too late. One of the mages, a young girl, called a fireball into existence the size of Ethan's head and threw it at him with such venom that he almost wanted to allow it to hit him so that her anger wasn't wasted.

But Ethan couldn't allow that to happen; he had a task to carry out. He didn't want to fight these mages, though he seldom came up against an opponent who could best an Archmage. But this wasn't about winning or losing; he needed these mages; he needed them to come to the King's birthday celebrations so that they could witness the end of an era and the redemption of the wielders of the Cyclonic Essence.

Ethan had been present when the air mages had taken down the Brotherhood of the Flame. He had witnessed the destructive power that they managed to conjure, but he didn't feel threatened by the four mages who stood defensively in front of the rest.

Calling upon his Cyclonic Essence, Ethan pushed the fireball off course by a couple of feet, and it sailed past him harmlessly. He didn't have time to rest, though, when another, and another flew at him in quick succession.

Ethan deftly manoeuvred through the onslaught of fireballs, his mastery over the Cyclonic Essence allowing him to manipulate the air around him and deflect the attacks. He focused his mind, channelling his mana into a protective barrier that shimmered with a golden aura.

The fire mages watched in astonishment as their fiery assault met with nothing but air resistance. Their expressions wavered between surprise and concern, unsure of how to proceed. Ethan seized the opportunity to address them, his voice strong and determined.

"I am Ethan, an Archmage of the Cyclonic Essence," he declared, his voice carrying across the parched landscape. "I come not as an enemy but as a messenger. We have a plan to bring an end to the tyranny that has plagued our lands."

The fire mages exchanged glances; scepticism etched on their faces and within a moment, their onslaught recommenced. Clearly they had either not understood what Ethan was saying, or simply didn't believe him.

This time though, one of the boys of the group, which he could now see consisted of two red-haired girls, a young teenager with unruly dark hair, and a smaller, thinner boy with no hair atop his head at all, began to cast a new spell. As he did so, Ethan remembered that this exact spell had been cast at the battle against the Brotherhood.

From one of the boy's fingertips, a jet-black mist spewed into the space all around them, instantly blotting out the hot sun and plunging Ethan into a world of darkness.

As the black mist engulfed Ethan, his vision was rendered useless, shrouded in an impenetrable darkness. His heart raced, and his instincts kicked in as he focused on his other senses, relying on his intuition and magical awareness to navigate the unknown.

Ethan extended his senses, feeling the subtle shifts in the air currents and listening for the faintest whispers of movement. He remained vigilant, ready to react to any potential attack from the fire mages concealed within the darkness. His mana ebbed and flowed within him, pulsating with raw power, ready to be unleashed when the time called for it.

But a thought occurred to Ethan, and with a flick of his wrist, he willed a gust of wind to blow the smokescreen away and clear the battlefield. He did not want to be shrouded like this; if the fire mages couldn't see him, then they couldn't see his sincerity or listen to what he had to say.

"I am not your enemy!" he called through the smoke whilst his spell came into effect. But the response was simply more fireballs arriving through the smoke.

Ethan let his spell go and felt the effect of the wind immediately. As always, it was cool against his skin, and as it built in power, the smoke began to be carried away from his vision and off into the distance. The problem though, was that he didn't want to put too much power into the spell in case any of the fire mages mistook it for an attack, and by the way the smoke kept refilling, he guessed that the boy casting the spell was continuing to do so without stopping.

Ethan had but one more choice: to push more mana into the spell.

"Please! I have not come here to fight!" he begged, though no reply came. Instead, his words were greeted by a jet of white-hot flames that cut through the smoke and impacted his golden mana shield.

The fire spells were powerful for sure, but Ethan had no trouble in deflecting them or allowing his shield to absorb them. He was an Archmage of the Cyclonic Essence, and that was something that was not achieved without merit or power.

Deciding to change tactics, Ethan cast a new spell. One that he hadn't practised for a long time but one that he thought could at least make a little difference here. Feeling the mana flow through him, he enacted the spell that would get his point across to the fire mages without the danger of committing them harm.

Within a second, a ten-foot-tall, golden replica of Ethan stood within the smokescreen, and it didn't matter how black or how dense the smoke was; his clone, manufactured from the very air that surrounded them all, shone through as clear as daylight.

"I am not here to harm you," the huge golden Ethan bellowed. "I have come to tell you of the ploy to overthrow the tyrant King! Listen to me; I am not fighting against you…"

But something happened that Ethan had not been expecting. He felt it before he saw or heard anything, the massive inferno that was approaching, and before he could let his spell wash away in order to defend himself, the smoke around him, in every direction and including his golden clone, exploded into orange flame.

Ethan raised his hands to form a quick shield to defend himself from the new attack that was, without question, magnitudes stronger than anything he'd experienced from these mages so far. But something told him that it wasn't going to be enough.

Had Ethan taken a second longer in calling his hasty shield into existence, the flames might've killed him on the spot. But thankfully, his shield took a good portion portion of the inferno, then shattered with the sound of breaking glass, sending Ethan flying back through the air and away from the battle, only to land on his back, burnt, broken and unable to move.

Ethan coughed. He could only look straight upwards, but he knew that he was in a bad way. The fact that his body didn't hurt was a bad sign, and he knew that when he had coughed, there had been blood.

But then a shadow fell over Ethan, and in a moment, filling his vision, was the young mage who he now recognised. This boy, this unimpressive young man with not a single hair atop his head, was the same fire mage that had ended the battle between the King's armies and the Brotherhood of the Flame.

The boy's eyes, now that he was closer, Ethan could see, were entirely absent pupils and shone with a red deeper than any he had seen before. It was clear at that moment that Ethan's own power as an Archmage had been soundly dwarfed.

"My name is Kai," the boy said. "And I am the last thing that you will ever see."

Despite his injuries and the overwhelming power of the fire mage, Ethan refused to succumb to despair. He had come too far and fought too hard to let it all end here. His mind raced, seeking a way to turn the situation in his favour, to find a path towards unity rather than destruction.

With great effort, Ethan forced himself to look up at Kai without fear or anger, pain searing through his body. He looked into Kai's eyes, the intensity of the young mage's gaze not enough to quell the determination within Ethan's own.

"Kai," Ethan spoke with a rasp, his voice filled with exhaustion, but also unwavering resolve. "You may be the last thing I see, but I refuse to believe that this is the end. We are mages, wielders of immense power. There is strength in unity, in setting aside our differences and fighting for a greater cause."

Kai's expression wavered, his fiery mana flickering with uncertainty. He had expected fear or submission, not defiance. He had grown accustomed to the idea that his power was unmatched, that he was the ultimate force in this desolate land. But Ethan's words, though wounded and weak, resonated with a truth that struck a chord within him.

"You speak of unity?" Kai's voice carried a hint of scepticism. "We fire mages have been isolated, hunted down. We have seen our comrades fall, our homes destroyed. What hope is there for us to unite with those who have stood against us? With the air mages who sought to kill us all?"

Ethan struggled to speak, his body protesting with every movement. His voice was filled with earnestness. "Hope lies in the possibility of a future where our elemental differences do not divide us," he said. "In recognising that the true enemy is the tyranny that has engulfed our lands, not each other. Together, we can rewrite the narrative and forge a path towards freedom and justice."

Kai's solid red eyes flickered again. The flames within him seemed to waver as if caught in a tempest of conflicting emotions.

"And why should we trust you? Your kind, and your Captain Ren," Kai said. "These are the mages who have fought against us on the front lines. These are the mages who have killed more of my friends and family than I care to count. These are the mages who fall in line with the King and do as he commands."

Ethan understood Kai's scepticism and the deep wounds that had been inflicted upon the fire mages by his own kind. He knew that trust would not come easily, that it would require more than just words to bridge the divide between them. He took a moment to gather his thoughts, his gaze never wavering from Kai's intense eyes.

"You're right, Kai," Ethan admitted, his voice filled with genuine remorse. "There have been mistakes made on both sides, acts of violence and betrayal. But I stand here before you as an individual, not as a representative of a group. I acknowledge the pain and loss you and your fellow fire mages endured."

He paused, his tone becoming softer but resolute. "But if we continue down this path of division and vengeance, we will only perpetuate the cycle of suffering. We have the power to break free from this cycle, to rise above our past grievances and work towards a future where our elemental gifts can coexist in harmony."

Ethan's words hung in the air, the weight of their meaning palpable. The fire mages surrounding Kai remained silent, their gazes shifting between Ethan and their leader. Kai's face contorted with conflicting emotions, the flames within him flickering with uncertainty.

Slowly, Kai lowered his hands, his fiery mana diminishing to a gentle glow. "I have seen enough destruction and death," he said, his voice laced with weariness. "If there is a chance, however small, to bring about a different outcome, then perhaps it is worth considering."

"Then I need to tell you about what we have planned. And there is something that you should know about Captain Ren," Ethan said slowly. "But first. Please, is there anyone amongst you that can help me to my feet?"

Chapter 18 – Party

As the day of the King's birthday celebrations had arrived, the streets surrounding the palace came alive with an air of excitement and anticipation. Decorations adorned every corner, cascades of vibrant ribbons and colourful banners fluttering in the gentle breeze. The aroma of freshly prepared delicacies wafted through the air, enticing passers-by with the promise of delectable treats.

People from all walks of life poured into the streets, their faces filled with smiles and laughter. Musicians played lively tunes, their melodies weaving through the air as dancers twirled and spun with grace and exuberance. Stalls and market vendors lined the pathways, offering an array of trinkets, crafts, and sweet confections.

From the steps of the grand palace, the King stood, resplendent in his royal regalia. The golden crown atop his head glimmered in the sunlight, symbolising his authority and power. His royal guards, dressed in pristine armour, stood to attention, forming an unyielding wall of protection.

Beside the King, Theodore, still in his guise as Captain Ran, exuded an air of loyalty and unwavering devotion. He watched the bustling festivities unfold with a facade of admiration, his eyes scanning the crowd for any signs of potential threats. The weight of his responsibility, the dual roles he played, pressed upon his shoulders.

But he knew that eventually, there would be just one person who would bring about the end to this terrible regent, and he did not have to search the crowds for him.

Theodore approached the King, a smile gracing his features, concealing the truth behind his guise. "My Lord, the celebrations are truly a sight to behold," he said, his voice filled with practised admiration. "The joy and happiness of your subjects are a testament to your wise and benevolent rule."

The King's eyes sparkled with satisfaction as he surveyed the vibrant scene before him. His voice carried a regal tone, tinged with pride. "Indeed, Captain Ran," he replied, his gaze sweeping across the crowd. "It warms my heart to see my people come together in celebration. It is a testament to the unity and prosperity of our kingdom."

Theodore nodded, feigning agreement. "The performers and entertainers have outdone themselves this year, My Lord," he added, his voice laced with false enthusiasm. "Their talents and dedication have truly brought the festivities to life."

The King chuckled, his expression one of delight. "Yes, they are the best in the kingdom for sure," he said, his eyes following the graceful movements of the dancers. "They remind us of the beauty and artistry that exist within our kingdom. Tonight, we shall revel in their performances and forget the worries of the world, if only for a moment."

Theodore concealed a flicker of concern behind his facade, contemplating the weight of the plan that rested upon his shoulders. He knew that beneath the veneer of celebration, danger loomed, and the time to act would soon come.

"As always, my Lord, your wisdom shines through," Theodore said, his voice laced with admiration. "May this day be a testament to your greatness, and may it pave the way for a brighter future for all."

The King turned his gaze towards Theodore, a glimmer of gratitude in his eyes. "Thank you, Captain Ran," he said sincerly. "Your loyalty and dedication have not gone unnoticed. Together, we shall continue to build a kingdom where peace and prosperity reign."

Theodore bowed respectfully, his heart heavy with the weight of his hidden motives. "I am honoured to serve you, my Lord," he replied, his voice carrying the weight of a carefully crafted facade.

Then the King's expression darkened somewhat. "Tell me, Captain. Do you think that the people are happy?"

Theodore's facade of admiration faltered for a moment as he sensed a hint of unease in the King's words. He chose his next words carefully, concealing his true intentions behind a mask of loyalty.

"My Lord," Theodore replied, his voice steady. "The people appear joyous and engaged in the festivities. Their smiles and laughter echo throughout the streets, giving the impression of contentment and happiness."

The King's gaze remained fixed upon the crowd, his expression contemplative. "Appearances can be deceiving, Captain," he said, his voice tinged with a touch of concern. "There is unrest brewing beneath the surface, whispers of dissatisfaction and doubt. I fear that despite our best efforts, there are still those who question my rule."

Theodore's heart quickened slightly, sensing an opportunity to gather insight into the King's thoughts. "My Lord, every ruler faces challenges and dissent. It is the nature of leadership," he said, his voice carefully measured. "But you have always been attentive to the needs of your people, striving to ensure their welfare and happiness."

Of course, it was a lie, but Theodore knew not to insult the King by saying that, as they both knew, the kingdom was poor, and the majority of the people were standing on the brink of poverty.

The King nodded, his expression regaining a semblance of confidence. "Indeed, I have dedicated my reign to their prosperity," he said his voice firm. "And that is precisely why I have decided to make an announcement tonight, something that will alleviate their worries and reaffirm their faith in our kingdom."

Theodore's curiosity was piqued, but he maintained his facade, his voice curious. "An announcement, my Lord? May I inquire as to its nature?"

A faint smile played on the King's lips, his eyes glimmering with anticipation. "Not just yet, Captain," he replied, a note of secrecy in his voice. "But rest assured, it is something grand, something that will make every citizen proud to be a part of our realm. Tonight, we shall give them a reason to celebrate, a promise of a brighter future."

Theodore's mind raced with possibilities, his thoughts consumed by the potential impact of the King's mysterious announcement. He knew that this revelation could be the key to their plan, the moment to seize upon and rally the people against the tyrant's rule.

"As always, my Lord, your foresight is commendable," Theodore replied, his voice carefully masking his excitement. "I am certain that the people will be filled with hope and gratitude upon hearing your announcement. Our kingdom will prosper under your wise guidance."

The King's smile widened, satisfaction evident in his features. "Thank you, Captain," he said, his voice filled with genuine appreciation. "Your unwavering support and counsel have been invaluable to me. Together, we shall shape the destiny of this realm."

Throughout the day, the party went from strength to strength without so much as a hitch. Theodore had remained vigilant, watching the crowds of people for any signs of the rebellion or the mages that his allies had been sent out to petition for their aid, but in the end, there were simply too many people with so many motives for their attendance for him to keep a proper track of.

Some of the citizens were there for the festivities, of course, all smiles and happily joining in with the entertainment. Some were clearly there because they knew that it was expected of them, and some were there because Theodore could tell from the look of them that this could be their only chance in a long time to get something decent to eat.

As evening fell, the King's command echoed through the city, carried by the voices of heralds and messengers. Citizens were summoned to gather before the palace gates, their anticipation palpable as they responded to the call. Theodore watched from beside the gates, his keen eyes scanning the growing assembly.

The air buzzed with excitement as people from all walks of life converged upon the designated area. Families stood hand in hand, their faces lit with anticipation, while merchants and craftsmen paused their daily routines to join the amassing crowds. The atmosphere crackled with curiosity, hope, and a shared desire for change.

Amidst the crowd, Theodore's sharp eyes caught glimpses of hooded figures moving with purpose and discretion. These were the telltale signs of the rebellion, the work of his comrades in bringing like-minded individuals to the festivities. Theodore's heart swelled with pride and gratitude, knowing that their efforts had not been in vain. But he was also reminded of what had to happen next, the dark deed well juxtaposed to the happiness that the King sought to spread for his birthday.

The crowd swelled, their voices rising in a chorus of chatter and anticipation. Friends and neighbours exchanged excited whispers, speculating about the nature of the King's announcement. Rumours spread like wildfire, carrying a sense of hope and curiosity.

The wooden platform, positioned prominently before the palace gates, stood as a stark reminder of the King's authority. It had once been used for public executions, a chilling spectacle of power and control. Theodore's gaze shifted from the platform to the King, observing the calculated choice of location.

The King, regal and composed, emerged from the palace surrounded by his Royal Guard. His presence commanded attention, drawing the collective gaze of the crowd. As he ascended the platform, a hush fell over the assembled citizens, their anticipation palpable.

Theodore watched from within the crowd, his heart pounding with a mixture of trepidation and determination. This was the moment they had been waiting for, the opportunity to seize the attention of the people and reveal the truth about the King's tyranny. He knew that their plan hinged on this pivotal juncture.

The King raised his hands, a gesture to silence the murmurs that still lingered in the air. His voice, strong and commanding, carried across the gathering men, women and children. "Citizens of our great realm," he began, his words resonating with authority. "Tonight, I stand before you to share the news that will shape the course of our kingdom's future."

The crowd leaned forward, their eyes locked on the King, their expressions filled with anticipation. Theodore felt the weight of the moment, the delicate balance between revelation and the risk of exposure.

"As your King, it is my duty to ensure your happiness, prosperity, and safety," the King continued, his voice carrying a blend of grandeur and calculated charisma. "I have listened to your hopes, your dreams, and your concerns, and I stand here tonight to address them."

Theodore's breath caught in his throat, his eyes darting between the King and the hooded figures amidst the crowd. He knew that they were poised to seize upon this moment, as soon as Theodore made his move.

The King's words carried on. "I am no fool! I can see the hardships that many of you face in your day-to-day lives, but I come to you now with a message of hope that there is something better for you all!"

The crowd's initial excitement shifted into a palpable tension, the air growing heavy with apprehension. Theodore's eyes narrowed as he watched the King, his mind racing to anticipate the direction of his words. This was the turning point, the moment when the King's true intentions would be revealed.

"I have decided," the King continued, his voice resonating with authority and what could only be false compassion, "that in order to secure the future of our kingdom, one member from every household shall join our noble army."

Theodore's heart sank, disbelief and outrage welling within him. The crowd murmured, a wave of confusion and apprehension rippling through their ranks. Families exchanged worried glances, their hopes of a joyous celebration shattered in an instant.

The King's words hung in the air, an eerie silence enveloping the crowd. The initial excitement had turned to unease as the weight of the King's decree settled upon them. Theodore's mind raced, contemplating the implications of the King's plan. It was a thinly veiled attempt to expand his kingdom, to use the strength of its citizens for his own conquests.

Theodore's gaze shifted again to the hooded figures within the crowd. Their eyes met, and he could see the fear, anger, and determination reflected in their hidden faces. They, too, understood the gravity of the situation, the need for action against the King's tyrannical rule.

As the silence lingered, the King's expression shifted, his eyes scanning the crowd for a reaction. Theodore sensed a cruel satisfaction in his gaze, an indication that the King had expected this announcement to be met with total compliance, perhaps even gratitude. But the air was thick with uncertainty, the crowd grappling with the harsh reality of the King's demands.

Theodore's mind raced, his thoughts consumed by the need for a swift response. The rebellion had planned for such a moment, a call to action against the King's oppressive regime. The time to rally the people was now. To fight back and ignite the spark of resistance.

Summoning his courage, Theodore took a deep breath and began his march towards the platform that the King stood upon, still giving his speech. As he walked, the Royal Guard moved aside to allow him passage, and it seemed to Theodore like everyone in this place wanted this to happen.

Theodore's steps were measured, his heart pounding in his chest. His hand gripped the hilt of the sword the King had bestowed upon him, a symbol of trust and loyalty, now transformed into a weapon of justice.

All eyes turned to Theodore as he ascended the steps of the platform, his gaze fixed upon the King. The King's expression shifted from one of confidence to mild surprise, his eyes narrowing in scrutiny as he beheld Theodore's determined countenance.

Theodore's voice rang out, firm and unwavering, capturing the attention of every person in the crowd. "Your Majesty," he began, his voice carrying the weight of truth and rebellion, "your reign has brought suffering and oppression to our people. Your decree to conscript their loved ones into your army is nothing more than a thinly veiled attempt to further your own power and dominance."

A ripple of murmurs spread through the crowd as Theodore's words struck a chord within them, igniting a flicker of defiance against the King's iron fist.

The King's face contorted with anger and disbelief, his voice laced with venom. "Captain Ren, what is the meaning of this treasorous interruption?" he demanded, his authority wavering under the weight of Theodore's accusation.

Theodore stepped forward, his grip on the sword tightening. "I am no longer Captain Ren, loyal servant to your reign," he declared, his voice steady and resolute. "I am Theodore, a member of the rebellion, a force that stands against your tyranny. Your days of oppression are over!"

The crowd watched in awe and trepidation, their collective breath held as they witnessed the confrontation between Theodore and the King. The hooded figures within the crowd began to slowly inch forward, their numbers growing, their support swelling with each passing moment.

Theodore's gaze never wavered as he continued, his voice projecting across the platform. "I bear witness to the suffering of our people, to the hunger, poverty, and fear that has plagued our land under your rule. But tonight, we stand united, ready to cast off the chains of oppression and build a future founded on justice and equality."

The King's face twisted in fury, his hand reaching for the weapon at his side. "Guards! Seize him!" he bellowed, his voice filled with desperation.

But the Royal Guards hesitated, their loyalty shaken by the words Theodore had spoken, by the resonance of truth that had sparked within their hearts. The atmosphere grew tense, a standoff between loyalty and dissent.

At that moment, Theodore raised the sword high, its blade gleaming in the fading light of the day. The crowd remained silent, sensing the weight of history hanging in the balance.

"This sword," Theodore's voice boomed, filled with determination, "was given to me as a symbol of trust and loyalty. But today, it becomes a weapon of justice, a tool to free our people from your grip."

With a swift motion, Theodore brought the sword down, the blade slicing through the air with a resounding clash against the wooden platform. The impact echoed through the silence, a powerful declaration of rebellion.

The crowd erupted into cheers and applause, their hope rekindled by Theodore's bold act of defiance. The rebellion had been sparked; the people awakened to their collective power and the possibility of a better future.

The King stood frozen, his face a mask of disbelief and fury. The once-unquestionable authority he had wielded now crumbled before the rising tide of rebellion. The time for change had come, and the destiny of the kingdom hung in the balance.

Roderick looked down at the deep cut that the sword had made through his regal outfit, blood already spilling from his mouth.

But then he smiled.

Theodore could see the blood staining his teeth and the wound that he had inflicted that should no doubt have been fatal. But still the King was smiling.

And then King Roderick laughed.

Chapter 19 – Rebellion

"You think I never saw the change in you, Theodore?" The King asked, apparently unfazed by the blood still spilling from his mouth. "You think that I am a fool who cannot tell when those close to me are hiding the truth of who they really are?"

Theodore's eyes widened in astonishment, his grip on the sword tightening. The King's words cut through the jubilant atmosphere, casting a shadow of doubt over the rebellion's moment of triumph.

"What do you mean?" Theodore stuttrered, his voice laced with uncertainty. The crowd around him fell silent, their cheers fading into an uneasy murmur. Again, nobody moved.

The King's laughter filled the air, a chilling sound that sent shivers down Theodore's spine. "Oh, Theodore, my dear Captain Ren,' the King said, his voice dripping with amusement. "Did you truly believe that I was unaware of your true identity? That I couldn't see through your guise?"

Theodore's mind raced, memories flashing before his eyes. The careful planning, the secret meetings, the intricate web of deception they had woven. How could the King have known? Had there been a traitor within their ranks?

The King took a step forward, blood trickling down his chin as he spoke. "You see, Theodore, I am so much more than you know, and I know so much more than you comprehend, and that is why I am the King, and you are nothing but a dead mange."

The crowd shifted, uneasy murmurs turning into fearful whispers. Theodore's heart pounded in his chest, his mind grappling with the implications of the King's revelation. The rebellion had been exposed, and their hopes of a swift and victorious uprising shattered in an instant.

"But fear not, dear Theodore," the King continued, a sinister smile playing on his lips. "Your little rebellion ends here tonight. Your comrades, your hopes, all shall crumble before the might of my kingdom."

Theodore's grip on his sword tightened, his knuckles turning white. He had hoped for a swift and decisive strike against the King's rule, but now they were trapped, exposed before the very ruler they sought to overthrow.

The King's eyes glinted with a cruel satisfaction. "Guards!" he bellowed, his voice echoing through the square. "Seize them all! Let them taste the consequences of their betrayal!"

The Royal Guards twitched and the crowd immediately erupted into chaos, panic and confusion spreading like wildfire. People scattered in all directions, desperate to escape the clutches of the Royal Guards closing in. Hooded figures within the crowd removed their cloaks to reveal their bright eyes; reds, greens, and gold littered the masses, and they all prepared to protect themselves and their fellow rebels, their determination undimmed even in the face of imminent danger.

Theodore knew that their only chance now was to fight, to resist the King's forces with every ounce of their strength. Dropping the sword to the ground, he faced the approaching Royal Guards and left the King behind him to deal with the more significant threat, his mind clear and resolute. Immediately he called his Cyclonic Essence into being, creating an impenetrable barrier of wind to separate himself and the King from the rest of the soldiers. He had pushed so much of his mana into the spell that the barrier was so thick and dense that he couldn't see through it, truly leaving him alone with the tyrant King, who somehow was still standing.

Theodore stood face to face with the King, their eyes locked in a battle of wills. The air crackled with tension, the world outside the barrier fading into a distant backdrop.

"I may be alone, King Roderick, but I am far from powerless," Theodore declared, his voice filled with defiance. "Your reign of tyranny ends here tonight."

The King's laughter echoed within the confined space, his eyes ablaze with a mad arrogance. "Oh, Theodore, you always had a flair for the dramatic," he taunted, his voice dripping with disdain. "But your Cyclonic Essence is no match for what is a part of me. For what I became all those years ago."

"The people have seen your true nature and they will rise against you no matter what or who you are. Your reign will crumble, and the kingdom will be free."

With a flick of his wrist, Theodore directed the wind within the barrier to swirl and twist, creating a vortex that whipped around them. The force of the wind buffeted against the King, threatening to knock him off balance. But the King stood firm, a wicked smile gracing his lips.

"You underestimate me, Theodore," the King sneered, and in that moment, something clicked in what the King had said: 'What he became all those years ago'.

"What did you become?" Theodore practically had to shout over his own whirlwind. Both he and the King's clothes were being whipped back and forth as the magical storm swelled around them both, but the King did not seem afraid.

"You are so naïve," King Roderick practically spat. "That day, so long ago… the day that my father fell at the hands of the death mages… that was the day I experienced true power. The Arcani Soul that touched me was nothing short of wonderous, and it resides within me today, fuelling my ambitions and allowing me to gain the strength I need to carry this kingdom forward into greatness through death to all who oppose me."

Theodore's eyes widened, his heart pounding in his chest. The revelation sent a chill down his spine, a deep understanding of the immense power that the King possessed. The Arcani Soul that resided within the King could not have been so different from his own passenger, Captain Ren. He wondered if they had known of each other's presence, though he had no recollection of it if that was the case.

As the wind continued to swirl around them, Theodore's mind raced, searching for a way to overcome the King's newfound strength. He knew that he had to dig deep within himself to tap into the essence of the Cyclonic Energy that had guided him throughout his life.

With a surge of determination, Theodore called upon the Cyclonic Essence within him again, his mana pulsating with raw power. The wind intensified, forming a cyclone that close in around the King, its force increasing with every passing second. But still, Roderick stood defiant, his own power of defiance seemingly unyielding.

"You may have tapped into dark forces, King Roderick," Theodore shouted above the howling wind, "but true strength lies not in domination but in the ability to unite and uplift others. Your path of tyranny will only lead to your downfall."

A glimmer of doubt flickered in the King's eyes, his arrogance wavering for a fleeting moment. Theodore seized the opportunity, channelling his mana into a final surge of wind, unleashing it with a forceful blast directed towards the King.

The blast slammed into Roderick, the power of the Cyclonic Essence colliding with the darkness within him. The barrier around them shattered, the wind dispersing high into the darkening sky.

Theodore stood, breathless and weary, his gaze fixed upon the fallen King.

Roderick lay sprawled on the ground, his body battered and broken. The arrogance that once filled his eyes had faded, replaced by a mixture of pain and defeat. Theodore approached him cautiously, still ready to call his mana back into action if he so needed it.

"Your reign ends here, Roderick," Theodore declared, his voice filled with sorrow. "May the kingdom find solace and healing in the wake of your tyranny."

Theodore picked up the shining sword from the ground and raised it above his head, prepared to deliver the final blow. A surge of conflicting emotions coursed through him. He had wanted to end the King's reign, to bring justice to the people and restore freedom. But now, faced with the moment of truth, he couldn't help but feel a pang of sorrow for the man who had fallen into darkness, just as he had.

Theodore's grip on the sword tightened as he fought his own mind. He wrestled with the conflicting emotions, torn between the desire for justice and the weight of compassion. The fallen King lay before him, vulnerable and broken, a mere shadow of the tyrant he had once been.

As Theodore hesitated, the King's eyes sparked in defiance. In an unexpected burst of energy, Roderick pushed himself up from the ground, his body battered but his will unyielding. Ignoring the pain, he stumbled to his feet and turned, desperate to escape the clutches of his impending fate and ran.

"No!" the King roared, his voice filled with desperation. He sprinted towards the palace, his every step driven by a primal instinct for self-preservation.

Theodore's resolve solidified. He knew that he couldn't allow the King to escape, to continue his reign of tyranny. With a determined grit, he chased after Roderick, his footsteps echoing off the ground.

The palace loomed ahead, its grandeur a stark contrast to the chaos that enveloped the streets. Theodore pushed himself harder, fuelled by adrenaline and the unwavering conviction that he had to see this through to the end.

Theodore's breaths came in ragged gasps as he closed the distance, his determination overriding the strain on his body. With a final burst of speed, he lunged forward, his outstretched hand barely grazing the King's tattered cloak.

In that fleeting moment, the King's eyes met Theodore's.

"You will never take me alive!" Roderick spat, his voice filled with venom.

"It is not your life I seek," he replied, his voice steady and resolute. "It is justice for the people, for the countless lives you have tormented and oppressed."

But the King's cloak began to rip and then tore in two before Theodore could enact his final, killing blow, and the King barrelled through the huge wooden door into the palace.

Theodore sighed and followed Roderick inside. The King was stalwart in his dedication to remaining alive, but Theodore knew that he had no choice but to see this through to the end.

Back in the courtyard where the rebels had gathered, the battle had begun. Most of the citizens of Avondale who had no stake in this fight, who did not want to be caught up in a battle between the Royal Guard and the rebel mages had quickly disappeared, and all that was left were the hooded figures standing upon the hard cobblestone square, the Royal Guard holding their weapons to the ready, soldiers of the King's army, and the air mages who the King had controlled for so long.

The air mages, though, were no longer under the influence of the King.

Some in the crowds and some standing along with the soldiers, the wielders of the Cyclonic Essence made their allegiance very clear.

"We stand as one!" Zephyr shouted.

"Open your eyes!" Ethan called from the centre of the square. "Let them all see who we truly are!"

More calls came, and with them, the eyes of the mages were each revealed as they stared at the Royal Guard and the soldiers, daring them to make their moves. But without the support of the air mages – the powerful Archmages that they were – the guards hesitated.

The King, though, had instilled something into his men that would not be easily swayed.

"Surrender to us now!" one of the Royal Guard announced loudly. "And know your place!"

Those were apparently the wrong words, and they signified the beginning of the battle for the freedom of Avondale.

Ethan, still in the crowd and his body clearly still not healed from his battle against Kai, was the first to prove that he offered more than just words.

Ethan stood in the centre of the square, his body aching from his recent confrontation with Kai but his determination unwavering. He raised his hands, drawing upon the Cyclonic Essence that coursed through his veins. The air around him crackled with anticipation as a swirling vortex of wind formed above his outstretched palms.

With a fierce shout, Ethan unleashed his newfound spell, a manifestation of his unwavering spirit and untapped potential. The winds roared to life, twisting and spiralling with incredible speed and precision. They coalesced into a concentrated cyclone, its force magnified beyond anything Ethan had ever conjured before.

The cyclone shot forth with explosive power, tearing through the air with a resounding boom. It weaved through Ethan's allies and struck the Royal Guard and soldiers with unrelenting force, sending them flying backwards, their weapons scattering across the courtyard. The impact was immediate and devastating, as bodies crashed into walls and fell to the ground, overcome by the sheer force of the cyclone.

Gasps of astonishment and fear echoed through the square as the rebel mages and remaining citizens watched in awe. They had never witnessed such a display of raw power, an embodiment of the untamed might of the Cyclonic Essence.

The Royal Guard, stunned and disoriented, struggled to regain their footing. But before they could mount a counterattack, the other air mages joined the fray.

Some of them used their Cyclonic Essence to push the Guard and soldiers back, causing them to stumble and fall. Others used their spells to push their dropped weapons away from their searching hands, but then one of the mages took matters more seriously.

This mage, who had yet to cast a spell, refined his mana into a tiny, condensed ball of air no bigger than a garden pea. Then he sent it at a supersonic speed at the Royal Guard who had called for their surrender, and the tiny projectile tore through his armour plate, in one side and out the other leaving a small pea-sized hole that immediately started bleeding as the man dropped to his knees with a confused look on his face. First blood had been spilled, and it was of the Royal Guard by one of their previous allies.

This was all of the convincing that the green-eyed earth mages and red-eyed fire mages needed to join in this battle. It was not like the last time that the mages, rebellion and soldiers had clashed when the air mages had helped to thwart their uprising; this time, they all stood on the same side as brothers and sisters, ready to enact their revenge. Ready to reduce the King's power to nothing.

The earth mages manipulated the very ground beneath them, causing it to tremble and crack. Stone pillars erupted from the earth, forming a defensive wall around the rebel mages and citizens. The pillars served as both protection and vantage points, allowing the elevated mages to rain down their spells upon the remaining Royal Guard and soldiers.

Meanwhile, the fire mages unleashed torrents of flames into the soldiers; their mana channelled into searing infernos that engulfed the enemy ranks. The soldiers' armour melted under the intense heat, their once-formidable weapons reduced to nothing more than twisted metal. The fire mages weaved through the chaos, their flames guiding their every move as they fought with fierce and unrelenting determination.

The air, earth, and fire mages had come together as a united force, their individual powers intertwining in a symphony of destruction. They fought with a shared purpose, fuelled by the injustices they had endured under King Roderick's rule.

The square became a battleground, the clash of elements reverberating through the air. The rebel mages and the newly joined forces of the earth and fire mages overwhelmed the Royal Guard and soldiers, their combined strength proving too much for the remnants of the King's once-mighty army.

Ethan, despite his injuries, continued to tap into the Cyclonic Essence that surged within him. He commanded the winds, shaping them into razor-sharp blades that cut through the air, slicing through armour and leaving the enemy in disarray. His Cyclonic Essence combined with the powers of the other mages, creating a formidable synergy that turned the tide of battle in their favour.

As the clash continued, the rebel mages and their newfound allies pushed forward, gaining ground inch by inch. The Royal Guard and soldiers, once loyal to the King, were now forced to retreat, their ranks thinning with every passing moment. The square, once filled with chaos and fear, became a battleground of hope and defiance as the rebels commanded the upper hand.

The mages pressed their advantage, following the defenders through the palace gates, and as they had done once before, more guards filed back from the interior of the walls and joined their comrades in their retreat.

The palace gates swung open, revealing the grand courtyard beyond. The defenders, both soldiers and the remaining members of the Royal Guard, hastily retreated, their footsteps echoing against the stone floors. The mages and rebels pursued, their determination unyielding.

But as the defenders reached the courtyard, they quickly regrouped, forming a disciplined line in front of the palace. The soldiers, each wearing a uniform adorned with the King's emblem, reached behind their backs and from their waists, retrieving small crossbows. The sound of metal sliding against wood filled the air as they armed themselves.

The courtyard fell into an eerie silence as the mages and rebels halted in their tracks. The air crackled with tension, anticipation, and a sense of foreboding. All eyes were fixed upon the defenders, who stood with their crossbows raised, aiming towards the incoming threat.

The soldiers' movements were precise and calculated, their training evident as they positioned themselves shoulder to shoulder. Their disciplined formation was a stark contrast to the chaotic power of the mages, yet it exuded an unsettling sense of order and purpose.

The crossbows gleamed in the sunlight, their mechanisms ready to release a storm of projectiles. The soldiers' fingers tightened around the triggers, tension radiating through their bodies as they prepared to fire.

The rebels and mages felt the weight of the impending danger, realising the vulnerability of their position. The elemental forces that had brought them this far seemed momentarily overshadowed by the imminent threat of the oncoming barrage.

Ethan, his breath caught in his throat, gazed at the soldiers before him. His body, still weakened from the previous battles, trembled with exhaustion and adrenaline. He knew that if the soldiers unleashed their crossbow bolts, the devastating hail of ammunition could decimate their ranks and shatter their hopes of victory.

The mages shared a silent understanding, a collective recognition of the perilous situation they faced. Their eyes locked, communicating a resolute determination to overcome this new obstacle. They had fought too hard and sacrificed too much to be halted at the precipice of their goal.

In that charged moment, Ethan's mind raced, seeking a path to turn the tide once more. He called upon the depths of his Cyclonic Essence, tapping into a well of power that lay dormant within him. A surge of determination flowed through his veins as he focused his mana with unwavering intensity.

But the guards sensed it too, and with a synchronised click and twang of the taught strings that held their bolts in place, the deadly volley launched towards the mages and rebels, and for a second, nobody knew what to do.

In the midst of the tension and uncertainty, Elara sprang into action. With a fierce determination shining in her eyes, she raised her hands towards the oncoming volley of bolts. Her connection to the earth surged forth, a wellspring of power waiting to be unleashed.

As the bolts raced through the air, time seemed to slow. Elara closed her eyer and focused her mana, channelling the essence of Gaia's Grace within her, nurturing the seed deep inside her like never before. Beneath her feet, the ground trembled, responding to her call. Vibrations spread outward, the very earth itself obeying her command.

From the cobblestones, thin tendrils of roots emerged, reaching upward with a tenacity that defied their delicate appearance. They weaved and intertwined, entangling themselves with each other, creating an intricate lattice of natural defences.

Vines snaked through the air, their thorny tendrils stretching out to form a protective barrier. Thick branches extended, intertwining with the weaving roots, forming a formidable wall. Leaves unfurled, creating a shield of foliage that blocked the path of the incoming bolts.

The volley of bolts then struck the impromptu fortress of earth and nature, but they found no purchase. The projectiles embedded themselves into the sturdy wood and twisted vines, their lethal force rendered impotent against the impenetrable defence.

Gasps of astonishment filled the air as the mages and rebels watched in awe. Elara's mastery over the earth had created a shield that stood unyielding against the enemy's assault. It was a testament to the resilience of Gaia's Grace and the power that could be harnessed through a connection with nature.

The soldiers, their confidence momentarily shattered, faltered in their advance. Their expressions twisted into a mixture of frustration and disbelief. The crossbows remained trained upon the new wall, but their trigger fingers hesitated, unsure of the effectiveness of their weapons against this unforeseen obstacle.

Within the ranks of the mages and rebels, hope sparked anew. Elara had given them a momentary reprieve, a chance to regroup and plan their next move. They looked to Elara, gratitude and determination etched upon their faces.

Elara, her gaze unwavering, maintained her focus on the shield she had created. She could feel the pulse of the earth beneath her, the interconnectedness of all living things. It fuelled her resolve, assuring her that they could overcome whatever challenges lay ahead.

The courtyard, once filled with the looming threat of the soldiers' crossbows, now held an aura of defiance. The rebels and mages stood united behind the impregnable wall of earth and vines, their spirits reignited by the display of Elara's mastery.

But then one of the Royal Guard shouted to reload their crossbows, and a flurry of activity followed.

Now was the time for Kai to show what the fire mages of the Brotherhood of the Flame could do.

From behind the solid wall, Kai peered through his blindfold with his mana vision. Of course, none of the soldiers nor the Royal Guard had any mana within them, but that didn't mean that Kai wouldn't be able to see what was happening through the residual mana within the world. He could see that their enemies were preparing another volley of crossbow bolts, and although he could see that Elara's wall of earth mana was formidable, it would only take one of the small bolts to find its way through to end the life of one of his allies. And that was something that he could not bear.

Feeling the mana flow through his very body, ebbing, flowing and then surging, he felt his feet leave the ground beneath him as he began to float into the air. Higher and higher, he floated until he breached the top of the wall, where the soldiers and guards would see him, his eyes burning a deep red even through his cloth blindfold.

As soon as the men reloading their crossbows saw Kai, they immediately and all as one, changed their aim so that they were all pointing their weapons at the young fire mage.

Kai, however, did not care.

He raised his hands, palms facing outward as if beckoning the assault to begin.

With a synchronised release, the soldiers fired another volley of bolts towards Kai, their weapons aimed to strike down the audacious fire mage. The projectiles whistled through the air, hurtling towards their target with deadly precision.

But Kai was prepared. He tapped into the depths of his fiery mana, igniting a blazing inferno within him. As the bolts neared him, an intense heat radiated from his body, rippling through the air in shimmering waves.

In a display of mastery over the element of fire, Kai channelled his mana to generate a localised heat so intense that it defied the laws of nature. The bolts, mere inches away from him, disintegrated into ash, their once-lethal forms reduced to nothingness.

Silence fell upon the courtyard as the remnants of the bolts settled like a fine mist around Kai before falling slowly down to the ground beneath. The soldiers and guards stared in disbelief, their faces etched with disbelief, and then fear. They had witnessed an impossible feat, a display of power that defied their understanding.

Emboldened by his success, Kai directed his mana towards the soldiers and guards who stood before him, their weapons held at the ready. His fiery essence reached out, enveloping each weapon in an intense heat that surpassed any forge or flame they had ever encountered.

Spears turned brittle and crumbled to ash, their wooden shafts disintegrating in the blink of an eye. Crossbows, once lethal instruments of warfare, met the same fate, reduced to smouldering remnants of charred wood.

Swords, held tightly in the soldiers' hands, grew unbearably hot, their metal surfaces glowing with an otherworldly heat. The guards yelped in pain, dropping their weapons as the metal warped and twisted under the force of Kai's mana. The once-sharp blades melted away, pooling on the ground as liquid metal.

The courtyard became a scene of chaos and confusion as soldiers and guards recoiled, their weapons rendered useless. Panic and fear gripped their hearts as they realised the futility of their resistance.

In a moment of clarity, the soldiers and guards exchanged glances, an unspoken understanding passing between them. They dropped to their knees, their remaining weapons clattering against the ground. Surrender echoed through their collective actions, a recognition of the overwhelming power that stood before them.

Kai lowered himself back down to the ground, behind the wall and nodded wordlessly to Elara, who allowed her wall to fall and as it did so from the top down, unwinding itself and receding back into the ground, the rebels and mages could all see that the battle had finally come to an end. The Royal Guard and the soldiers, to a man, had soundly surrendered.

Chapter 20 – Forgive Me

As Theodore stepped through the threshold of the palace, he was met with an eerie stillness. The air felt heavy, laden with the weight of history and the echoes of power. Shadows danced along the grand hallways, their shifting forms adding to the disorienting atmosphere.

Theodore's footsteps echoed through the vast expanse of the palace, but there was no sign of the King. He moved cautiously, his senses alert to any sound or movement that could betray Roderick's presence. Yet, the palace seemed to play tricks on his mind, its labyrinthine layout becoming a maze of uncertainty.

Suddenly, the sound of the King's voice reverberated through the corridors, echoing off the ornate walls. "You thought you could defeat me, Theodore?" Roderick's taunting words filled the air, seemingly coming from all directions at once.

Theodore's grip tightened on his sword, his brow furrowing in frustration. The King's manipulative tactics were clearly designed to keep him disoriented, to sow doubt and confusion. But Theodore knew he couldn't succumb to the King's mind games. He had to stay focused to find his way through the maze of echoes.

Theodore pressed forward, his steps measured and deliberate. He listened intently, his ears attuned to the faintest whisper of movement or the echo of a distant voice. But the palace remained shrouded in silence, broken only by the hollow sound of his own footsteps.

Time seemed to stretch, minutes blending into eternity as Theodore navigated the twisting corridors. The weight of his duty bore down upon him, urging him to find the King, to bring an end to the tyranny that had plagued the kingdom for far too long.

Then, just as Theodore's determination wavered, a faint sound caught his attention. It was the softest of whispers, a murmur carried on the gentle breeze that swept through an open doorway. Following the sound, Theodore quickened his pace, his heart pounding in his chest.

He turned a corner, his gaze fixed on the end of the hallway. There, bathed in the dim light filtering through stained-glass windows, stood the figure of King Roderick. His back was turned, his stance defiant and unwavering.

Theodore's breath caught in his throat as he approached, his grip on the sword tightening with anticipation. This was the moment he had been waiting for, the final confrontation that would determine the fate of the kingdom.

But as Theodore stepped closer, the figure before him flickered, its outline dissipating like smoke. The King's mocking laughter filled the air, echoing through the halls. "You can never catch me, Theodore," Roderick's voice taunted, seeming to come from all directions at once.

Theodore's frustration grew, his patience wearing thin. He refused to be swayed by the King's tricks. With renewed determination, he pressed on, moving deeper into the palace, guided by his unyielding resolve.

The echoes of the King's voice continued to follow Theodore, a constant reminder of the task at hand. He knew he had to stay focused, to trust his instincts and overcome the challenges that lay ahead. The palace might be a labyrinth of deception, but Theodore was determined to navigate its twists and turns until justice was served.

Theodore's footsteps echoed through the palace, each stride bringing him closer to the elusive King.

As Theodore ventured deeper into the palace, the air seemed to grow heavy with a palpable tension. His footsteps echoed off the opulent walls, reverberating through the grand halls. The remnants of the King's voice lingered, a haunting reminder of the taunts that had plagued him.

Suddenly, an ethereal whisper reached Theodore's ears, faint yet distinct. It called out to him, a familiar presence that stirred deep within his being. It was unmistakably the Arcani essence of Captain Ren, a force that Theodore had thought he had been long rid of.

The essence swirled within Theodore's core, its energy pulsating with a desire to be unleashed. It whispered promises of power, of dominance and control. Theodore felt its tendrils winding through his thoughts, his body, seeking to influence his actions.

A sly chuckle resonated through the hallways, the voice echoing with a mischievous tone. "Theodore, my dear vessel, don't you long for the taste of true power?" The King's voice echoed from around corners, amplified by the acoustics of the palace. "Embrace me again, Captain Ren. Together, we can reshape the kingdom in our image."

Theodore's heart raced, his mind engulfed in a tempest of conflicting emotions. The allure of power tugged at him, luring him towards the path of darkness. He had felt the intoxicating surge of energy that Captain Ren's essence could offer, but he had also witnessed the devastation it could unleash.

"No, I won't succumb to your manipulation," Theodore muttered through gritted teeth, his voice filled with resolve. He knew the risks, the danger of allowing Captain Ren's essence to gain control. He had seen first-hand the destruction it had wrought.

But the King's taunting continued, the echoes growing stronger and more persistent. "Think of the possibilities, Theodore. The kingdom could be ours, a realm shaped by our will. Embrace your destiny as my vessel, and together we will wield power beyond your imagination."

Theodore's steps faltered as doubt seeped into his thoughts. The whispers of Captain Ren's essence grew louder, its promises tempting him with visions of dominance and supremacy. The line between Theodore and Captain Ren blurred, their identities melding in the face of temptation.

His grip on the sword was now so tight that the metal bit into his palm. He could feel the essence of Captain Ren stirring within him, demanding release. But Theodore fought against it, calling upon his own sense of self, his own values and ideals.

"I am not your vessel, Captain Ren," Theodore declared aloud, his voice trembling with determination. "I will not be swayed by your empty promises. The kingdom deserves a better future, one free from tyranny and darkness."

The echoes of the King's voice wavered, a flicker of surprise breaking through the taunts. For a moment, Theodore felt a glimmer of hope, the belief that he could resist the allure of Captain Ren's essence.

Then it hit him all at once. The surge of power that the Arcani Soul pushed through his very being caused his entire body to tense, and his mouth opened to allow a scream to leave his open mouth.

Theodore's scream echoed through the palace halls, a visceral release of the internal battle raging within him. His body trembled under the weight of Captain Ren's essence, the arcane soul surging forth with an intensity that threatened to overwhelm him.

But Theodore refused to yield. With every ounce of strength and willpower, he fought to regain control, to suppress the rising tide of darkness that threatened to consume him. He clenched his fists, digging his nails into his palms, grounding himself in the physical pain to resist the allure of power.

The echoes of the King's taunting laughter bounced off the walls, reverberating through Theodore's mind. They twisted and distorted, the voice taking on an eerie quality that disoriented his senses. The palace seemed to warp and shift, its grandeur now a labyrinth designed to ensnare him.

Disoriented and disheartened, Theodore stumbled forward, his steps unsteady. The whispers of Captain Ren's essence clawed at the fringes of his consciousness, tempting him with promises of unstoppable power and the realisation of his deepest desires.

But in the midst of the chaos, a flicker of clarity ignited within Theodore's core. He remembered the faces of the rebels, the innocent lives that had suffered under the King's tyranny. He recalled the sacrifices made in the name of justice and freedom. It was their unwavering spirit that fortified his resolve.

"I will not be controlled by you, Captain Ren," Theodore gritted his teeth, his voice carrying a newfound strength. "You may have once held sway over me, but I refuse to be your pawn. The kingdom deserves a future free from darkness, and I will be the one to ensure it."

With his declaration, Theodore channelled his inner Cyclonic Essence, a swirling storm of determination and resilience. He visualised the winds sweeping away the suffocating darkness, clearing a path of clarity and purpose.

As he continued his journey through the palace, Theodore fought against the echoing taunts, his steps guided by an unyielding conviction. He manoeuvred through hallways and chambers, relentless in his pursuit of the King, his unwavering spirit cutting through the fog of deception.

Theodore's heartbeat echoed in his ears, a constant reminder of his own humanity, his own free will. He somehow knew that Captain Ren's essence would always be a part of him, an ever-present temptation, but he refused to let it define him. He would control his fate, his actions driven by compassion and justice and he would press down on the Arcani soul for as long as he had the energy.

With each turn, each step, Theodore drew closer to the King's lair. He knew that their final confrontation awaited, a battle of wills that would determine the fate of the kingdom. The echoes of the King's voice may continue to haunt him, but Theodore was determined to emerge victorious to usher in a new era of hope and light.

But then blinding pain dropped Theodore to his knees as he felt the essence of Captain Ren within him shift. It was like the Arcani Soul had taken a hold of his spine from within his very body, and there was nothing he could do to fight back against it any longer.

Then he felt it. The King had appeared and wrapped a single hand around Theodore's neck, picking him up from the ground easily, despite being mortally wounded and still covered in his own blood which was still flowing from him loike some unending spring.

As Theodore dangled helplessly in the grip of King Roderick, his vision blurred and his senses dulled. The weight of the King's hand on his neck was suffocating, choking the life out of him. His struggle to maintain control over Captain Ren's essence seemed futile in the face of the King's overpowering presence. He simply couldn't deal with them both at the same time.

Theodore's gaze met Roderick's, and in that moment, he saw a glimmer of satisfaction and triumph in the King's eyes. The realisation struck him like a bolt of lightning — the King had anticipated this outcome, and had deliberately pushed Theodore to the brink of succumbing to Captain Ren's essence.

Theodore gasped for breath, his throat constricting, but he refused to allow fear to take hold. He focused his thoughts, his remaining shred of willpower, on severing the connection with Captain Ren, on reclaiming control of his own destiny.

But the struggle within him intensified. Captain Ren's essence surged forth, its influence intertwining with Theodore's own consciousness. Memories, thoughts, and desires clashed, melding together in a tangled web. Theodore fought to distinguish his own voice from that of Captain Ren's, to preserve his own identity amidst the turmoil.

The King's voice, dripping with derision, cut through the haze. "Oh, Theodore, how delightful it is to witness your inner turmoil," Roderick sneered. "You see, Captain Ren and I have shared a deep connection, a bond that transcends the mortal realm. Together, we are unstoppable."

"We're here to help!" a shout rang out that took both the King's attention as well as Theodore's.

They both looked around to see three mages. The two earth mages, Elara and Rylan, and the young, blindfolded fire mage, Kai.

And then Theodore felt it. His control over his own body had all but disappeared, and once again, he was stuck within his own mind, staring out through the eyes of Captain Ren, and no matter how hard he screamed, there was nothing that he could do about it.

Theodore's eyes glowed an intense gold the moment they fell upon the mages, and he began summoning his spell.

"Move!" Kai shouted, seeing the build-up of mana within Captain Ren, and he pushed Elara and Rylan to the side so that the needle-fine jets of air that Theodore had cast at each of them simultaneously missed the earth mages by mere millimetres. The single blade of mana that was headed towards Kai, though, was met with an equally powerful wall of heat that disintegrated Captain Ren's spell before it struck.

The King was nowhere to be seen, and Ryland and Elara could only watch as the two Grandmaster-level mages faced each other.

"I thought you had changed sides!" Elara shouted. "I thought you called us here so that we could help you kill the King!"

"There is something there, something inside of him," Kai announced, seeing the foreign presence within Captain Ren's mana. "I think… I think that he is being controlled again."

"Can we help him?" Elara asked, panicked.

"Ha!" Captain Ren let out a loud laugh. "You think that you can stand up to me? You think that you are anything more than an annoyance to me?"

Then without another word, Ren sent a hurricane of air mana at the group, knocking them all back and to the ground with such a force that Kai hadn't even seen coming.

Kai then watched as Captain Ren prepared his next spell. The mana within him swelled, and as Kai made his own attempt to call his mana into action, he felt something change within him. His connection to his mana, the source of all his power, had been severed.

'Azar?' Kai thought. 'are you there?'

'Yes," The Eternal Flame that resided within Kai answered. 'I am still with you, but this mage is so powerful. We may be able to save him yet, removing the Arcani Soul from his body… but it will not be easy, my friend.'

Kai was used to things being difficult, though, and mana or not, he still had to do whatever he could to take Captain Ren down. The future of the rebellion and everyone he had ever cared about relied upon that very fact.

"I can see what is inside of you," Kai said slowly. "I know that it is not your will or your way. The things that you are being forced to do. I see you trapped inside."

Rylan and Elara looked on, knowing that neither of them was powerful enough to make a difference in this battle.

Captain Ren's laughter echoed through the chamber, his voice dripping with arrogance and malevolence. The mages, battered and disoriented, struggled to regain their footing, their determination unshaken despite the overwhelming power of their adversary.

Kai, his connection to his mana severed, reached deep within himself, drawing strength from the Eternal Flame that resided within him. He locked eyes with the Captain and spoke with unwavering conviction.

"I know you're in there," he declared, his voice resolute. "This is not who you truly are. We won't let this essence control you. We'll find a way to free you from his grip."

Elara and Rylan, though shaken, now joined Kai's side, their expressions filled with determination. Together, they formed a shield of unwavering support around Theodore, refusing to let him face this battle alone.

Captain Ren's expression twisted with rage as he unleashed another onslaught of destructive mana. The mages braced themselves, but all three now felt that their powers were not working. Once again, Captain Ren had suppressed all mana except his own.

Kai glanced at Elara and Rylan, their eyes filled with determination. They shared a silent understanding, a bond forged through countless battles and shared hardships. They knew that the future of the rebellion and the fate of their loved ones rested on their shoulders.

But Captain Ren was so powerful. With another blast of mana, the three young mages found themselves pinned against the stone wall a foot off the ground, and no matter how hard they struggled, there was nothing they could do.

Captain Ren then slowly walked over to them and peered at each of them in turn.

"It is such a shame to have to waste such potential," he sneered. "But you have always been nothing to me. Power is all that I care for, and in losing to me here once more, you have proven yourself to be weak.

'Weak…' Kai heard the distant voice of Azar whisper from deep down inside of him as he had heard once before. It reminded him of the time when he actually had been weak, unable to even stand on his own two feet. But then, something occurred to him. He used to be weak. In fact, he was even weak for a short while when he and Azar had first been acquainted. He was even weak when he stole the Eternal Flame from Marcus. But he had never been weak since the third Eternal Flame he had absorbed had become a part of him. He was the vessel of three Eternal Flames, and two of them were at the level of Grandmaster.

With that realisation, Kai felt the mana within him surge. The air around him seemed to pressurise, and he forced it into a tiny ball, no bigger than an apple. He knew that he couldn't release a spell like the last time he had fought Captain Ren; these two earth mages would not have survived it being so close to him. And if he wanted to free whoever this person was from his malevolent puppet master, then he couldn't kill anyone. Instead, he concentrated on the ball of mana and began to slowly feed it more and more as Captain Ren spoke.

"You think that you can make a difference when faced with more power than you could have ever imagined possible? I am the one to be afraid of. I am the all-powerful; I am your God!"

And with those words, Kai moved the small orb of energy that he had been nurturing to an inch off Captain Ren's chest. It was clear that the air mage couldn't detect anything and was still confident that his spell to suppress all mana was in effect, so Kai simply smiled.

"What are..." Captain Ren managed to say before the orb of energy detonated. The blast that followed was directed straight at the Captain and struck with the energy of the very sun in the sky. The corridor shone so bright that Elara and Rylan had to shut their eyes as tightly as they could, and even when they had fallen down to the ground, they could still tell that the spell hadn't yet been completed.

Eventually, the orb of light and directional heat dissipated, and Elara and Rylan both opened their eyes to see what had happened.

Captain Ren, a smoking crater in his chest, was slumped against the opposite wall of the hallway. Somehow he was still breathing. Presumably, the Arcani Soul within him was keeping him from death, but his eyes were closed, and it was clear that he was unable to move.

Immediately, Kai walked over to the slumped form of the air mage,

Kai knew what to do this time. He focussed on the mana deep within the Captain. Again, as he had done with Grandmaster Orthos, Kai focussed everything he could on the Captain's power and drew it into himself. Every last piece of it without prejudice. He could feel a combination of Cyclonic Essence as well as an Arcane Soul, but he took it all.

It felt good. He didn't leave a single shred behind.

Captain Ren looked as though he had aged a lifetime in that very moment, his skin becoming wrinkled and pale, and as Kai turned to look at the two earth mages, they saw through his blindfold that his eyes flashed golden and then a deep purple before returning to their usual bright red, and then nothing at all.

'Leave me... to work...' Azar's voice echoed in Kai's mind. He could tell that this power was going to be a challenge for Azar to overcome, but this time it felt different. His entire body tingled with the feeling that it wanted nothing to do with these essences; it was as though they were being rejected, and Kai slumped to the ground as his body weakened to almost nothing, once again unable to stand under his own power.

His eyes closed, and his mind went blank. Kai was alone again, though he knew that it was just a matter of time before the powers within him would overcome these unwanted souls.

Elara and Rylan looked at each other in confusion at the still form of Kai as he lay on the floor, and then a new sound sent chills down their spines. The sound of footsteps and clapping.

"I truly did not think anyone would have the power to feel our dear Captain Ren," King Roderick said mockingly. "But now what? I still live, and while I do so, the kingdom is all mine. You have failed, and now you shall both die. I wonder, though," he added quickly and turned his attention to Rylan. "Yes, I can see it. The love that you two share for each other. It is almost sweet, but that is nothing more than a distraction, and something that you are about to find out, can be most painful in itself."

The King's eyes shone a deep purple, and he held both his hands out before him. Elara and Rylan both watched with wide eyes as the skin on his hands melted away to reveal two skeletal hands that morphed and reformed into two very deadly-looking clawed appendages.

Elara froze, not ever having seen anything so gruesome in all her life.

With fear coursing through her veins, she struggled to find her voice. The sight of the King's transformation sent shivers down her spine, and the realisation that their lives hung by a thread ignited a fierce determination within her.

Rylan, his expression hardened, stepped forward, placing himself protectively in front of Elara. The bond between them fortified their resolve, giving them the strength to face the monstrous King.

"We will not be intimidated by you, Roderick," Rylan spat, his voice filled with defiance as he purposefully left out the word 'King' from his retort. "Love and friendship are not weaknesses — they are our strength. We will fight for each other and for the freedom of this kingdom. And that is something you will never know or feel."

Elara rallied her own courage, her hands trembling as she summoned her earth magic. She drew upon the energy of the earth beneath her feet, channelling it into a protective dome of roots and vines around herself and Rylan. She couldn't let fear paralyse her, not when their lives depended on their ability to stand against the King's onslaught.

The King's twisted grin widened as he observed their futile attempts to shield themselves. His elongated claws flexed, and he lunged forward with incredible speed and power, aiming to strike at the heart of their defences.

But Elara was ready. With a focused determination, she released her magic in a torrential surge, manipulating the earth to rise up and form even more thick, protective walls of roots and branches as she had once been taught by her dear friends. The walls encased her and Rylan, creating a fortress of Gaia's Grace that would withstand the King's relentless attacks.

As the King's claws scraped against the unyielding walls, chipping them away, Elara channelled her magic once more, sending a wave of jagged spikes surging forward from the walls. This time she had Landon to thank, and the memory of her friends caused her eyes to well up with tears. But this was no time for mourning; she willed more mana into the spikes, aiming to pierce the King's flesh. She summoned every ounce of strength within her, fuelled by her care for Rylan and her unwavering commitment to the cause they fought for.

The King's eyes widened in surprise as the spikes tore through his skeletal form, piercing his very essence. He recoiled in pain, his monstrous facade fading as his true vulnerability was exposed. He screamed, and the sound made Rylan Smile.

Rylan then seized the moment, summoning his own earth magic. He commanded the ground beneath the King to crack and rupture, ensnaring the King in an inescapable web of earth mana. Tendrils from unknown and unseen trees and plants broke through the ground, tossing stones aside as though they were nothing. They snaked their way around the King's feet and ankles before weaving upwards against the thrashing outraged King. The King's struggles grew feeble as nature's grip tightened around him, immobilising his monstrous form.

Elara and Rylan exchanged a brief but resolute glance, their unspoken understanding conveying their next move. With one final surge of combined power, they unleashed a concentrated blast of earth mana, Gaia's Grace pulling the essence of the very world around them to inflict its revenge. Every soul that had fallen, everybody that had given their life to the cycle that the earth maintained to keep in equilibrium, lent their power to this final blow, this one attack that would obliterate the King's physical form.

Silence fell upon the chamber, broken only by the heavy breaths of Elara and Rylan. They stood amidst the wreckage, their bodies weary but their spirits unwavering. The threat of King Roderick had been vanquished, and they had emerged victorious.

But then a shadow rose from behind Elara. A shadow so huge and terrible that Rylan's eyes widened in surprise. And then it lunged.

Without thinking, Rylan shoved Elara out of the way of the oncoming spectre and did the only thing he knew to do on an instinctual level: he reached to his side and drew his wooden sword.

Rylan's wooden sword, a symbol of his unwavering spirit and connection to the natural world shimmered with latent power as he raised it to defend against the looming shadow. Time seemed to slow as the spectre descended upon him, its grotesque form enveloping him in darkness.

With a primal roar, Rylan thrust his wooden sword forward, aiming to impale the spectre. The blade pierced through the shadowy form, but instead of meeting resistance, it slid between the fog and bones, passing through as if they were nothing more than ethereal wisps.

A surge of determination coursed through Rylan's veins. He knew he had to tap into the depths of his own power to overcome this formidable foe. Gripping the hilt of the sword tightly, he channelled his mana, his connection to the earth, and forced it into the blade.

As he did, a wondrous transformation unfolded before his eyes. The wooden sword began to grow and expand, sprouting roots, branches, and leaves in a dazzling display of vibrant green. The blade elongated and thickened, turning into a living extension of the very forest itself.

With a mighty heave, Rylan unleashed the full force of his mana-infused sword. It tore through the spectre, ripping it apart with raw, primal energy. The creature let out a piercing shriek, its form dissipating into the air like smoke.

But Rylan's power didn't stop there. The mana within the sword surged, spreading throughout the room and infusing the very structure of the palace. The roots of the enchanted sword burrowed deep into the ground, cracking through floors and tearing through walls.

Above them, the palace roof shattered, revealing a star-filled night sky. The wooden sword continued to grow, its trunk reaching upward like a colossal pillar. As it extended, the bones of the defeated King, once scattered across the chamber, were drawn into the growing tree, becoming intertwined and held within its branches.

The transformation was awe-inspiring. What was once a battleground now bore witness to a majestic sight—a towering tree of immense proportions, its branches spreading wide, infused with the remnants of the King's essence.

Rylan, still holding the hilt of the sword, stood in silent awe, his chest heaving with exertion. The magnitude of what he had accomplished washed over him, and a sense of profound fulfilment filled his heart.

Elara, who had managed to regain her footing, approached Rylan, her eyes filled with admiration and wonder. She reached out to touch the trunk of the tree, her fingertips grazing the bark and she felt a surge of life and connection.

"This... this is incredible," Elara whispered, her voice filled with reverence. "I knew you could do it, Rylan. You have not only defeated the King, but you have created something... something magical! Just like that time back in the forest!"

Rylan nodded, his gaze fixed on the magnificent tree before them. "It is a symbol, Elara. A symbol of the victory we have achieved and the new beginning we will forge. The bones of the tyrant now serve as a foundation for growth and renewal."

Together, Elara and Rylan stood in the presence of the towering tree, their hands clasped, their spirits intertwined. They knew that their journey was far from over, but they also knew that as long as they stood together, guided by the power of their friendship and connection to the earth, they would be unstoppable.

As they looked to the future, they could already see the seedlings of hope sprouting from the branches of the magnificent tree — a testament to their unwavering courage and the indomitable spirit of the kingdom they had fought so fiercely to protect.

Chapter 21 – A Great Council

The soldiers and the guards had all been placed on their knees with their hands behind their backs, facing away from the palace. The rebels and all of the the mages stood over them, though even in this position of power, each of them felt like if the shoe had been on the other foot, the guards would have been far less lenient with them.

Then the huge wooden front roof of the palace took everyone's attention, and after a moment, out stepped Elara and Rylan, carrying the unconscious form of Kai in their arms. Around Rylan's wrist, he carried to shining golden crown that once sat atop the tyrant King's head.

The soldiers and guards, now subdued and powerless, turned and stared in awe as the victorious mages carried the unconscious form of Kai between them. The weight of their triumph and the immense responsibility they now bore was palpable in the air.

Elara's eyes shone with determination as she held Kai close, cradling him gently in her arms. Rylan, his grip firm yet tender, displayed both exhaustion and pride as he clutched the golden crown that once adorned the head of the tyrant King. The crown seemed to emit a faint glow, symbolising the newfound hope and the dawning era of liberation.

Silence fell over the palace grounds as the rebels and their prisoners looked upon the group with gratitude and awe. The mages, now embodying the ideals of justice and freedom, had shattered the chains of oppression and brought down the tyrannical ruler who had held their lives in his iron grip.

With a solemn expression, Elara addressed the gathered crowd, her voice ringing with a sense of resolve and determination. "Today, we have witnessed the fall of a tyrant, the dawn of a new era. But our fight is far from over. We must rebuild, heal, and forge a future that embodies the principles of unity, equality, and compassion."

Rylan then spoke, the golden crown glinting in his hand, and he held it high in the air, a symbol of their collective victory. "This crown, once worn by a tyrant, now serves as a reminder that power resides within the people, and it is our duty to wield it wisely and with humility. Let this crown represent our commitment to building a kingdom where justice prevails and the voices of all are heard."

A ripple of applause and cheers spread through the crowd, an outpouring of gratitude and renewed hope. The rebels, once prisoners, now found themselves standing tall, their spirits lifted by the triumph they had achieved together. They looked to Elara, Rylan, and the unconscious Kai, recognising them as the embodiment of their collective strength and resilience.

As the cheers subsided, Elara's gaze shifted towards the soldiers and Royal Guard still on their knees, their hands still behind their backs. She approached them with a mixture of compassion and understanding, her voice resonating with a quiet authority.

"To the soldiers of the army of the kingdom of Avoncale and the King's Royal Guard," Elara began, her words carrying across the silent courtyard. "You have served under the banner of a tyrant, compelled by oaths and promises that were built on deceit and oppression. But today, the kingdom stands on the precipice of change, and with it comes the opportunity for each of you to redefine your purpose and reclaim your own freedom."

She paused, allowing her words to sink in, and then continued, "Know that you are not bound by the sins of your former leader. The choice to stay or to leave lies solely in your hands. If you wish to depart from the service of the kingdom, you are free to do so without repercussions. You have the chance to choose a new path, one that aligns with the values of justice and fairness that we now strive to uphold."

A murmur spread through the soldiers and Royal Guard, their faces reflecting a range of emotions — doubt, uncertainty, and the glimmer of hope. Some glanced at their comrades, silently weighing their options, while others cast their gazes downward, deep in contemplation.

But then, one among the soldiers stood up and stepped forward, his voice firm and resolute. "We have sworn oaths, not to a tyrant, but to protect and serve the people of this kingdom," he spoke on behalf of his comrades. "We recognise the magnitude of the injustices that have occurred, and we are willing to atone for our past by awaiting your orders or the orders of those you all deem worthy. We pledge ourselves to the cause of justice and the rebuilding of a better kingdom."

Elara's heart swelled with admiration for their courage and dedication. She nodded, a small smile playing on her lips. "Your loyalty to the people does not go unnoticed. You have shown the strength of character and the capacity for change. Together, we shall forge a new path, rebuilding this kingdom on the foundations of trust, equality, and compassion."

With those words, the soldiers and Royal Guard rose from their kneeling positions, no longer prisoners but allies in the fight for a brighter future. Their transformation symbolised the transformative power of hope and the potential for redemption.

United in purpose and filled with determination, the gathered mages, rebels, soldiers, and former Royal Guard stood as a collective force. The weight of responsibility and the task of deciding the kingdom's future now resting upon their shoulders.

Amidst the murmurs and exchanged glances, a voice rang out from the crowd. It was a member of the Royal Guard, standing tall with a newfound resolve. "But who will rule?" he called out, his voice carrying the curiosity and uncertainty that echoed in the hearts of many. "Are we to follow you now, as the ones who brought forth this new age?" He asked, clearly uncertain if he wanted to pledge his life to three young mages.

Elara stepped forward, her presence commanding attention. She surveyed the faces before her, her gaze unwavering. "In a kingdom without a rightful royal line of succession, where the power is reclaimed by the people, it is only fitting that the rule be entrusted to the collective wisdom and guidance of all those who call this land home."

A hushed anticipation settled over the courtyard as Elara's words sank in. "We shall form a council," she declared, her voice steady and resolute. "This council will be composed of representatives from each magic school, the citizens of Avondale, and the soldiers who have pledged their allegiance to the cause of justice. Together, we will craft a governance structure that reflects the diverse needs and aspirations of our people."

A murmur of agreement rippled through the gathered assembly as whispers of hope and possibility mingled in the air. The notion of shared leadership, guided by principles of fairness and inclusivity, resonated with many who had long yearned for a voice in the decision-making process.

Elara continued, her voice carrying a sense of conviction. "This council will ensure that the voices of all are heard and considered, that decisions are made in the best interest of the people. We will establish a framework that upholds justice, protects individual rights, and fosters unity and cooperation."

As her words settled, Elara felt a sense of collective purpose washing over the crowd. The formation of this council, born out of the desire for a fair and just society, held the promise of a future where power was shared and the people were empowered rather than just one man.

She extended her hand, inviting others to join her in this endeavour. "Let us come together, united in our commitment to rebuild Avondale. Let us weave the threads of our individual strengths and talents into a tapestry of harmony and progress. Together, we shall forge a kingdom that stands as a beacon of hope and a testament to the indomitable spirit of its people."

But then, someone took Elara's outstretched hand from behind. It surprised her so much that she almost dropped Kai to the ground, who she and Rylan still carried.

Turning to see who it was, she was met with the tired, weary and very old-looking face of Captain Ren.

"My name is Theodore," Theodore said. "And I have to thank all three of you for what you did." His voice was tired and lacked any power that the Captain had ever portrayed. "But this young fire mage .." he indicated to Kai, "he has done something that I would never have thought possible. Once, I was a powerful air mage, ascended to the level of Grandmaster, but now… now I have nothing within me. This young mage has stripped me of my mana, not temporarily or just in part, but in its entirety... the entity controlling me, the one who committed all of these awful crimes has finally gone, forever and completely."

Elara's eyes widened in astonishment and relief as she listened to Theodore's words. The weight of his transformation, the release from the grip of Captain Ren's essence, resonated deeply within her. She could sense the genuine exhaustion and vulnerability emanating from him, a stark contrast to the once powerful and manipulative figure he had been. But she could also see the damage that his body had suffered, and she wondered how exactly he had survived, let alone had managed to walk on his own.

She lowered her hand, her expression filled with empathy and compassion. "Theodore, we are grateful for your presence and your words," Elara spoke softly, acknowledging the profound change that had taken place within him. "You have shown tremendous strength and resilience, and it is a testament to the power of redemption and the capacity for change."

Rylan, still holding the golden crown in his hand, spoke up. "Theodore, you have witnessed first-hand the devastating consequences of succumbing to darkness and losing oneself. But now, you have been freed, liberated from that burden. What will you do with this newfound chance at a different path?"

Theodore's tired eyes searched the faces before him, his gaze finally settling on Kai's unconscious form in Elara and Rylan's arms. A faint smile touched his lips, a glimmer of hope shining through the weariness. "I will join you," he answered, his voice carrying a blend of determination and gratitude. "I will use whatever remains of my strength and experience to contribute to the council, to help rebuild Avondale and ensure that the mistakes of the past are not repeated... that is, if you will have me."

Elara nodded, her respect for Theodore growing. "Your presence and wisdom will be invaluable, I am sure, Theodore. Together, we will forge a future where redemption and forgiveness can flourish."

As Theodore joined the ranks of the mages, rebels, soldiers, and citizens before the palace, the collective purpose and determination that had infused the crowd earlier seemed to intensify. The formation of the council and the inclusion of Theodore marked another step forward on the path toward healing and unity.

Elara turned her attention back to the crowd, her voice resonating with renewed energy. "Let Theodore's journey serve as a reminder that change and redemption are within our grasp," she declared. "Together, we will harness the strength of our diverse talents and perspectives and create a council that leads with integrity and compassion. Avondale's future will be shaped not only by our actions but by our collective will to create a better world."

A surge of applause and cheers erupted, filling the air with a palpable sense of hope and determination. The soldiers, the rebels who had fought for freedom, and the mages who had wielded their powers for justice now stood united, ready to embark on the journey of rebuilding their beloved kingdom.

Hand in hand, they moved forward, carrying the unconscious Kai and the shining golden crown that symbolised the dawning era of shared leadership and the unyielding spirit of Avondale. The challenges ahead were great, to be sure, but the collective resolve burned bright, fuelled by the belief in a future where the mistakes of the past would be redeemed and a new legacy of unity and progress would be forged.

The night passed quickly, and a new day arrived before anyone really knew what they were going to do. Most of the mages and rebels who did not have a home in the city slept within the great palace, spreading themselves about the place in the ample space it provided.

As the new day dawned, casting a gentle light upon the gathered assembly, a sense of anticipation filled the air. The weight of responsibility and the task ahead loomed large, and the members of the council-to-be began to engage in earnest discussions about how to proceed.

The citizens of Avondale, unsure of what to expect to happen next, gathered before the great palace and the huge tree that symbolised all of their freedoms. Mixed amongst them all as equals stood soldiers, Royal Guardsmen, mages from all schools of magic as well as the non-magical residents of the kingdom.

The group that had finally ended the reign of the tyrant King stood on the steps of the palace and debated their plans so that all could see and, more importantly, listen.

Kai, having regained consciousness, stood under his own power once more, his fiery gaze reflecting determination and purpose. He knew that he had a role to play in shaping the future of Avondale, and he was ready to embrace it.

"I have spoken with my Eternal Flame within, and I have been assured that the Arcani Soul is no more. But now we move on to more important issues. We must ensure that each school of magic is represented in our new council," he spoke up, his voice resolute. "Every affinity brings a unique perspective and set of skills that will be vital in making well-rounded decisions. Let us select mages who embody the virtues and principles of their respective schools to join the council. Let us have equal representation so that nobody is left behind. Azar has told me this has always been an issue in past kingdoms: one faction rises to power, and the rest are left unrepresented. I believe that if we solve this issue, we can build a future for all of the residents of Avondale."

Elara nodded enthusiastically. "I am humbled to be entrusted with this responsibility by the rest of the earth mages, and of course, I will offer my service to the kingdom if it will have me," she said, her voice steady. "I will bring the perspective of the earth affinity to the council, but we must also ensure that the voice of the people is heard. Theodore, I must ask, although you have been clear that you have no affinity today, but with your experiences and your deep understanding of the kingdom's past, I believe you would be an ideal representative for the people."

Theodore, his weary face displaying a mix of gratitude and uncertainty, met Elara's gaze. "I have seen the consequences of power wielded without regard for the people," he acknowledged, his voice filled with sincerity. "If you are willing to accept me, I will stand as their advocate, doing my best to ensure that their voices are heard and their needs are prioritised." Then he added slowly in almost an undertone. "But I know what I have done, and some may not look kindly on this position if I am allowed it."

"The people, as we all here now do, will understand what has happened to you," Elara replied. "But some may take some convincing. Either way, Theodore, we count you among our equals here, and the people need a strong and caring voice, but one that is filled with knowledge. This is the voice that I believe you shall bring."

Theodore thought for a moment, then simply nodded.

Then as though it had already been agreed by the Archmages of the Cyclonic Essence, Ethan, with a contemplative expression, interjected. "The realm of air magic embraces adaptability and strategic thinking," he proposed. "I offer myself as a representative of the air affinity, with a focus on the practicality of our decisions and ensuring that we anticipate and address challenges from all angles."

Theodore looked at Ethan with a sense of pride. He had always known that Ethan would step into a great role, and he knew that this would be one that he would excel in.

Elara looked at Theodore as though to ask if this was a good choice, and again Theodore nodded, although almost imperceptibly this time. Elara knew that they would need guidance from Theodore in many matters relating to the air mages, though she didn't want to appear to be begging for help already, seeing as the council had not yet even been formed.

The gathered assembly fell into deep discussion, considering the merits and qualifications of each potential council member. The mages, rebels, soldiers, and even the citizens debated the selection process, emphasising the importance of inclusivity and diverse perspectives. But in the end, nobody else offered to stand in the council, and nobody could provide a more appropriate candidate for each of the seats in the council.

"And so let it be known," Elara finally said, "that Avondale, from this day forward, shall be ruled not by a tyrant King. Not by one individual who seeks power and riches, but by a council, who will do nothing other than their utmost to help their citizens grow and prosper."

"We have chosen a path of shared leadership, recognising that no single person or group should hold absolute power," she proclaimed, her voice carrying the weight of conviction. "Together, we will strive to create a council that listens to the voices of all, upholds justice and fairness, and promotes Avondale's well-being and progress."

The crowd that had gathered erupted into applause, their enthusiasm echoing throughout the palace grounds. The new council members shared a moment of unity, knowing that the real work lay ahead. They embraced the challenges and uncertainties, fuelled by the collective belief in a future where redemption, unity, and progress would flourish.

"Tell me why you didn't want to be the leader again?' Elara mouthed to Rylan whilst the crowds cheered loudly.

"Ah, you know I always preferred actions over words," Rylan replied. "Besides, this is what you were born to do, right? You were the one who got us all together, the one who led us through the forest and into a better life… you deserve this, Elara, and I'll be by your side every step of the way."

Eventually, the crowd settled again, and Theodore spoke.

"Then let me make a proposal!" he announced. "Let us take this palace, this place of opulence and status and give it back to the people. Let us all use this as a forum for teaching, learning, discussions and trade. Let us forget what this place has meant for the rulers of the past. Let it stand as a testament to what we all believe in!"

Again the crowd cheered, and Theodore could feel nothing but acceptance from them all.

It was clear to everyone that the kingdom of Avondale had its council. Kai, Elara, Ethan, and Theodore would form the core of the council, and behind them stood both of Elara's parents, as well as Kai's, who would offer them guidance and wisdom – not because they needed it, but because they wanted it. Theodore stood for the people and promised to lend his voice to those who needed it the most. He thought of his friends back on the farm, Jack, Maia and Malek, and how he would be a pillar of hope for people like them, people who worked tirelessly and had, in the past, had to give everything to the King whenever he had asked.

Kai was filled with determination for the future. He had discussed this council in detail with Azar, and the Eternal Flame within him assured him that this would be the only way for the kingdom of Avondale to truly flourish; without greed, without power given to one individual, and with equality for all people.

But it was Ethan who remained silent, lost deep in his own thoughts. For Ethan knew what needed to happen next, his people had lived apart from the city, the kingdom and the surface for too long, and if the air mages truly wanted to be seen as an equal part of the council, then he knew that for the first time in many, many years, the Sky City would finally have to come home.

Finally, the council members and the people of Avondale were ready to move forward, ready to shape a destiny that would be guided by their shared aspirations and unwavering commitment to building a better kingdom. This day would be filled with discussions, planning, and a renewed sense of purpose, as Avondale embarked on its journey of rebirth and transformation. But first, there were reparations to be made, citizens to be fed, and mages to be rehomed.

Elara sighed at the thought of the mammoth task that lay before her, but she smiled, knowing that she could finally close the chapter on this dark time that had cast a shadow over so many people who she now saw as friends, family and equals.

Epilogue – Skyfall

One year had passed since the formation of the council in the kingdom of Avondale, and the changes that had taken place were nothing short of remarkable. The oppressive rule of King Roderick had been replaced by a new era of shared leadership, where the voices of the people, mages, and citizens alike were valued and heard. Under the guidance of Elara, Kai, Ethan, and Theodore, the council had worked tirelessly to transform Avondale into a thriving, just, and harmonious society.

The first and most significant change came in the form of a redistribution of wealth and resources. The council recognised that the kingdom had long suffered from social and economic inequality, with the majority of wealth concentrated in the hands of the elite. Determined to rectify this, they implemented a series of policies aimed at providing equal opportunities for all citizens. The land was redistributed fairly to farmers, ensuring they could cultivate their fields and provide sustenance for themselves and their communities. Wealth was no longer hoarded by the few but rather invested in infrastructure, education, and healthcare for all. And above all, the stringent taxation was abolished, leaving the people able to work, grow and keep what they earned.

Education became a cornerstone of the council's efforts. They established academies across Avondale, where mages and citizens could come together to learn and share knowledge. The mages, once isolated within their respective magical disciplines, now found themselves collaborating and embracing the diverse forms of magic that existed within their kingdom. Earth, air and fire mages worked side by side, sharing their wisdom and learning from one another. The barriers that had once separated them crumbled, and a new era of magical understanding and cooperation flourished.

The council also championed the importance of cultural exchange and unity. They celebrated the richness of Avondale's diverse population, encouraging festivals, performances, and gatherings that highlighted the traditions, music, and art of different regions and communities. The once-divided citizens now saw themselves as part of a greater whole, embracing their shared identity as citizens.

But it was in the healing and reconciliation process that the council's work truly shone. The scars of the past were deep, and the wounds inflicted by King Roderick's reign were still fresh. The council established truth and reconciliation commissions, giving victims of the previous regime a platform to share their stories and seek justice. They created support networks and counselling services to help individuals and families rebuild their lives and find solace in a community that stood united against the injustices of the past.

The people of Avondale, once plagued by fear and uncertainty, now lived in a society where their voices mattered. The council listened and acted upon their concerns, ensuring that decisions were made collectively and with the well-being of all citizens in mind. No longer did the people feel silenced, persecuted or marginalised; instead, they were active participants in shaping their own destiny.

Under the council's guidance, Avondale flourished. The once desolate streets were filled with the sounds of laughter, the aroma of freshly baked bread, and the sight of children playing freely. The economy boomed, driven by innovation and entrepreneurship, as the council fostered an environment that nurtured anyone who strived for the better and encouraged them to keep pushing for more. The kingdom had become a beacon of prosperity and hope, a testament to the resilience and spirit of its people.

As the council members looked out upon the transformed kingdom, they felt a deep sense of pride and fulfilment. Avondale had undergone a profound metamorphosis, emerging from the darkness of its past into the light of a promising future. The mages, once segregated and isolated, now stood as beacons of unity and progress. The people, who had suffered under tyranny, now revelled in their newfound freedoms and shared prosperity.

But amidst the achievements and progress, the council knew that their work was far from over. They continued to tackle challenges such as environmental sustainability, addressing the needs of marginalised communities, and planned to strengthen diplomatic relations with neighbouring kingdoms. The council remained steadfast in their commitment to constant improvement and the pursuit of a more equitable and just society.

Environmental sustainability became a focal point for the council. Recognising the importance of preserving their natural resources, they implemented policies to protect the kingdom's forests, rivers, and wildlife. Efforts were made to promote sustainable farming practices, encouraging farmers to embrace organic and circular economical methods and minimise their impact on the environment.

To ensure that no one was left behind, the council placed great emphasis on addressing the needs of marginalised communities. Programs were established to provide access to quality education and healthcare in underserved areas. Efforts were made to bridge the gap between rural and urban communities, improving infrastructure and connectivity to promote equal opportunities for all.

The council recognised the importance of creating strong diplomatic ties with neighbouring kingdoms. They planned that through open dialogue and peaceful negotiations; they would foster alliances that promoted trade, cultural exchange, and mutual understanding. Avondale would quickly become known as a kingdom that valued diplomacy and cooperation, extending its hand in friendship to other realms and working collaboratively to address shared challenges.

In their pursuit of a more just and inclusive society, the council confronted the shadows of the past head-on. They supported initiatives to honour the memory of those who had suffered under King Roderick's reign, erecting memorials and organising events to commemorate their sacrifices. These gestures of remembrance served as a reminder of the kingdom's collective commitment to never forget the injustices of the past and to continually strive for a better future.

"From the sky, it's coming!" A young man was shouting as he entered the council chambers.

Elara was the first to speak in an effort to calm the man down. "It's alright; take a deep breath," she said.

The young man took a breath as instructed, his chest heaving with excitement and anticipation. He composed himself and spoke with a mixture of awe and urgency. "You won't believe it! The Sky City — it's descending! The balloons are deflating, and the fans are slowing down. It's coming towards Avondale!"

Theodore's eyes widened. He had known that one day this day would come, that his people would return to the surface to reunite themselves with the kingdom. And he knew that the Archmages had been working on this for a very long time; it seemed that finally the Sky City had come to believe that the kingdom of Avondale really had changed.

A wave of astonishment and curiosity washed over the rest of the council members. The news of the Sky City's descent filled the room with a renewed sense of wonder and intrigue.

Ethan, the representative of the air mages, stood up, his eyes filled with excitement. "This is a momentous occasion," he exclaimed. "For too many years, the Sky City has remained aloft, detached from the affairs of the kingdom. Its descent signifies a willingness to rejoin the Avondale community."

The council members exchanged glances, their thoughts racing with the possibilities that this unprecedented event held. The coming together of the air mages with the rest of the kingdom could pave the way for a new era of collaboration and shared knowledge.

Elara nodded, her voice filled with anticipation. "We must extend a warm welcome to our brothers and sisters from the Sky City. Let us show them the progress we have made, the unity we have fostered, and the potential for growth and harmony that awaits us."

The council swiftly sprang into action, dispatching messengers to spread the news throughout Avondale and make preparations for the arrival of the air mages. The city buzzed with excitement as citizens gathered in the streets, eager to witness this historic moment.

Minutes turned into hours as the Sky City slowly descended, guided by the steady hands of the air mages. The massive balloons that had kept the city afloat for so long gently deflated, one by one, while the colossal fans that propelled it through the skies slowed their rotation.

Finally, the Sky City touched the ground; its graceful descent met with cheers and applause from the awaiting crowd. The council, dressed in their plain robes, stood at the forefront, ready to greet their long-lost kin.

As the air mages stepped onto Avondale soil, their eyes filled with wonder and curiosity. They beheld a transformed kingdom, one that had embraced progress, unity, and the pursuit of justice. The council members, led by Elara, approached the air mages with open arms, extending the hand of friendship and reconciliation.

Theodore, his voice filled with gratitude, spoke on behalf of the air mages. "We have witnessed the incredible journey that Avondale has embarked upon. The unity and determination you have displayed have inspired us, and we are eager to contribute to the growth and prosperity of our shared home."

The air mages, having lived in seclusion for years, were humbled by the warm reception they received. They marvelled at the advancements in magic and the harmonious coexistence of different magical affinities.

"Brother," Volnus replied as he took hold of Theodore's wrist, and Theodore smiled warmly in return. The years had not been kind to Theodore; his skin cracked and wrinkled. Volnus, on the other hand, looked the very same as the last time Theodore had seen him, his bright long hair flowing down his back.

"There are many things that I have to tell you," Theodore explained slowly, seeing Volnus' concerned gaze at Theodore's appearance. But for now, come to the palace, and we will see what we can do to all work together in this new world."

Time, as it so frequently does, passed, and the kingdom of Avondale grew in both strength and happiness.

As the council convened in their chambers, engaged in a discussion about the future of Avondale, a sudden commotion erupted outside the doors. The sound of hurried footsteps echoed through the hall, growing louder with each passing moment. Before anyone could react, a citizen burst into the room; his face flushed with excitement and urgency.

"Forgive my intrusion, esteemed council members," the citizen gasped for breath, his voice filled with a mix of excitement and apprehension. "There is an unknown mage who has arrived in Avondale, seeking an audience with the council. He claims to possess unique and extraordinary powers."

The council members exchanged glances, their curiosity piqued by the unexpected arrival of this mysterious mage. Theodore, ever vigilant, felt a familiar tingle of recognition as if a dormant memory had been awakened.

Elara stepped forward, her voice filled with a sense of caution. "Who is this mage, and what does he seek from us?"

The citizen caught his breath, his eyes darting around the room. "He did not reveal his name, but he spoke of a great revelation — a discovery that could reshape the very fabric of our magical world. He insists that his intentions are pure and that he wishes to share his knowledge and abilities for the betterment of Avondale."

Ethan, the air mage representative, spoke up, his curiosity evident in his voice. "We must exercise caution when encountering unknown and potentially powerful mages. We have learned from the past that unchecked power can lead to dire consequences."

Theodore, his mind again focussed, nodded in agreement. "We must approach this with prudence. The actions of mages in the past have left scars on our kingdom. We cannot afford to repeat those mistakes."

Elara's gaze hardened, her resolve unyielding. "We will meet with this mage, but on our terms. We will ensure that his intentions are pure and his powers are not a threat to the stability and well-being of Avondale."

With a shared understanding, the council members left the chambers, making their way towards the grand hall where the unknown mage awaited their arrival. As they entered the hall, the atmosphere was tinged with anticipation and uncertainty.

The mysterious mage stood before them, his presence radiating an air of enigma and power. His silver hair shimmered under the soft glow of the chamber's lights, and his eyes sparkled with a dark otherworldly intensity.

Elara approached the mage, her voice steady but cautious. "You have requested an audience with the council. Speak your purpose, and we shall listen."

The mage inclined his head to reveal his entire face and the deep purple of his eyes, his voice carrying a sense of intrigue. "I have travelled far to bring you tidings of a discovery — an ancient form of magic that has been long forgotten and is absent from this kingdom, persecuted just like all of yours once was. It possesses the potential to harmonise the different magical affinities, uniting them in a way that has never been done before."

The council members exchanged glances, their curiosity piqued by the mage's words. Theodore stepped forward, though, his memories guiding him. "I… know you," he said slowly. "Back out there on the battlefield…"

The mage inclined his head downwards respectfully. "You must have me mistaken, good sir," the mage replied, but Theodore was certain.

"No, I am afraid that I do not," he said flatly. "When the world was filled with death and destruction, and my memory had failed me… you told me that I would remember myself, and then I should find you. Well, I tell you now that I remember myself more than I ever have done before, and it is clear to me that you were speaking to my Arcani Soul… you were one of the death mages who cast the spell to have my body taken from me, were you not?"

The atmosphere in the grand hall grew tense as Theodore confronted the mysterious mage. The council members exchanged glances, their curiosity mixed with concern. Elara, ever composed, gestured for calm. She knew that the truth of Theodore's accusation needed to be addressed, regardless of the potential implications.

"I tell you, good sir, you have me mistaken," the mage replied, but Theodore knew that he was right. He knew that this master of the Arcani

Soul could not have been in the city with good intentions.

Theodore's voice held a firm resolve as he met the mage's gaze. "I have no doubt in my mind, for my memories have returned to me. I remember the conversation we had, the promises you made, and the power you wielded. You were one of the death mages who stripped me of my body, forcing within me the Arcani Soul that these people came to know as Captain Ren. I am Theodore, and I am a puppet no longer."

The council members exchanged shocked glances, their eyes darting between Theodore and the mysterious mage. Elara's voice, tinged with a mixture of concern and caution, broke the silence.

"If what Theodore says is true, then we must proceed with the utmost care," Elara declared, her gaze fixed on the mage. "Your presence here raises questions of trust and accountability. We cannot ignore the pain and suffering that has been inflicted upon our people."

"Tell me, Council," the mage replied. "Do you even know what the Arcane Soul is or what it does? How it helps people as they move on to the afterlife?"

The council members looked at each other in confusion but didn't offer a response.

"Then let me enlighten you," the mage said. "People need somewhere to go once their mortal soul has been freed from their body; without such a place, they would be destined to walk this place lost and afraid. The Arcani Soul and the wielders of its power are there to aid those souls. We show them the way they must follow to be free and live out all of eternity in the afterlife." He smiled as though all of this was a very noble cause, and by all accounts, it didn't seem like it was a terrible thing.

"And the power you wield," Ethan was the first to reply. "You simply use it to help others?"

"No, they do not!" Theodore interrupted. "These death mages want nothing more than pain and suffering to fill the lands because that is where they get their power from. The more death, the greater their power. That is why they placed their Arcani Souls within the king and me, and that is why this once magnificent kingdom descended into hardship and war."

Elara's voice cut through the tension, her resolve unwavering.

"We have witnessed the devastating consequences of the Arcani Souls and the power wielded by the death mages," Elara stated firmly. "Our duty as the council is to protect Avondale and its people from further harm. We cannot allow the cycle of death and destruction to continue."

The mysterious mage's expression shifted, a flicker of conflict crossing his features. "I understand the pain that has been caused, but I assure you, there is more to this story. The Arcani Souls are not inherently evil. They possess the potential for both darkness and light, and it is our choices that determine their true nature. Is that not the same for any sentient being and all of us present in this place right now?"

Theodore's voice dripped with scepticism as he locked eyes with the mage. "Your words hold little weight. We have witnessed the havoc wrought by the Arcani Souls. Innocent lives were lost, and the kingdom was plunged into chaos. How can we trust that you are any different?"

The mage's gaze softened, revealing a look of regret. "I bear the weight of the past upon my shoulders, but I am here to make amends. I seek redemption not only for myself but for the legacy of the death mages. I offer you a path forward, one that can bring harmony and healing to Avondale."

Ethan, his voice laced with caution, spoke up. "What path do you propose? How can we ensure that history does not repeat itself?"

The mage took a step forward; his voice filled with a sombre earnestness. "I propose a path of understanding and reconciliation. I will share my knowledge and guide those who possess the Arcani Soul, but under strict supervision and with the aim of healing rather than destruction. Together, we can learn to harness the power of the Arcani Soul for the greater good."

The council members exchanged uncertain glances, grappling with the weight of the mage's proposal. The wounds of the past were still fresh, and the scars ran deep within their kingdom. But in the mage's words, there was a glimmer of hope — a chance to break free from the cycle of darkness that had haunted Avondale for far too long.

Elara then addressed the mage. "We cannot ignore the pain and suffering that has been inflicted upon our people, nor can we forget the lives lost. Your proposal raises important questions of trust and accountability. We must tread carefully and ensure that the welfare of our citizens remains our top priority."

The mage nodded, a solemn acknowledgement of the council's concerns. "I understand the magnitude of the task before us. I am prepared to demonstrate my commitment to healing and redemption through actions, not just words. Let my deeds speak for themselves, and together we can build a future that is fair and just for the people."

"I will not allow this," Theodore interrupted sternly, sensing the council's acceptance of his words. He turned to Elara and the other council members with a look of pleading on his face. "You do not know how these mages work. They lie and trick so that they can insert their will into the people. The things that I saw… the things I was forced to do… and the kingdom, too, so many killed over so many years and for what? Just for these mages to gain their power? I will never trust them, and I know that they are planning something terrible with all of this. Please, I beg you all, do not fall for these words."

"I see that the light in your eyes that yearns for a better future has gone," the death mage said quietly to Theodore. "I see that you no longer possess the desire to push this kingdom forward into growth and prosperity. I weep for you, brother, and I weep for your everlasting Arcani Soul."

"I HAVE NO ARCANI SOUL!" Theodore practically bellowed, and his voice echoed through the grand hall, his anger and frustration reverberating in the air. The council members exchanged troubled glances, torn between Theodore's impassioned plea and the mage's offer of redemption. Elara, her voice filled with empathy, stepped forward to address Theodore directly.

"Theodore, we understand the pain and trauma you have endured. Your words hold weight, and we value your perspective. We will not make any hasty decisions that could endanger our people..."

"My mind will not be changed!" Theodore interrupted her. Had he still been an air mage, he would have called upon his mana at that point and ended this death mage's life. But he was a mage no more. He was a man, and he did the only thing he could think to do at that very moment. He punched the death mage on his jaw. Hard.

The mage fell back, shocked at the sudden attack, and the grand hall erupted into chaos as Theodore's fist connected with the mage's jaw. Gasps filled the air as the council members watched in stunned silence. Elara quickly regained her composure, her voice ringing out with authority.

"Stop!" she commanded, rushing forward to intervene. The council members, alarmed by the unexpected turn of events, moved to restrain Theodore and the fallen mage. The atmosphere crackled with tension as emotions ran high.

The mage, holding his jaw, rose to his feet, his eyes burning with a mixture of surprise and anger. "You dare strike me, mortal?" he hissed, his voice laced with indignation. His eyes flashed a deep purple, and within them, Theodore saw a power that he had not yet seen from the man.

Theodore, his own anger still simmering, locked eyes with the mage. "You deserved it," he replied, his voice filled with bitterness. "For the pain you caused, for the lives lost, and for the manipulation and deception."

Elara, her voice firm but measured, addressed the chaos that had erupted. "Enough! Violence will not solve anything. We are here to find a path forward, one that brings healing and justice to our kingdom. Let us calm our emotions and proceed with reason."

The council members, their initial shock giving way to a sense of responsibility following Elara's words, began to separate Theodore and the mage, keeping a careful distance between them. The tension in the grand hall was palpable as Elara turned her attention to Theodore.

"GET OUT OF THE WAY!" the shout came from Kai, as peering through his blindfold, he could see the mana swelling within the death mage as the anger fuelled his retribution. The council members as one leapt back away from the man as his eyes began to shine so brightly that they looked like two burning balls of Arcane fire.

"In truth, it does not matter what you say now!" The mage raised his voice so that everyone could hear clearly. "If you will not allow the Arcani Soul representation at this council, then we will take it from you."

Then, as Theodore had seen before, the ground beneath the mage trembled, responding to the raw magical energy being channelled through the man's fingertips and with a swift motion, the man thrust his hands forward, and a purple shockwave rippled through the air. A vortex of swirling energy formed before him, crackling with a bright, intense purple light.

Again, as Theodore had seen before, the vortex expanded in a wide circle, but where once ethereal wisps of light began to detach from the lifeless bodies littering the ground on the battlefield he had awoken in, this time the wisps, again clearly representing lost souls flowed outwards from the spell itself, searching for vessels.

Turning to look at the rest of the council, Theodore's eyes were wide with fear. He wanted to tell them to watch out, to not let these wisps touch them for fear of what they could become, but in his moment of panic, his mind took over. All he could do was look directly at Ethan and practically whisper: "You can do this."

Ethan looked back at Theodore first in surprise and then in understanding. Captain Ren and Theodore had been known for their ability to dispel mana by using his Cyclonic Essence, and although nobody else had been able to achieve similar results on the same scale, Ethan closed his eyes and called upon his mana.

Elara and Rylan fell backwards instinctively, and Kai watched through his blindfold as the golden mana pulsed from Ethan's soul, clashing like a firework against the glowing purple orbs.

And then it happened; Ethan's spell, through sheer determination and willpower, froze the wisps where they were in mid-air. It hadn't entirely dispelled the mana of the Arcani Soul, but it had done enough, and Kai stepped forward, sighing as he anticipated the power that he, Azar and the Grandmaster's Eternal Flame would have to sap from these beings and then from the death mage himself. It would be difficult, painful and tiresome, but Kai knew that he was not the only person in the entire world that could remove this threat caused by these dead mages. He just didn't know how many of them there were out there and how far their tendrils reached.

Once the death mage had been suppressed and placed under guard, and Kai was taken to his bed to rest so that he could conduct his internal fight, it left Elara, Rylan, Ethan and Theodore to discuss what had happened and how they should proceed.

"Our kingdom has been reforged into one of equality,' Elara said. "If we ban these death mages, then are we no better than the tyrant King Roderick?"

"But the tyrant King searched for innocents and killed them because he was a ruthless tyrant, not because they posed a threat to his people," Ethan replied.

Theodore, his voice filled with conviction, added to the conversation. "We cannot turn a blind eye to the actions of these death mages. They manipulated and caused great suffering, using innocent lives as pawns in their pursuit of power. We have seen first-hand the devastation they can bring."

Rylan, his face etched with concern, interjected. "We must ensure the safety of our people. Allowing unchecked power and influence within the council poses a risk to the very foundations we have built. We cannot afford to repeat the mistakes of the past."

Elara nodded, her gaze steady as she considered the weight of their decisions. "We must strike a balance between justice and mercy. We cannot ban all death mages outright, but we must have strict regulations and oversight. Those who seek redemption and demonstrate a genuine commitment to change should be given an opportunity to prove themselves. But we must remain vigilant, and if any show signs of returning to their dark ways, we must take swift action to protect our kingdom. After all, they can't all be alike, can they?"

Ethan, his gaze focused and determined, spoke up. "I agree with Elara. We cannot let fear dictate our actions, but we must not allow ourselves to be naïve either. We will establish a system of checks and balances, ensuring that those with the Arcani Soul are closely monitored and that their actions align with the values and principles we hold dear."

The council members nodded in agreement, a shared understanding settling among them. The path forward would be challenging, but they were united in their resolve to protect Avondale and its people. They would forge a new era, one where the mistakes of the past would serve as lessons and where justice and compassion would guide their decisions.

But this one particular death mage, this one wielder of the Arcani Soul, would be held to account for his actions. That would be, of course, once Kai had removed his ability to practise magic once and for all.

~The End~

A Thankyou

Again, your investment of your own time and money is always well appreciated and again, I ask that you **rate** and **review** everything that you read – and not just this book, so that lesser-known authors can grow their audience and gain the credibility that they deserve for their hard work.

Also, check out my website, it's usually kept up to date with current works, reviews and a few extra little bits. You'll find it at:

www.davidlingard.com

Thank you

9 781739 386658